INNOCENT TEMPTRESS

He kicked the door shut.

"Richard, please, let me explain."

"Explain? What is there to explain?" He advanced on her, ignoring the fear in her eyes. "That you prefer a gypsy to your own husband? That you lock me out of your room but run to the arms of that—that Romany swine?"

Serena backed away, but he stalked her, like a lion stalking his prey; she would not get away from him this time. She backed into a chair and stumbled; he grabbed her arms and pushed her toward the bed.

"Richard, it isn't like that."

"No, then what *is* it like?" he snarled, backing her closer to the bed. "Didn't you like being in his arms? You damn well seemed to be enjoying it."

"No!" she cried, shaking her head. "No!"

"And did you enjoy his bed, Serena?"

"No, Richard. Please, I never—"

Taking her arms, he lifted her and tossed her onto the middle of the bed. "All these nights I've wanted you, but I waited while you played the frightened child," he said, wrenching off his neckcloth and unbuttoning his shirt. "Damn you to hell, Serena! *I* am your husband and *I* am going to have you!"

ZEBRA'S REGENCY ROMANCES
the Lords & Ladies you'll *love* reading about

THE ROGUE'S BRIDE (1976, $2.95)
by Paula Roland

Major Brandon Clive was furious when he returned to England to find the wrong bride foisted off on him. But one look at Alexandra, and Brandon instantly changed his mind.

SMUGGLER'S LADY (1948, $3.95)
by Jane Feather

No one would ever suspect dowdy Merrie Trelawney of being the notorious leader of smuggler's band. But something about Merrie struck Lord Rutherford as false, and though he was not in the habit of seducing country widows, it might make an interesting change at that . . .

CRIMSON DECEPTION (1913, $2.95)
by Therese Alderton

Katherine's heart raced as she observed valuable paintings mysteriously disappear, but her pulse quickened for a different reason in the Earl's company. She would have to get to the bottom of it all—before she fell hopelessly in love with a scoundrel.

A GENTLEMAN'S MISTRESS (1798, $2.95)
by Mary Brendan

Sarah should have been grateful that Mark Tarrington had hired her as a governess. Instead the young widow was furious at his arrogance and her heart's reaction to him. Sarah Thornton was obviously going to require patience which was the one quality the earl had little of.

FARO'S LADY (1725, $2.95)
by Paula Roland

Jessamine arrived at a respectable-looking inn—only to be mistaken for a jade that night by a very drunken gentleman. She vowed revenge and plotted to trap Hugh Hamilton into a marriage he would never forget. A flawless plan—if it hadn't been for her wayward heart.

SAPPHIRE TEMPTATION

BY JANIS LADEN

ZEBRA BOOKS
KENSINGTON PUBLISHING CORP.

ZEBRA BOOKS

are published by

Kensington Publishing Corp.
475 Park Avenue South
New York, NY 10016

First printing: February 1987

Printed in the United States of America

For my husband, Michael,
with love
"Tell me, Muse, of the man of many wiles—"
— *The Odyssey*, Homer

ACKNOWLEDGEMENTS

My deepest gratitude to Marjorie Miller for her invaluable guidance, and for making me believe. To Diane Bouchard for her helpful insights into the Regency period, and to the Westwood writers, past and present, for all their suggestions. Special thanks also to my agent, Florence Feiler, to my editor, Wendy McCurdy, and to my typist, Mabel Mossman. And finally to my husband, Michael, who listened for 1001 nights.

Diamonds, rubies, and amber studs
Tempt not mine eye nor stir my blood,
But the deep blue jewel my soul doth fill —
Its hidden fires elude me still.

—Sir Isaac Mariner

Chapter One

"Father, surely you are not serious! You cannot mean to hold me to this." Richard Gower, the Marquis of Egremont, abruptly stopped pacing the floor, ran his fingers through his dark hair, and regarded his parents with astonishment.

"But I'm afraid I *am* serious, Richard; never more so," responded the Duke of Luntsford softly. He sat comfortably in his favorite leather chair, his wife perched on its arm, his hand casually encircling her waist.

"But it—it's preposterous! Why, it's medieval! To have effected a betrothal when I was yet in short coats and the girl yet in her cradle! Mother, surely *you* can see that this will not serve."

"Oh, you'll get no quarter from me, my dear son. I met your father but three days before our own wedding, and here I am, twenty-three years later with, shall we say, very few complaints." The Duchess of Luntsford favored her husband with a gentle smile, and Richard saw a gleam of mischief light his father's eyes as he returned her look. "And now, I think I shall leave you two gentlemen to continue this discussion without me." She rose with a natural litheness and grace that was undiminished by her years. Richard did not miss the lingering squeeze his father gave her hand as she did so.

"Richard," she said as she glided to the door of the study, "you must not be angry. It is the way of the Gowers, and has been for four centuries. Truly, it is all for the best."

"Your mother is right, Richard," Luntsford said when she'd gone. "Why don't you sit down?" Richard heaved a tense sigh and sat down opposite the duke. "I will confess that I was as skeptical as you all those years ago, but as you see, I was wrong."

"Father, with all due respect, I know well that you and Mother are devoted to each other, but, if you will excuse me, I believe I am not far off the mark when I conjecture that 'twas not always so."

"I beg your pardon?" Luntsford demanded, his bushy graying brows converging in a frown.

"Well, I—I only meant that—" Richard paused, knowing he was overstepping his bounds but determined to make his point, "that I am two and twenty and it was five years after my birth that Livvy came along, and I do remember once hearing Grandmama saying—"

"You are impertinent, young man!" bellowed his father.

"Forgive me, Father," Richard said, his lips twitching.

"And that has nothing to say to the matter. There are many reasons why a woman—oh, hell!" The duke suddenly grinned. "It wasn't five years, you must know—our—er—estrangement. After all, it takes nine months for a babe to grow. But truth is, your mother and I—well—we both had an excess of pride. Which I am afraid you've inherited, Richard, more's the pity! But we mended our fences, right and well, and you shall do the same. All comes out right in the end, you'll see."

"Oh, Father, 'tis a good deal easier to say that three and twenty years later than to be in my position, looking ahead. I respect the family traditions, and I am sensible of my duties as your heir. In truth, I should not cavil overmuch were my affections not already engaged."

"Ah, yes. The lovely Miss Lister. I am sorry, truly sorry, my son, that political affairs kept your mother and I so long in town. For had I known of your interest in Miss Lister, I should have reminded you of your betrothal and perhaps saved you any distress. You were told, by the by, as a youth."

"That was a very long time ago, Father. And I never actually believed—but that doesn't signify. The fact is that I am most sincerely attached to Miss Lister and I—"

"A veritable beauty, I'll grant you that," mused the duke. "And her situation is rather straitened, if my information serves. She and that wastrel brother of hers forced to close down the family seat and take up residence here in greatly reduced circumstances. Yes, I can see how a young man might—"

"This is *not* a passing fancy, Father," Richard interjected, leaning forward in his chair, hands clasped between his knees. "Caroline is—oh, how can I explain it—she is like the sunshine to me," he finished with a broad smile and a sweep of his hand.

"Yes, I've no doubt she is, my boy," the duke replied, flicking a bit of dust from his black coat. "But you know, it's a funny thing about the sunshine. A man can take just so much of it, but after a while—well—he begins to chafe under it."

Richard regarded his father steadily for a moment, then leaned back, rubbing a hand over his eyes. "And what of my prospective bride? What is *she* like?"

"Well, I have not met her, of course, but—"

"Haven't met her? Then how—"

"Richard, you cannot expect me to have gone to inspect her as one does cattle at auction. But my intermediaries assure me that she is quite unexceptionable. Charming, witty. A most unusual young woman."

" 'Unusual!' Oh, Lord. A veritable antidote, I'll wager."

"Nothing of the kind, boy. But then, not every girl can look like Caroline Lister. But that is hardly of prime importance in marriage, you know."

Richard raised his eyebrows. "Spoken by a man married to one of the most beautiful women in the kingdom."

"Nonetheless, Richard, I think, from all reports, that you and the Lady Serena shall suit admirably. I have let you go your own way in many things. To Cambridge when it is our tradition to go to Oxford. To study and collect your insects when other young men perfect their boxing stance at Gentleman Jim's. But this is different, and you will do what is expected of you."

"And if I refuse, Father?" Richard was leaning forward again, his voice deceptively calm.

"Gowers have married Wexleys since the Fifteenth Century, Richard," the duke intoned, rising majestically and looking down at his son. "It is a blending of two of the foremost families in all England. We have produced great statesmen and even several royal princesses." Centuries of pride sounded in that voice, and then his father came to him and put a hand on his shoulder. The voice softened but the duke did not meet his eyes. "You are my only son and heir, Richard. But if you defy me in this, I shall disown you."

"I see," his son said heavily, and stared bleakly ahead of him.

"I don't care a rush whether I shall one day be a duchess or a shop girl! I refuse to wed a man I have not met!" Lady Serena stamped her small foot on the blue Aubusson carpet and frowned at her parents. The Earl of Stoneleigh sat in a highbacked wing chair and his wife stood before the gilt mantel.

"Serena! You will kindly comport yourself appropriately. You are eighteen years of age and it is high time your learned to curb your temper," the earl rebuked her sternly. "You have no right to refuse anything. You are my daughter and shall wed according to my wishes."

"And do not spurn the state of duchess, Serena. You shall be very wealthy and wield a great deal of power in society. Not to mention being mistress of Luntsford Court," the countess added.

"But don't you understand, Mama?" Serena entreated, moving toward the countess. "I'm not interested in those things. It is the man I care about, not his titles and dignities."

"Nonetheless, a coronet is not to be despised," her mother countered stiffly.

Without thinking Serena blurted, "It is not a coronet that will join me in bed at night, Mama. It is a *man*."

"Oh! How—how dare you speak in such a manner!" spluttered the countess, clutching at her thin breast. "Stoneleigh, *do* something!"

The earl strode to the pair and abruptly handed his wife her vinaigrette. "Here, Madam, take this. And as for you, Serena, you will apologize to your mother for such an unseemly outburst!" he demanded.

"I'm sorry," she mumbled, not meeting her mother's eyes, for inside she was seething. They just couldn't do this to her! They wouldn't!

"Now, we will all be seated, if you please," the earl commanded in steely tones. When they had each seated themselves in the straight highbacked chairs surrounding the ornate sofa table, he continued. "I will attribute your excess of feeling to your youth, Serena, but do not try me further. I realize this is all very sudden but you will soon accustom yourself to the idea."

"Of course she will," said her mother briskly. "And you need not sit in each other's pockets, you must know. After you have presented Lord Egremont with

14

an heir you may each go your own way."

"Does that mean that I can have affairs?" asked Serena before she could stop herself.

"Serena!" the earl's gray eyes blazed and Serena lowered her own. "Woman, do you not monitor her reading material?" he demanded, now glaring at his wife. "What your mother means," he intoned, "is that you may pursue separate interests, friends and the like. As she and I have done. Many successful marriages are patterned thus."

Serena gazed bleakly at the two of them, not daring to ask what they thought a "successful marriage" was. She had long known that her parents were not happy together and had vowed that she would not suffer a similar fate.

"Could I not have a Season, as other girls do, Papa?"

"There is no need for such an expenditure," her mother answered brusquely. "Your husband can take you to London if he is so inclined."

"But, Mama, Papa, I — I want to — to fall in love with a man." An image of such a man rose in her mind's eye. He would be very tall, with golden hair, not unlike a Viking. "And I—"

"Love! What is wrong with you, child?" railed the countess. "You are not some dairy maid casting eyes at the farmer's son. You are the daughter of the Earl of Stoneleigh and you shall behave as such."

"It's those damned books she reads," growled the earl, folding his arms across his portly frame.

"Stoneleigh, please, mind your tongue," his wife reproved. "Now then, Serena, we shall very shortly pay a visit to Luntsford Court."

"But is it not customary for the man first to visit

the—the woman's home?" Serena asked desperately.

"Only for the purpose of courtship, Serena. Since there is no need of that, I see no reason to stand the expense of an extended visit by the Gowers," the countess replied, her nose high and her thin lips pursed.

"But, perhaps it would give Lord Egremont and me a chance to decide—"

"There is nothing to decide, daughter," her mother interrupted coldly. "We have, I believe, made that quite clear. We shall, as I said, soon journey to Luntsford Court. We shall stay less than a se'ennight—such visits are awkward at best. After that you need only concern yourself with bridesclothes and the like. You will, of course, be married here at Stoneleigh."

Serena's heart raced as a feeling of horror overtook her. "And if I—if I refuse this marriage?" she whispered.

"You will not gainsay me, Serena," the earl commanded, rising from his chair. "But if you do, I shall disinherit you. And though you will be a wealthy woman in your own right someday, you may not touch a shilling of your grandmother's legacy until your twenty-first birthday. Until then you will starve," he said brutally. "Think well on it, Serena. And remember that no honorable man will have you after I repudiate you."

Serena fought to hold back the tears, but as she gazed at the earl and countess, she was met by a cold stare from each.

Serena sat nervously beside her mother as the car-

riage turned into the massive circular drive of Luntsford Court. Despite her dread of the moment, she
could not help admiring the stately Palladian mansion,
its symmetry and simplicity a welcome change from
the forbidding gothic aspect of Stoneleigh. And with
that admiration came a ray of hope—perhaps the
marquis would be an amiable man, one with whom she
might share—

"Do not gawk, Serena," her mother commanded
sharply, breaking into her thoughts. " 'Tis not at all the
thing. The house is well enough—not so grand as
Stoneleigh, of course, but, 'twill serve."

"Yes, Mama," Serena murmured, her dread mounting as she saw a cadre of liveried servants amassing on
the marble staircase.

"Stoneleigh, do wake up! We have arrived!" her
mother snapped.

"No need to shout, Madam. I know well enough
where we are," the earl muttered, pulling his ample
frame upright and smoothing the sleeves of his coat.
"Serena, for pity sakes, put a bit of bloom in your
cheeks! You look like a frightened rabbit," he said with
irritation. "You are not being marched to the guillo-
tine, you know." She could only hope he was right and
resolutely lifted her chin and straightened her back.

"Your father is correct, Serena," her mother put in.
"You must not appear too timid. But neither must you
be too forthcoming. You must keep your eyes downcast
and speak only when spoken to, else you shall give
Lord Egremont a disgust of you."

Serena had little time to ponder how to observe these
conflicting strictures, however, for the carriage drew to
a halt and the door was swung open. There followed a

flurry of activity, as one footman after another conveyed Serena and her parents up the great marble staircase to the front portico.

An hour later she could not recall a single detail of the huge entry lobby, nor the faces of her prospective in-laws. She remembered only a friendly smile from the duke, a rather stiff greeting from Lord Egremont's younger sister, and the warm green eyes of the duchess. And then she had been presented to Richard, Marquis of Egremont, her betrothed husband. He was tall, dark and unsmiling, his greeting polite but distant. She had gazed up at him in frank curiosity until her mother hissed a warning, whereupon Serena obediently lowered her eyes and dropped the requisite curtsy. A moment later they were ushered up to their rooms, and now, lying wide awake on her bed, Serena could not even recall the color of Lord Egremont's eyes.

They were brown, she thought glumly, seated next to him at dinner. Dark brown to match his scowling brows, and remote, to match his manner toward her. He treated her with the polite deference one might expect of a distant cousin or casual acquaintance, and discouraged any but the most impersonal talk between them. The most intimate question he asked her all evening was whether she cared for the stuffed artichokes, or would she prefer the creamed asparagus, or both?

"Creamed asparagus, please," she murmured, and wondered why she seemed so tongue-tied. It was not her wont, but somehow the piercing eyes of her mother and the aloofness of the marquis overwhelmed her.

The rest of the company, she noted, was having no better time of it. The duke and duchess made a valiant effort to keep conversation flowing, but they did not receive much help. Lord Egremont contributed little but his forbidding countenance, and his sister Olivia was either extremely timid or by nature taciturn. This Serena put down to her youth—with her delicate face and soft blond hair, the girl looked hardly out of the schoolroom. Serena hoped she might further her acquaintance later.

As for her parents, the earl joined the conversation only when the subject turned to horses. And her mother seemed bent on emphasizing, at every turn, the superiority of Stoneleigh over Luntsford Court.

"Luntsford is a very gracious home, I am persuaded, my dear Duchess," said her mother with exaggerated sweetness in between bites of braised goose, "but, of course, nothing can compare to the grandeur of generations. Stoneleigh Manor is much older, you must know, the earl's title dating back nearly several centuries prior to the dukedom, is that not so?"

Serena wanted to sink under the table, but the duke replied affably, his dark eyes twinkling, "Indeed, you are correct, Lady Stoneleigh. Our title only dates to Charles I. We are mere upstarts, I fear."

The countess turned rather pink and Serena nearly choked on her mirth and her wine. But she sobered soon enough when she noted that Lord Egremont's expression had not changed; he had none of his father's sense of humor, it seemed.

Her mood brightened when, after coffee in the drawing room, the duchess suggested that the marquis show Serena the conservatory. Perhaps now they might become acquainted. But her hope was momentarily dashed as her mother rose to accompany them.

"Ah, Lady Stoneleigh, perhaps you might stay to hear Olivia sing," the duchess ventured quickly.

"I hardly think they should be allowed—" began the countess haughtily, but the duke, rising as well, interrupted firmly.

"Yes, stay, pray do, Lady Stoneleigh." And then he added more softly, "They are betrothed, after all."

Her mother's rather gaunt body stiffened. "With all due respect, your grace, I—"

"Yes, wife, do stay," her father seconded with a meaningful look, and to Serena's amazement, her mother acquiesced.

Not that her presence would have signified, Serena thought helplessly, as she and the marquis strolled the aisles of the conservatory a few minutes later. For Lord Egremont was more interested in his father's orchids than in his prospective bride. He went on about them at some length, yet without a hint of passion. Serena, who normally loved flowers, found herself forming a rapid distaste for orchids.

"And do you like horses, my lord?" she interjected at one point, eager to draw him out.

"Why, yes," he replied woodenly, "I believe them to be an effective means of transport." To which quelling reply the normally garrulous Serena could vouchsafe no rejoinder, and lapsed into miserable silence.

The marquis then shifted the talk to hybrid roses. And so it went until, without so much as taking her arm, he ushered her back to the company in the drawing room. She could not fault his manners, for he was unfailingly polite, yet his remote indifference

20

dismayed her. How, she wondered in despair, could she ever marry such a man?

"And you expect me to marry *that*?" demanded Richard of his parents, flinging his hand toward the heavy door of the library, through which the Lady Serena had but lately passed. As country visits went, this one, but two days old, was in his opinion an unmitigated disaster.

"Now, Richard, I really do not think you are giving the girl a chance. Stalking the corridor with that fierce scowl. Why, she must be terrified of you." The duke was sprawled comfortably on the leather tufted sofa, his wife tucked under his arm.

"Oh, fine thing," continued Richard, pacing the floor. "A mouse into the bargain. Father, you simply cannot be serious about this. She's—she's—oh, it's hopeless, I tell you. She has not a modicum of conversation, nor charm. Her hair is a veritable bird's nest, her manner of dress ludicrous, her—"

"Oh, I grant you her wardrobe needs a bit of doing. But you must not lay it all at her door. Her parents, particularly Lady Stoneleigh, are a bit nip-farthing, I should say," interjected the duchess with a twinkle in her eye. "But as to the rest, I tell you she has wit *and* charm. And she is an artist, you know."

"Oh, Mother, every girl who has ever suffered a governess paints watercolors," Richard retorted, exasperated.

"That is *not* what I meant, Richard. She has an artist's eye and, I believe, depth of feeling. You really must make an attempt to get to know her, my dear."

"I should say she has rather a comely face, under all that hair," mused the duke. "And she has very nice eyes, you know."

"Perhaps," admitted Richard grudgingly, slowing his pace. Her eyes *were* rather striking, an unusual shade of deep blue, that is, when they were visible beneath the mounds of dark brown hair she wound so casually about her head. "But still you must see it will not do. Why, I cannot imagine her ever becoming mistress of Luntsford. She has neither the carriage nor the bearing to command the servants, to be hostess to—"

"You forget, Richard," his mother put in gently, "that she is the daughter of an earl, trained, no doubt since childhood, to assume this very role. And you are wrong, you know. She *does* have the presence—one need not have golden ringlets in order to have proper carriage and bearing."

Richard flushed at this reference to Caroline Lister and sank down into a chair across from the sofa. He knew he had not been quite fair to Lady Serena. But he could not help it. "Still and all—"

"Still and all, Richard," echoed his father, "your mother and I have a suggestion for you. You and Lady Serena are, of course, welcome to make your home here. But such a situation can sometimes prove trying for a young couple." He paused and glanced pointedly down at his wife. Richard had vague memories of his grandmother as something of a tartar. "You might want to set up an establishment of your own. Wheatfield Hall is quite beautiful and has been standing empty too long. I should be happy to have it opened for you, should you wish it. It's smaller than Luntsford, of course; not nearly as daunting for a young bride, I should think."

For the first time a glimmer of a smile came to Richard's face. "You are very kind, Father. I am persuaded it would—er—mitigate matters—but I have not yet—"

"Yes, I am certain it would, Richard. Do speak to Serena about it," the duchess chimed in, patting her husband's hand.

Richard frowned. "You have not been very encouraging to her, Richard," the duke said. "Nor has Livvy been, come to think on it."

"So I've noticed," Richard said with a sigh. "Livvy is quite taken with Caroline, you see."

"Oh, dear. I suppose I had ought to speak to the child," the duchess said, looking up at her husband, who nodded and then spoke once more to his son.

"Has it ever occurred to you, Richard, that Lady Serena might be as—shall we say—hesitant about this marriage as you are?" inquired the duke.

Richard's eyebrows shot up. "You think that *she* doesn't want to marry *me*?" His voice held unabashed amazement.

"Oh, such modesty, such humility," drawled his mother dramatically, her green eyes twinkling.

"Now Mother, that is not at all what I meant. 'Tis simply that I've yet to meet the girl who would not give her right arm for the coronet."

"You *did* say this one was different, did you not?" asked the duke, and Richard grimaced.

Serena stood before her parents in the sitting room of the beautiful guest suite at Luntsford Court.

Somehow she had to talk them out of this dreadful betrothal. "But Mama, Lord Egremont is—is positively forbidding! Why, he hardly talks to me. I do not think he likes me at all!" she wailed, wringing her hands.

"Stuff and nonsense, Serena. You must simply exert yourself to be more agreeable to his lordship," said Lady Stoneleigh, standing before the gold damask draperies of the large picture window. "You must find out what his interests are and try to draw him into conversation."

"He studies insects," Serena said bluntly.

"Insects?" the countess shuddered.

"Insects?" echoed the earl from his stance at the mantel.

"Yes, insects," Serena replied implacably. It was not, she told herself, that she had anything against insects. It was simply that she thought that any man with the slightest claim to a romantic nature would at least be handy with his fives, or have a mad passion for horses, but—insects?

"Nonetheless, you might at least show some degree of animation. Certainly you might praise his home. It is quite impressive, though furnished a little too simply for my tastes," snapped Lady Stoneleigh.

Luntsford *was* a lovely home, Serena thought miserably, but he didn't want her here. Only today the marquis had informed her, in the most wooden of tones, that if she wished they might take up residence at the family home in Hertfordshire instead of here in Kent. He had said it was her choice, but it was clear from his aloof manner that he had no wish to install her as his bride at the family seat. But all she said now was,

24

"Yes, Mama," and then her gaze shifted to her father.

"Yes, you must acquaint yourself well with Luntsford Court, Serena," he declared. "And as for Lord Egremont, he exhibits the natural reserve of an Englishman, born and bred to one of the highest positions in the land. You will accord him the proper respect at all times. And he is, you know, rather handsome," the earl ended with a hint of a smile.

Serena supposed he *was* handsome enough in his own way. But with his dark hair, even darker eyes, and hawklike nose, he reminded her more of a gypsy than a Viking. But a very cold gypsy, she thought miserably.

"He is a cold man, Father," she said, before she'd thought better of it. "Not at all what I—"

"Enough of this nonsense, Serena," interrupted her mother acidly. "You are merely being missish. You are young, so it is understandable that you should be frightened of—certain things in marriage. But you will become accustomed to men and their ways soon enough." She gave a shudder of distaste and Serena glanced from her to the earl. "You will do your duty," her mother continued in a chilly voice, "just as I did; just as all women do."

Serena tried to catch her father's eyes, but he turned away from her, his expression bleak. And suddenly she realized that he, too, was trapped. They all were. There was no hope for it.

Serena stood stoically before her vanity, nearly oblivious to the two maids at her feet, fiddling with last minute tucks of the lace and fastening of loose pearls on her wedding gown. In truth, had she closed her eyes she would have had a great deal of difficulty describing the gown she was even now wearing, so little interest had she taken in its design. At first she had suggested that the gown was far too fussy for her, but her mother waved her objections aside as another bit of fustian. And so a mask of indifference had settled on Serena. And besides, how could one take pleasure in the design of a wedding gown or bridesclothes when one was marrying a cold, aloof stranger? She, who had never in her life been at a loss for words, could not seem to hold a three minute conversation with the man. She realized that he was probably no more happy about the marriage than she. But, as she had heard dozens of times in the past weeks, Gowers had married Wexleys for centuries, and so it would be.

But dammit, he might make some effort to be conciliating! She remembered asking him, during her brief visit to Luntsford, about his study of insects. What was it that he found so fascinating about them? she'd asked. He had replied in polite, remote tones that it was very serious work, not anything likely to interest a woman and would she care to see the picture gallery?

She thought now, despairingly, that that was the most interesting conversation she'd had yet with this man who would be her husband within a few short hours. It did not augur well for the future.

Richard ventured a glance at his bride as they stood before the altar. Her gown was so weighted down with flounces and pearls that it was a wonder her small frame could carry it. There seemed to have been some attempt made to discipline her hair, but still, long dark

26

brown wavy strands escaped at every opportunity.

He could not help the picture of golden ringlets that flashed before him and quickly squelched it, bringing his mind back to the present. Serena's eyes *were* rather extraordinary, he noted, but his thoughts were arrested by the look on her face. My God, did he look as glum as she did? This would not do at all.

"Smile," he whispered to her. "We must put a good face on it." She turned her lips into a smile that did not reach her eyes, and he was once again glad her clutch-fisted parents had disparaged the idea of a grand wedding at St. George's in Hanover Square. He would not want all the *ton* to bear witness to this sealing of his fate.

Serena stared out the window as the coach lumbered south toward the coast. The wedding and the days preceding it had passed in a complete blur. Even now she could recall only bits and pieces. She remembered dancing with the duke at the wedding breakfast; he had tried to make her laugh with amusing stories of her husband's childhood. Lord Egremont's three young cousins had made a great effort to be solemn and polite, though she knew they were itching to be away again at play. The duchess had been all that was gracious, but Olivia puzzled Serena. She had hoped to find a friend in her new sister, who was only one year her junior, but for some reason Olivia seemed to have taken her in dislike. Serena could not think why; they hardly knew each other.

It was then that her thoughts shifted back to her husband of a few hours. She hardly knew him, either. When the carriage had rolled away from Stoneleigh he had asked if she were comfortable. Would she care for a cushion, or a bite of apple tart from the hamper that had been packed for them? He had been all that was polite, saying nothing more, nothing less, than was proper. He had made occasional impersonal comments about the passing landscape, but otherwise had remained silent, his face unreadable. Serena, whose inclination it was to be anything but silent, to say, in fact, exactly what she thought, was at a complete loss. She had tried several times to engage him in conversation, but his formal replies had quite discouraged her. Would she ever break through his impassive mask?

She turned her head and gazed covertly at her husband. He was really very striking looking. He was quite tall, not perhaps of the stature of a Viking, but a full head taller than she. His hair, almost the color of her own, fell in perfect waves that hers would never achieve. His nose and jawline were strong, unyielding, and his dark brown eyes were ever cold. His mouth was generous, though, his lips full, and she wondered whether there was any hidden warmth in him, after all. Probably not, she thought irritably, and gazed once more out the window.

They were to spend then next three weeks in "a charming little seaside cottage," the duchess had said. "A perfect place for a young couple to get to know one another, much better than racketing about the Continent the first few weeks of marriage, I should say. The duke and I love Gateshead Cottage; we have used it as a hideaway many times over the years." Serena recalled the duchess' words now in abject misery. She doubted that she and Lord Egremont would ever make use of a "hideaway" cottage, and as for the next few weeks — she had no notion of how they would ever pass the time. But even that was not as daunting as the one thought that began to loom larger the closer they came to Gateshead. Lord Egremont hardly spoke to her, but tonight was their wedding night, and surely he would expect . . . Desperately she pushed her thoughts in another direction.

Chapter Two

Serena stood at the window of her bedchamber clad in a white lawn nightgown buttoned up to her chin. Her new maid, Hannah, had left her but a few moments ago, and she knew that in a short while the connecting door between their rooms would open and her husband would come through. She shivered in spite of the warm September night. It was one thing to share a carriage ride, or even a formal, four course dinner, with a cold, aloof stranger. It was quite another to share a bed with him!

She heard the soft click of the door and watched him approach. He wore a burgundy dressing gown and walked slowly, deliberately toward her. She was glad the room was dark save for the moonlight streaming in. Oh, she thought, if only she knew what was to happen now, she would not be so unaccustomedly frightened!

Richard regarded his bride steadily as he slowly

traversed the room. She looked absurdly young and innocent in that nightgown, which covered nearly every inch of her body. Trust Lady Stoneleigh to choose such a garment for her daughter's wedding night, he thought wryly. Serena's deep blue eyes were wide and luminous in the moonlight as he came to stand before her. But it was her hair that caught and held his gaze. The same hair that looked disheveled when caught up in a travesty of a bun yet looked luxuriously thick and rich cascading past her shoulders.

"Good evening, Serena," he said, and reached a tentative hand up to grasp a lock of her hair.

"Good evening, my lord," she whispered, and he felt her tense at his touch. He looked into her eyes and saw her fear, and though instinct told him to be patient, gentle, yet he felt a stab of annoyance, or was it disappointment? Caroline would not have been frightened. He had only kissed her several times, but she had always responded warmly, though modestly.

But this was not Caroline, he told himself angrily, and wound his fingers through the hair that was the wrong color. Slowly he lowered his lips to hers. Serena stood rigid, unmoving. The lips beneath his were cold and unyielding. He encircled her waist with his free hand and pulled her closer. She did not resist, nor did she offer the least encouragement. It was like kissing a stone pillar. Never had he met with such lack of response, the fact that his partners had all been experienced women notwithstanding. That he should be shackled to a woman who obviously did not want him filled him with despair, and then anger. Abruptly he pulled away from her.

"I will not force my intentions where they are not wanted," he said icily. "I never have and I do not intend to start now. I shall not come to you again until you indicate that you wish me to. I bid you good evening, ma'am." He bowed formally, turned on his heel and strode from the room, ignoring her astonished spluttering.

The minute he attained his own room and slammed the door behind him he knew that his action had been rash, even unjust. It was not Serena's fault that she was not Caroline. And as to the rest—well—the chit was probably terrified of him. They hardly knew each other, and he did not suppose she knew very much about marital intimacy either. Who would have told her, after all? Certainly not her clutch-fisted, thin-lipped mother. He was appalled at his own insensitive behavior and thought he ought to go back, to talk to her and soothe her fears. But his pride would not let him, nor would the sudden image of Caroline, her eyes filled with tears the day he'd told her of his impending marriage. Besides, he told himself, Serena would not welcome him now. She was probably relieved that he had gone, with his promise not to return.

Serena had stared wide-eyed at her husband's retreating back, unable to do more than stammer the beginnings of a protest. She stood baffled now he had gone, wondering what she had done wrong. Indeed, she had no idea what she was supposed to have done. Contrary to her father's belief, she had read only a few books of a romantic nature. And those when she was fourteen or fifteen, when her friend Elspeth had smuggled them to her. But then Elspeth had been sent away to school (of which her own mother did not approve as allowing too much freedom) and that had ended.

There had been very little in Elspeth's books to further her education in such matters at all events. Of late she had read a novel by the new authoress, Jane Austen, and several other works, and so she had some idea of love, of the communication of spirit between two people. But she knew very little of passion and nothing at all of the marriage bed.

But there was one thing she did know — no heir could come of that cold, unfeeling kiss. And suddenly Serena was very angry. He hadn't even given her a chance! Damn him! Did he expect her to have the experience of a lightskirt? Well, she was not about to indulge in a fit of the sulks for his sake. Though they had arrived at dusk, she had seen that the cottage was beautifully situated. She would draw and paint and enjoy the scenery, with him or without him! She would act, in fact, as if nothing were amiss. And did he really expect her to invite him back to her chamber? Hah! So much, she thought, for the precious Gower heir!

Serena glided into the breakfast room with an easy smile and light step.

"Good morning, my lord," she chirped, as if she had never slept better.

Blast it all! thought the marquis, for he'd slept fitfully at best. Didn't she feel the slightest bit overset about last night's events, or lack thereof?

Apparently not. She advanced to the sideboard and, remembering his manners, Richard stood up. "May I help you?" he managed.

"No, I'm right; do — do sit down," she said, but he didn't. He remained standing, studying her as she heaped her plate. She wore a midnight blue muslin dress, the simplest garment he had seen her in to date. For the first time, without all those overskirts and flounces, he could see that her figure was quite lovely — slim and supple and rounded in all the right places.

He seated her when she was ready and poured her coffee. Then he sat down opposite and regarded her intently, as she buttered her bread. An arrested look came into his eyes as he realized that she actually looked quite pretty, and he wondered why the simple expedient of a dress should make it so. Certainly its hue brought out the magnificent deep blue of her eyes, but it was more than that. His gaze took in her creamy, glowing complexion, her small, perfectly formed nose and the soft pink lips that did not look nearly so cold as they'd felt last night. Her hair was as hopeless as ever, but somehow this morning it looked almost charming in its disarray. He looked again at her dress and then suddenly he understood. The simplicity and color of the gown suited her, and it was as if she had come alive. Only yesterday, in the carriage, she had looked like a drowning cat in a hideous olive green carriage dress embellished with layers of lace and gewgaws. He felt now as if he were seeing her for the first time. He remembered what his mother had said about her artist's eye and knew she had chosen the dress herself.

"Your dress is lovely," he ventured, strangely hesitant.

"Thank you, my lord," she said quietly, and sipped her coffee.

"Did you choose it yourself, Serena?"

"I — well — in a manner of speaking," was all she said, and then busied herself with her scrambled eggs. What the devil would it take to draw her out? He cocked his head in question and waited.

"I had to talk Mama round to this color at first stop. She—ah—prefers me in yellows and greens."

"So I'd noticed," he said dryly and caught a reluctant twinkle in her eye.

"And then I—well—I convinced one of the maids to help me tear off all the lace and furbelows and burn it all before Mama was the wiser," she added with a glint in her eyes.

He was surprised at that hint of mischief but answered in kind. "Your mother does seem to have—er—definite ideas about dress."

"Yes, and it has gotten worse of late. She was very firm about what manner of dress befit my new station in life."

The look in her eyes could only be called irreverent and Richard bristled. "You do not take your new station seriously, Serena?" he asked quietly.

The smile left her eyes and she put down her fork. "I do not take clothing all that seriously, Richard. As to my station—I hope I shall do what is expected of me, but, in truth, I have not thought much on it."

"Haven't thought much—do you realize, my lady, that you are a marchioness? That you will one day be a *duchess*?" he demanded.

"Yes," she replied in a soft but steady voice. "But I should think there are more important considerations when one enters into marriage."

"Such as?" he countered, not bothering to temper his annoyance.

"Such as the compatibility of the individuals involved," she retorted tartly and stabbed at her eggs.

They continued their meal in silence.

After breakfast the marquis had politely asked whether she would care to take a walk. She had tendered a guarded yes and would my lord mind if she took a sketch pad? No, he wouldn't, and would she mind if he took his spy glass?

The conversation had been inane in its formality and now as she awaited him at the cottage door she felt growing exasperation. She supposed they had made some headway at breakfast — they'd had what might be termed a conversation, but he had quickly ended it with his display of consequence. As to last night, it was obvious that that would not be discussed, for which she was most grateful.

"Where is your bonnet, Serena?" he asked as they stepped out into the sunshine.

"I do not like wearing a bonnet. I've too much hair for it, actually. And since there is no one here I did not deem it necessary."

He opened his mouth to say something but then thought better of it, contenting himself with a frown. She determined not to let him put her out of countenance and allowed him to lead her round the back of the cottage.

The view that greeted her made her gasp. "It's beautiful," she breathed. Gateshead was situated atop a grassy knoll overlooking the Channel. There was a fairly steep drop to the white sandy beach below and she had the sudden urge to scamper down and kick off her boots.

"We can take a picnic hamper down there tomorrow

if you like," he said, almost smiling.

"Oh, I should love it," she replied, and almost clapped her hands in delight. But she refrained; he would probably not think it befitting her station in life.

They walked around to the front again and onto a winding lane lined with carefully tended flowers. Cobbs, who with his wife served as caretaker at Gateshead, was an avid gardener, the marquis explained, and then proceeded to name some of the flowers and other vegetation as they passed. He led her through a grassy area and then to a small wood, all the while persisting in his monologue with all the animation of a tour guide addressing two dozen people. She remembered his father's orchids, and began to despair of the day, when she espied a bird's nest just ahead.

"May we stop here for a bit?" she asked.

"Yes, if you wish," he answered woodenly.

She murmured a thank you and crept toward the beech tree. Silently, she sank to the ground with her pad in hand. She could hear the squeaking of the chicks but none were visible. She would wait them out. It was not Serena's style to paint wide landscape vistas. She preferred to concentrate on small things—a cluster of berries and leaves, for instance, or tiny animals. She would sketch out-of-doors and later paint. She had once spent nearly two hours on her belly drawing a hedgehog, trying to get the swirl of his fur just right. Now she began to sketch the nest and surrounding branches, trying to memorize the shadings of color that she would later fill in. Her husband regarded her curiously, then shrugged and turned away. When finally a little yellow head bobbed up, she nearly forgot the marquis, so intent was she on her work.

She remembered when she heard him give a muffled exclamation. The chick disappeared and she rose and went to her husband. He stood just two yards away, spyglass aloft.

"What is it?" she asked softly.

"Nothing of interest. Just a caterpillar," he said brusquely. "Shall we go?"

She nodded, refraining from a tart comment about the unusual pastime of insect watching. She was very glad that she would have her painting to occupy her this afternoon.

And so she did, his lordship having announced at luncheon that he would spend the afternoon reading in the library. They met again at dinner, a formal, proper affair, after which he bade her a distant goodnight. At least, she told herself as she trudged up the stairs, they would never argue overmuch. He was too damned polite.

Richard viewed this morning's outing to the beach with mixed feelings. He could not understand why a man of his equanimity should so easily be put out of countenance by Serena. He did not quite know what to make of this wife he had acquired. She vexed him, but she also intrigued him, and then there had been those few moments yesterday morning when he'd felt the stirrings of attraction . . .

"I'm ready, my lord," Serena said, fairly skipping down the stairs, sketch pad and bonnet in hand. He could not help thinking that Caroline would *never* skip down the stairs . . .

"A bonnet, Serena?" he asked mockingly.

38

"There are no trees on the beach, you must know, and though I do love the sunshine — well — it *can* get a bit too hot," she replied. He frowned, remembering another speech about too much sunshine.

His eyes flitted over her; she wore a thin yellow muslin dress with too many ruffles.

"Mama is very partial to ruffles," she said ruefully.

He was immediately contrite. He did not wish her to feel the need to apologize. "Actually, Serena, I was thinking that you look rather charming," he countered, for the ruffles did not quite hide all her assets. "But should you wish to replenish your wardrobe when we go home to Wheatfield, I shall have no objection."

"Thank you," was all she said, and they proceeded on their way.

Richard elected to carry the picnic hamper himself, the steep descent to the beach being rather too much for old Cobbs to negotiate. He wedged the hamper into the shade of a boulder and then spread a blanket he had brought. He waited for Serena to be seated but she had other ideas. She rapidly kicked off her tiny boots and then bent over, her back to him, to remove her stockings.

"Serena, I —" he began, scandalized. But then he stopped, realizing she would think him absurd. They were married, if only in the legal sense, and so he supposed it was not all that improper. But he could not help thinking that Caroline would never have done such a thing.

Serena turned back and looked quizzically at him, a decided twinkle in her eye. "Care to join me?" she asked. His eyes travelled down to her bare feet and ankles, peeking out from beneath her skirt. Of course

39

he would not wish to—but as her feet sank into the sand, he remembered the feel of smooth sand between his toes, and water slapping at his ankles. It had been years . . .

Moments later they were both headed, quite barefoot, to the water's edge. They walked in surprisingly companionable silence for some time. The sun felt warm and soothing and the cool water tickled their feet. Every so often Serena would gather up her skirts and dart further into the water, letting it splash up to her calves. He found himself wishing she would not do so; it was disconcerting in a way he would rather not contemplate.

He felt a trace of sweat on his brow and shrugged off his black coat, throwing it over his shoulder. He rolled up his sleeves and watched Serena do the same. He found himself studying her covertly—the way her body moved when she bent to trace the water with her fingertips, the flash of naked calf as she flirted with the sea. At one time he caught her gazing quite steadily at him and when their eyes met she flushed becomingly. He thought it was time they went back, but it was Serena who spoke first.

"Oh, it is such fun, is it not? I had not thought the September sun to be so hot. I declare I should dearly love to swim!" she exclaimed, and then her eyes widened and she blushed crimson.

So, she had some sense of propriety after all. "I do not think that would be possible, Serena. You could not swim alone, for it is dangerous, and—"

"Oh, but I did it all the time at home!" she blurted, and her eyes lit with mischief. "Mama never knew, of course, but—" His eyebrows shot up. It seemed that his bride was not the meek little mouse he'd thought her to be. "But I am a very good swimmer." She stopped, seeing his look, and snapped, "Do you mean to stop here for three weeks, my lord, and *never* go swimming?"

"You are impertinent, Serena," he said sternly, but she didn't reply. She just stood there, water to her ankles, hands on her hips, waiting for his answer. There was fire in those deep blue eyes, and he knew, as he said the words, that they were ill-advised. "Well, I suppose I might—er—turn around until you are in the water."

"Certainly you might, and I shall of course wear my chemise."

His eyes flashed at such improper speech, but she was already racing to the blanket.

He kept several yards away from the blanket until she was safely in the water, all the while wondering what she would look like in a clinging, wet chemise.

"Why don't you join me, my lord?" she called. "It's lovely."

"No!" he barked, unaccountably vexed by the question. He sat down to watch her, but the sun was too damned hot. He recalled again his father's words about sunshine and assured himself that he loved the sunlight.

"I'm coming out now," she called after a time, and he quickly removed himself from the area. When he returned it was to find her standing beside the blanket, struggling with the buttons at the back of her dress.

"Here, let me help you," he said without thinking, and moved behind her. Most of her hair had come down and he had to push the thick wet locks aside to

41

reach the buttons. Her body felt warm under his touch, even through the layers of petticoats, and he found his fingers fumbling with the decidedly simple task. "There," he said when he had done, and turned her around to face him. Her dress had become wet, and it clung to her in a most revealing way.

Her color was high and involuntarily he reached a hand up and grazed her cheek with his fingertip. "Your hair is beautiful when it's down," he heard himself rasp.

"I—ah—thank you, my lord," she stammered, and swallowed hard. She took a step back from him and pulled the last locks free of their pins. She shook her head and her thick, heavy, mane spilled past her shoulders and down her back. She tried to wring it out, and then began to wind it about her head again. He could not help staring and at length she said, "I—ah—rather like my hair down as well. It is much more comfortable, you see, for it is too heavy to be constantly confined with pins. But Mama bade me put it up when I was fifteen."

"That seems a bit young."

"So I told Mama, but she said my hair was indecent and must be hidden. Is that not the outside of enough? Oh, and how often I have longed to run through the woods with not one single blasted pin in my head!" she concluded with an impish look in her eye that set alarm bells ringing in his head. He would not have thought Serena to be in the least mischievous, and he suspected there was much he did not know about his wife.

He opened his mouth to speak but his eye was caught by a crumpled wet bit of flimsy white fabric on the blanket. "Serena, is that not your—er—"

"Why, of course, my lord," she answered calmly,

following his gaze.

"Do you mean to say you took—that is—that you stood here—ah—" he stammered, quite beside himself.

"Of course, I did, my lord. You did not expect me to put my dress on over a soaking wet chemise, did you?"

Since that was exactly what he *had* expected, he said nothing, but glared fiercely at her.

"Why, I should catch a chill, or at the least be highly uncomfortable. And I do assure you the beach is quite deserted. Even *you* were nowhere to be seen."

That was hardly the point, he thought, running his fingers through his hair abruptly. She was just too damned innocent for her own good!

Serena awoke the next morning feeling more cheerful than she had in weeks. She had actually had *fun* yesterday. True, her husband had resumed his formal tone after their interlude on the beach, and she still could not breach the barrier he had erected between them, but there had been those moments . . . There had been other moments, too, that she did not understand. She blushed even now as she remembered how she stared at him in his shirtsleeves. She did not know when she had ever seen a man thus, and she had found it strangely disconcerting. She recalled his lean, muscled back and the way the black hair curled on his forearms . . . She was grateful when Hannah came to help her dress.

Richard suggested at breakfast that they spend the morning in the garden. He might read and she could draw. She agreed readily but asked if she might set up her painting easel outside. He wondered why she felt the need to ask permission for so reasonable a request.

They passed a rather agreeable morning, and though they spoke little, the silence was not unpleasant. In the afternoon they went for a walk, and he was not quite sure how it was, but he ended up talking about how caterpillars turn into butterflies. Amazingly, Serena seemed interested.

They were quite a way from the cottage when dark clouds suddenly rolled across the sunny skies and let loose a torrent of rain. Richard grabbed her hand and together they ran through the trees and down the lane toward Gateshead. Cobbs was nowhere to be seen when they pushed the door open and stumbled, breathless, into the vestibule. They were still holding hands, alternately laughing and gasping for breath as they leaned back against the closed door.

"My goodness, but that was fun! Oh, but we must be a sight!" she exclaimed, giggling and pulling a wet clump of hair away from her brow. His eyes widened at her idea of fun but she went on. "I am sure I look frightful and you—"here her voice softened in concern and she turned to face him. "Oh, my lord, here you have given me your coat and now you are drenched." Her eyes lingered quite a long time on his shoulders and chest, his white shirt quite plastered to his skin. She colored, and he thought she shivered.

"No more are you, my dear," he said softly, his eyes taking in her own form, the wet dress clinging to her contours despite his coat. Her blush deepened and he took a step closer to her and pressed her hand warmly. With his free hand he brushed the remaining hair from her face. "You'll catch a chill, Serena. I think we both need a warm bath and a hot fire. Do you not agree?" he whispered, smiling.

"Y-yes, I—I should like that, my lord," she stammered, and then looked down at their clasped hands as if noticing them for the first time. She quickly looked back up at him with an expression in her eyes that he could not quite define. Was it uncertainty, fear, or—or distaste? Abruptly, he dropped her hand and took a step back. "I suggest we retire to right ourselves," he said impassively.

They were polite and formal with each other for the rest of the day.

It was the next morning, the fourth day after their wedding, that the messenger arrived from Luntsford Court. Richard and Serena were seated at breakfast when Cobbs showed him in.

"It be urgent, my lord," the man said as he handed the missive to Richard.

Richard waited until he'd gone before breaking the ducal seal. His face was pale as he read his mother's scrawled hand.

"I—it seems my father has taken ill, Serena. Pneumonia. He's delirious with fever and they fear—well—my mother is quite distraught. I'm afraid we shall have to return immediately to Luntsford."

"Of course, my lord." She rose and came to him.

"I'm sorry to cut short our—"

"Nonsense, my lord," she said softly, putting a hand on his sleeve. "Of course we must go. Not but what it is very beautiful here; perhaps we may return at another time. For now, you are needed at home, and you could never relax here at all events."

He smiled gratefully at her and was not pleased at the thought that Caroline would never have reacted thusly. She would have pouted prettily and implored him with fluttering eyelashes to await further news before rushing home. And he would have felt a cad for refusing her.

Chapter Three

The carriage rolled into the sweeping circular drive of Luntsford Court and came to a halt before the great marble staircase. A footman appeared to let down the carriage step and Richard wasted no time alighting and then turning to help Serena down. When he turned back it was to see a flurry of servants descending the staircase, followed by three women: his mother, Livvy, and — good God! What the devil was Caroline doing here?

And then his mother was upon them, hugging them both. "Serena, Richard," she said in a tremulous voice, "thank you for coming." Richard thought she looked like hell, but it was Serena who spoke first.

"Of course we came, your grace," she said kindly. "How is the duke?"

His mother shook her head. "He is delirious with fever," she replied.

And then suddenly they seemed to be surrounded by a small army of servants, struggling with bandboxes, trunks, and a rather large painting easel. They moved aside to let them pass, and somehow Serena ended up several feet away, face to face with Caroline and Livvy.

"Hello, Serena," Livvy said coolly, slipping her arm through Caroline's. Richard stiffened and felt his mother's hand on his sleeve. "I'd like you to meet my very particular friend, Caroline Lister. She's staying here too, so we shall all be very cozy." There was a decidedly unpleasant note in Livvy's voice and Richard's eyes flashed.

"What the devil is she *doing* here, Mother?" he whispered fiercely.

"Oh, Richard, 'tis such a coil. That brother of hers left for the Continent, leaving her with none but an aging housekeeper, and she but eighteen years old. Livvy implored me to have her, and I really could not let her stay alone. You must remember that I had no reason to expect you—you were to go to Wheatfield after Gateshead."

"But, Mother, I—"

"Of course, I realize that now it will not serve," his mother interrupted. "Caroline was so distraught at first that she could not recall the name of a single relation, but she has since given me the direction of some distant cousins in Yorkshire, and I have written them. What else can I do?"

"Little enough, I expect," Richard said heavily, "except keep an eye on Livvy. I do not like her tone to Serena." He paused and then said, "I'm sorry, Mother. You have quite enough on your mind as it is. 'Tis just that—well—Serena knows nothing about Caroline, you see."

The duchess seemed about to speak but their attention was claimed by a trill of forced feminine laughter. "I cannot wear that color myself, but I own it is most interesting," Livvy drawled, and Richard decided it was time to step into the breach.

But when he came to Serena's side, and thus close to Caroline, he felt his breath catch in his throat. Caroline looked like a frothy confection in a pale lemon yellow gown of the flimsiest muslin decency allowed. Her perfect ringlets framed her chiseled face and Richard felt his heart lurch with almost physical pain. He was suddenly annoyed that Serena had worn her hideous green carriage dress, but he knew that was unfair. With difficulty he said, "Miss Lister is our neighbor, Serena. Miss Lister, may I present my wife, Serena, Lady Egremont."

"I am charmed, Lady Egremont. Livvy and Richard and I are such very good friends, you see, and now here *you* are. I am persuaded we shall all go on famously! Do you not agree, Richard?" Richard blanched at her use of his given name, chagrined that he had ever given her leave to use it. No more did he care for what she said. Had he not known Caroline's sweet temperament better, he would swear she was trying to make Serena feel the interloper. Serena's face was very still and he tried to think of a suitable reply. He was most grateful when his mother intervened.

"Oh, my dears, I own you must be positively fagged to death from your travels. We must not keep you standing about. Do come inside. Richard, perhaps you'd like to look in on your father, and I'll see Serena settled. I thought we might postpone the presentation of the servants until you'd had a chance to rest."

"Thank you, Mother," Richard said with a smile, and after a nod toward Caroline and Livvy, he propelled Serena and his mother up the stairs, before going on his way.

For some reason she could not quite define, Serena had found the scene of their arrival rather uncomfortable. Livvy had been decidedly cool, but it was more than that. Richard had seemed almost agitated and Miss Lister—well—Miss Lister's words had been friendly enough, but Serena's instincts told her that they were not sincere.

"Ah, here we are," said the duchess, and Serena realized that she had been so absorbed in her own thoughts that she had hardly noticed the majestic horseshoe staircase in the entry lobby, nor the rows of spacious apartments they had passed on their way. "I do hope you will be comfortable here," Lady Luntsford continued, throwing open the highly polished doors. " 'Tis a very spacious suite, and it has a lovely aspect."

Serena's eyes swept the large room with its intricately carved furnishings. It was done in shades of blue, the draperies and several chairs a deep blue to match her eyes. But she found the focal point of the room a bit disconcerting; it was a huge four-poster bed with carved cherubs that seemed to be hanging everywhere.

"It's beautiful, your grace," she said after a moment.

"Yes, I think the colors suit you. But I own I did not have time to prepare the room just as I'd liked. I daresay there is too much furniture, or perhaps it is simply arranged badly. But at all events, we can remedy that another day. It's just that I—" the duchess's voice lowered suddenly, and Serena thought her eyes filled. "I have been rather distracted and—and—"

"Of course you have, your grace. And you must not concern yourself with me. I shall be right."

The duchess put a hand up to Serena's cheek. Serena

was oddly touched by the gesture—she could not remember the last time her mother had touched her. "You are a dear. Still, I want you to feel welcome. Now, there is a dressing room beyond here and—"

"Oh, there you be, your grace. Begging your pardon. I'm not meaning to interrupt, but, er—" The medium-sized, pleasantly plump woman in a simple gray dress came bustling into the open doorway. Serena remembered her from her previous stay at Luntsford.

"Not at all," the duchess said. "Serena, this is our housekeeper, Mrs. Grayson. Perhaps you have met, have you not? Mrs. Grayson, may I present Lord Richard's bride, Serena, Lady Egremont." Serena acknowledged the introduction and the housekeeper welcomed her to Luntsford Court. "Now, then, Mrs. Grayson, did you need something?" the duchess asked.

"Yes, your grace. Excuse me, but Cook is needing to consult with you 'bout the menu for dinner."

"But I gave that to her yesterday."

"Yes, your grace. Of course." Mrs. Grayson looked down at her clasped hands. "But—er—it seems you have included two soups and no meat dishes for tonight. And we didn't think, Cook and I, that—"

"Oh, my word, I fear my wits have gone a-begging. Serena, my dear, will you excuse me? Your maid should be along straightaway, and I shall have a spot of tea sent up."

Serena assured her mother-in-law that she would be all right, and when the two women departed she closed the door behind them and turned to study her bed-chamber. The duchess was right, she thought. It was overcrowded with furniture. She slowly circled the

51

room, viewing it from different angles. She noted the two upholstered chairs drawn up to a skirted round table beneath the window, the large bureau, a gilt-leafed escritoire, and—suddenly it dawned on Serena that it was her mother-in-law's second impression that had been correct. The furnishings were simply misaligned. In fact, the whole room seemed a bit lopsided, and Serena's innate sense of balance was quite disturbed by it. And it was really quite obvious once she'd put a finger to the problem. Why, there were two cabriole-legged highboys standing side by side on the narrowest wall of the room, when of a certain they ought to be on opposite sides. And then, the delicate escritoire next the massive bed was—

Her thoughts were interrupted by a knock at the door. Ah, Hannah, she thought and called, "Come in."

But it was not her maid who entered the room; it was Livvy. "Hello, Livvy, do come in," she said graciously, and indicated a chair by the window that she might sit in. But Livvy simply ambled over to the bed and ran her hands over the blue floral coverlet. She smiled in a way that did not quite reach her eyes.

"I hope you like your room, Serena. Mama chose it 'specially, even though she has much to occupy her just now."

"Your mother is very kind," Serena replied, wondering what the girl really wanted.

"Yes, she has been *so* good to Caroline, treating her as one of the family. She's very beautiful, is she not?"

"Yes, the duchess is lovely."

Livvy made a face. "Not Mama, although I daresay she is rather well enough for her age. But no, I meant Caroline. She has a classic face, you know, and such beautiful hair. She is teaching me how to arrange *my* hair in just those ringlets."

Livvy's hair was very fine, not the golden, almost flaxen color of Miss Lister's, but a very pleasing honey blond that blended well with her dark brown eyes.

"I think you will look charming in ringlets, Livvy. And yes, Caroline, is very pretty."

Livvy clasped her hands on one of the bedposts and swung back and forth, a half smile playing at her lips. Then she ran her fingers over one of the naked cherubs. Serena stood next one of the highboys, waiting for Livvy to say her piece. The girl clearly had something on her mind. "Yes, everyone is taken with Caroline," Livvy said in a voice of calculated nonchalance. "Even Richard. He was to have married her, you know. But then, of course, he found out about his betrothal to you."

Serena stood very still, at first thinking she had not heard her right. But then she knew that she had, for it explained so much. Oh, so very much. But Serena was not an earl's daughter for nothing, and for once she was grateful for her mother's rigorous training. She lifted her chin a trifle. "Really, how very interesting," she remarked lightly, for all the world as if Livvy had just related some *on dit* about a third cousin from Bath.

Livvy's eyes hardened. "Yes, they were very much—"

"Oh, my lady, forgive me, but I seem to have lost my way," came a voice from behind a pile of bandboxes negotiating its way through the half-open doorway. Serena had never been so grateful to see a maid, any maid.

"Oh, Hannah, let me help you." She bounded to the

53

doorway and grabbed the two top boxes. Then she turned back to Livvy. "Livvy, if you'll forgive me, I have a great deal to do just now. And I own myself rather tired from our journey."

"Oh, of course, Serena. We can have a comfortable coze later on. I have so-o much to tell you," Livvy cooed and sauntered to the door. Serena was not at all sorry when the girl collided with two footmen staggering under the weight of a huge trunk.

Hannah went immediately to open a door next the dresser and deposit her parcels in what Serena knew must be the dressing room. Serena followed and for several minutes watched Hannah direct various liveried servants in the placement of bandboxes and trunks. She was glad of the distraction, but when all save the maid had departed, Serena felt suddenly very agitated. She began to pace the bedroom with the same frenzy with which her thoughts tumbled about her head. Now she understood only too well her husband's coldness, his seeming anger toward her. And she understood why the meeting with Caroline had been so strained. Oh God, she thought, stopping and leaning her head against the wall, whatever am I to do now?

Suddenly she felt as if she needed activity, any activity, to occupy her mind and her body. She looked around the room and then called to Hannah. The maid came out of the dressing room with two gowns draped over her arm. "Yes, my lady?" Hannah was a large pleasant-faced woman of indeterminate years who somehow always seemed to be smiling. Serena was grateful, not for the first time, that it had been the duchess, and not her own mother, who had chosen her maid for her.

"Hannah, I think perhaps we might unpack in just a few minutes. For now I should like to shift a few things around."

"Shift a few—uh—very well, my lady. I'll just put these things down . . . "

Serena was already pushing the escritoire away from the bed when the maid returned from the dressing room.

"Oh, my lady, you'll be strainin' yerself. A lady like you oughtn't t' be shiftin' furniture, I'll be bound. There are plenty of footmen about if you've a mind for—"

"Oh, no, Hannah, I should like the exercise. At all events, we shan't touch the dresser or the bed, and I am persuaded we can move the other pieces easily enough."

Which is exactly what they did for the next half hour or so. It was when they had the second highboy half way across the powder blue oriental carpet that the door flew open.

"Serena! What in the devil do you think you're doing?" the marquis barked, his large frame filling the doorway.

"Oh, Hannah, that will be all for now," Serena said hurriedly, turning to face her husband. The maid disappeared in seconds.

"Now, would you kindly tell me what in blazes you're about?" her husband demanded, slamming the door behind the maid and striding to Serena. "We are only just arrived and already you are turning the whole house topsy turvy!"

"Not the whole house, my lord. Just one room. *My* room," she retorted.

"No, Serena, not *your* room. *Our* room. Or did you

55

not bother to look? The room beyond the dressing room is a *sitting* room. *This* is the only bedroom."

Her eyes flew to his face. " 'Tis my mother's doing," he went on. "She believes married couples should be as close as possible." His voice was mocking, his expression grim. Was the idea so repulsive to him? But, of course, he had married the wrong woman.

"Well, I — ah — I suppose we may — ah — contrive, my lord."

He looked steadily at her for a moment and then sighed. "Yes, I suppose we may, Serena. There is a sofa in the sitting room. I shall sleep there."

"Oh, no, my lord. I would not think of discommoding you. I am smaller than you — I own I shall be the more comfortable on the sofa."

"I shall take the sofa, Serena! And I do not wish to discuss it further! Now sit down and tell me what the deuce my wife is doing moving furniture about like a common footman."

Serena sank into one of the two upholstered chairs that now stood several feet from the foot of the bed, the area in front of the window having been cleared for the escritoire and her painting easel. The marquis sat opposite her, glowering expectantly.

"Well, my lord, 'tis simply that — well — your mother did indicate that she thought there was something amiss with the room. And she was right. The furnishings were — well — the whole room was quite lopsided, you see. It had no symmetry, no sense of balance." She paused and noted her husband's frown. "But if you wish, my lord, I shall put it all back."

"No, Serena. We might just as well leave it. It does rather give one more of a feeling of spaciousness."

"Oh, I am so pleased that you think so, my lord," Serena exclaimed, leaning forward in her chair. "So if you'd just like to help me shift that highboy a few more feet over to the wall, we—"

"No, Serena. I shall send for a footman straightaway. Have the trunks arrived?"

"Yes, I think most everything is here. How—how is the duke, my lord?"

Her husband lowered his head and put a hand to his brow for a moment. The eyes that looked back at her were bleak. "He doesn't know me, Serena. His face is flushed, his eyes bright with fever."

"Has the doctor been to see him?"

"Yes. He came twice yesterday and once this morning. There is little enough we can do, though—bathe him and keep watch. My mother hardly leaves his side. She will not even let one of the servants stay with him at night."

"Perhaps I might be of help."

"Thank you, Serena. You are very kind. We shall ask, but I imagine she will decline. She came in while I was with him, insisted that I need not stay. She sat down beside him and—and it was as if they were in their own little world. I almost think he was aware of her." His voice had grown soft, and he stared into space.

"Perhaps he is. And I am persuaded that will help him to recover, you know."

He shook his head, his face grim. Then he ran his fingers through his hair. "It came on so suddenly, Serena. Two days ago he was fine. And I shudder to think—oh, God, he's so young. And my mother. She's all to pieces. I've never seen her like this."

"She loves him very much," Serena said quietly.

He regarded her intently. Something in the sad expression in his dark brown eyes made her say what she otherwise would not have done. "My lord, why did you not tell me about Caroline Lister?"

Richard's eyes widened as he stared at his wife. Good Lord, it needed only this. He sighed, knowing it was useless to dissemble, and unfair besides. "How did you find out?"

"Livvy told me."

"Damn!" he muttered. "That child should learn to keep a still tongue in her head."

"I would not have held you to our betrothal, my lord, had I known."

"I believe you, Serena. But there are more than just the two of us involved, and I think you know that. There are centuries of Gowers and Wexleys to account to." His voice sounded bitter in his own ears. Serena lowered her head and he cursed inwardly. What the hell was wrong with him? He softened his voice. "At all events, I knew that to tell you would distress you, and to no purpose. I—I am sorry that she is here, Serena. I certainly did not expect it, nor did my mother anticipate our coming here. Caroline is alone in the world, except for a ne'er-do-well brother who up and bolted for the Continent, probably running from his creditors. I only just met her this summer, you must know. That brother of hers mortgaged the family seat in Norfolk to the hilt and finally had to close it down. Their house here is smaller and easier to keep, though run terribly to seed." Richard stopped, aware that he was rambling but somehow needing to say it all. Serena listened in silence, her face very still and grave.

58

Richard thought it would have been easier had she cried or screamed reproachfully at him. As it was, he hardly knew what to say.

"Serena?" he coaxed, hoping for some reaction.

"Yes, my lord?" she asked, almost impassively, her eyes unreadable.

"I—well, I thought you should know that Caroline will be gone as soon as it can be arranged. Apparently she has some distant relations in Yorkshire—my mother has written them and we await an answer."

She merely nodded and rose. "You must be tired, my lord. You will want to rest before dinner, will you not?"

"Serena, I—" he began, standing as well. He took a step toward her, wanting somehow to touch her, as if to comfort her, but feeling he had not the right.

"Yes, my lord?" she asked quietly.

He gazed into those deep blue eyes and suddenly her face was an open book. There was a great sadness, almost a despair welling up in her eyes, in her very expression. But she was not angry with him, and that made him feel all the worse. "Serena, you must not worry about—that is— *you* are my wife. *You* belong here; Caroline does not. Do you understand me?"

"Yes, my lord." She sounded remote; her face was shuttered again.

He thought of his parents as he had seen them a short while ago, hands clasped together. He did not love Serena. How could he when he loved another? But suddenly he knew that he had got to build a life with her She was his wife. She, and not Caroline, would be the mother of his children. If he ever had any, he thought bitterly. Serena had shied away from his advances

59

before and now he knew there was little hope. Still, she was his wife and surely some day . . .

"I believe I hear someone in the sitting room, my lord," she said, interrupting his thoughts. "Perhaps the tea things have arrived."

"Yes, I—do let us go in to tea. And Serena, I—I should like it very much if you would dispense with my title and call me 'Richard'." He smiled, hoping she would be pleased. But she wasn't. A certain tightening of her mouth told him she was annoyed, or perhaps hurt. And then he remembered that, of course, she'd heard Caroline address him so.

"Yes, my lord—ah—Richard. As you wish," she said woodenly.

Damn! he thought. She had managed to turn a gesture of friendship into a demand for obedience! It was all such a coil, and she was not going to make it any easier.

They drank their tea in silence, each wrapped in his own thoughts.

Dinner was an ordeal. They sat in the family dining room, but neither the comfortable elegance of the rose-colored room nor the excellent food could make up for the empty seat at the head of the table. It seemed to cast a pall over everyone and, of course, having his wife and former love at the table together did not help matters any. Nor did Livvy. The girl seemed to think it her duty to extol Caroline's virtues to all and sundry. Serena said very little, but looked quite pale, and Richard wished to hell Livvy would cease babbling. Caroline was at her most charming, chattering on about fashions she'd seen in *La Belle Assemblee* and the latest list of marriages announced in the *Gazette*. Only Livvy responded with any degree of animation, however. Serena was polite but distant, and his mother seemed totally distracted. She hardly touched her food, and at one point when a footman asked whether her grace would prefer potato soufflé or cucumbers in white sauce, she looked at him quite as if she could not recall what a potato *was*.

When Caroline had exhausted the subject of announcements in the *Gazette*, she suddenly turned to Richard and asked his opinion of the Corn Laws. He chuckled inwardly to himself. She really was adorable. She obviously had no idea what the Corn Laws were all about. But she had undoubtedly seen the term in the newspaper and now thought to draw him into conversation. He replied blandly that though they had seemed a good idea at first, it was beginning to appear that they were doing more harm than good. She seemed quite impressed with his answer, but a certain look in her eye told him she had not the slightest idea what he was talking about. And so he quickly asked her what headdresses she thought the women would be wearing in London this year. Caroline seemed exceedingly pleased, even flattered by the question, and proceeded to expound on this fascinating subject for fifteen minutes.

He glanced once at his wife, seated next to him, and saw that her lips were most decidedly twitching in amusement. He felt suddenly piqued with Serena. It would not hurt her to glance at *La Belle Assemblee* on occasion. He looked down at her dress, a billowing concoction in a pale shade of lavender that made her

skin look positively swallow. The dress was cut un-
fashionably high across the bosom and smothered with
lace. He saw the obvious hand of Lady Stoneleigh, and
knew his annoyance at Serena to be unjust. But still, he
could not help the comparison to Caroline, who looked
delectable in a pink satin gown cut low across the
bosom to reveal the whitest skin he'd ever seen. Her
golden hair was smooth and fine and exquisitely
coiffed. Serena's hair looked like a sparrow and her
chicks might make a home there. And Caroline's
smile — God, but his heart lurched every time she
smiled at him, her amber eyes limpid with adoration.
Serena never looked at him like that, and he didn't
imagine she ever would.

Stop it! he told himself. He knew he would go mad if
he persisted in these futile comparisons.

And then Serena spoke, and his ruminations ceased.
"Your grace," she was saying with a soft smile, "the food
is quite delicious, but I am persuaded you have no
knowledge of what you have eaten. Pray do not remain
here for our sakes. I know you are wishing to be with
the duke."

The duchess's eyes seemed to well up. "Th-thank
you, Serena," she stammered. "If — if you will all excuse
me —"

She rose from her chair and hurried out and Richard
turned to stare at his wife. He was amazed at her
forwardness — she was, after all, a virtual stranger in
the house. But then he realized that she had put his
mother's feelings above the social niceties. Few people
would have done so; certainly not, he admitted ruefully, Caroline Lister.

Chapter Four

Watkins grumbled as he plumped the pillows and smoothed the sheets over the dark green sofa. 'Tweren't fittin', he thought, for his lordship to be sleepin' on a sofa in his own house. No more was it proper for himself, Thomas Watkins, gentleman's gentleman, to be makin' up beds like any common upstairs maid. But orders was orders. And no one in the household was to know. Watkins shook his head and stood up. He didn't know what was wrong between the master and his bride, but he knew it just weren't natural the way things were. Sleepin' in separate beds every night, and now the sofa! He could not understand how her ladyship could deny his master her bed. For he did not doubt that it was so — he knew his master's fondness for ladies too well to think aught. True, there'd been some talk about that blond filly — Lister was her name, he thought — but he didn't pay much heed. After all, his lordship had married the Lady Serena. And besides,

63

her ladyship was a taking little thing, not one a man 'd be like to resist, 'specially not when it was legal, all right and tight. So what in tarnation was wrong with her ladyship, to shut his lordship out?

He was not at all displeased to find her ladyship's maid in the dressing room when he proceeded there to finish arranging his lordship's things. He'd only just met Miss Hannah the day of the wedding, but Gateshead bein' as small as it was, he'd seen a good bit of her. She was what he called a sympathetic female — always smilin' 'stead of forever wearin' a Friday face. 'Course she *was* rather large, almost his own size, but still she didn't bowl a man over with a loud booming voice nor a heavy gait.

"Evenin' Miss Hannah," he said as she looked up from the gown she was smoothing out.

"Oh, Mr. Watkins, good evening to you," she replied pleasantly. "I see the master and the mistress are to share a dressing room."

"That they are, and it's like to be all they'll share," he said dryly, bending to one of his lordship's portmanteaus.

"Oh, dear," Hannah said, sweeping the gown up in her arms, "I'd so hoped that here, what with — well — there being only one bedchamber, you know . . ."

Watkins looked up to see Hannah flush becomingly. "'Twouldn't seem so, Miss Hannah. The master gave orders to make up the sofa in the sitting room," he said heavily, suddenly wishing that she had the familiarity with her mistress of a long-time servant. Then perhaps she could talk some sense into the young ladyship.

"Oh, that's dreadful, Mr. Watkins, just dreadful. And her ladyship so lonely and sad, and herself such a

64

sweet little thing."

"So lonely and—" Watkins blurted, exasperated. "If you'll pardon me, Miss Hannah, I dunno what call her ladyship has to be feelin' blue-devilled, when she's the one what locks her door at night!"

"Locks her—well, Mr. Watkins, I warrant she does not!" exclaimed her ladyship's maid in high dudgeon. Trust a woman to be unreasonable, he thought. Even a sympathetic one.

"Now surely, Miss Hannah, you aren't suggestin' that his lordship be the one who—well, ma'am, it just don't make sense! No sense at all."

"Sense or no, Mr. Watkins, my mistress ain't happy, and I'm not the one what is makin' her *un*happy." Hannah stalked to the cupboard to hang up the gown, and Watkins concentrated on folding his lordship's shirts. There weren't no sense arguin' with a female no how. Men were just too reasonable to ever win!

A few minutes later Hannah came over to where he stood arranging his lordship's cravats in one of the two bureaus. "Mr. Watkins, I've been thinking . . ." she began. Oh, Lord, he thought, a man 'd better watch out when a woman was thinking.

"Yes, Miss Hannah?"

"Well, mayhap you and I might—well—be of some help to my lord and lady. That is, if you've a mind to."

"Just what do you mean?"

"Well, I thought we might, well, kind of give things a bit of a push, don't you know."

Watkins closed the bureau drawer and turned to Hannah. He'd been with the master's family all his life, and he'd do just about anything for his lordship, even listen to some cork-brained female idea. Hannah was smiling and he thought that as females went, she weren't half bad.

His lordship opened the door of the bedchamber for Serena and then followed her in. She looked up at him curiously.

"I thought we should use the same door, Serena. We would not wish the servants to gossip, after all."

"No, of course not," she mumbled. Appearances, she thought, bristling. That was why he'd asked her to call him by his given name. It would simply not do for his wife to address him so formally, especially when a certain other person seemed so familiar with him.

Somehow her husband had ushered her to the center of the room, and they now stood only a few feet from the massive bed. The coverlet had been removed and the down comforter was turned down at the top corners, an unspoken invitation. Serena thought desolately that the bed was much too big for one person. But they would probable never share it, she reflected with an inward sigh, and then her gaze shifted to her husband. He looked very handsome, she decided, in a burgundy coat that spanned his broad shoulders perfectly. His black knee breeches hugged his muscular thighs, and Serena felt an unaccountable rush of warmth go through her.

"Serena," he said, interrupting her thoughts. "I just wanted you to know that I appreciate your thoughtfulness to my mother." His tone was gentle, his dark eyes kind. But she knew instinctively that there was no spark of desire in them. They were alone in their bedchamber and he had made no attempt to touch her.

Nor would he—not when he looked at Caroline Lister with the longing she'd seen at dinner.

" 'Tis nothing," she replied after a moment, hands clasped at her waist. "She was distressed and I noted it. I—I like your mother very much. I hope she will let me help her."

Her husband's eyes seemed to pierce hers and he took a step closer to her. "Thank you, Serena. I believe she is fond of you as well." She caught the flurry of his hand moving up, as if to touch her. But instead he abruptly ran his fingers through his hair and stepped back. "I—er—where is your maid?"

"I imagine she is waiting in the dressing room, as always," Serena said quietly, oddly disappointed.

His lordship strode to the door leading to the dressing room and opened it. "Yes, I suppose my man is here too. You must realize there is only one dressing room and so—Watkins? Watkins? Hannah? That's strange. And why is it so dark in here? Hand me a taper, will you Serena?"

She complied and followed him in as he lit the wall sconces. It was a rather large dressing room appointed with the requisite wardrobes, a wall of bureaus, vanity, a velvet chaise. But there was no sign of either servant. "That *is* strange," she murmured. Her husband frowned and opened the door to the sitting room.

"Blast!" he blurted when one sweeping glance revealed another empty room. "Oh, sorry, Serena. But where the devil *are* they?" He stalked to the bell pull in the dressing room and tugged impatiently at it. She wondered at his sudden irritability. "There, that should bring at least one of them running." He began pacing the floor, hardly glancing her way. "Now, as I was saying, there being only one dressing room, and our servants both needing access to it, I thought it would be most expedient if we each dressed in our own rooms."

"Yes, of course," she said dully, not bothering to ask what they were to do about the single vanity in the dressing room.

"And as to this vanity, I suppose we can contrive to use it at different times," he added.

"Yes, I suppose we can," she said a trifle wearily, thinking that they both sounded so reasonable — like two friends contracting to share rooms in Town for the season.

He stopped pacing. "Where in blazes is Watkins? Did you dismiss your maid?"

"No, of course not."

He tugged at the bell pull again and when several minutes brought no sign of a servant, he growled, "Well, fine thing. And I've no intention of combing the house at this hour looking for an errant servant. I suppose Watkins is halfway through a keg of rum by now. Don't know what Hannah's excuse is, but it doesn't signify. Can you do for yourself?"

"I — well — yes, I suppose so," she said, trying not to think about the row of tiny buttons at the back of her gown.

"Good. Then I suggest we each collect our night things and go to bed. It is late." He did not meet her eyes as he spoke, and she felt suddenly uncomfortable. She merely nodded in reply and each turned to their respective tasks.

Serena had no idea where Hannah had put any of her things, and so opened what seemed like endless drawers and wardrobe doors before finding what she needed. His lordship appeared to be having similar difficulty, but he slammed the drawers considerably louder than she did. Their clothing and toilet articles seemed to have been arranged with little rhyme or reason. One drawer might hold her things, the one directly under it his, instead of each having a separate bureau. At one point they both reached to pull open the same drawer. "You go ahead," she said.

"No, my dear. It's probably yours."

Serena shrugged. She opened the drawer and beheld row after row of lace pantalettes. She slammed the drawer shut, feeling herself turn scarlet and refusing to look at her husband.

He cleared his throat and loosened his cravat. "Don't know what they were about, Watkins and your maid, arranging things in such a harum-scarum manner," he growled and turned toward the wardrobe. Serena moved to the other bureau, not understanding why she was being so missish.

At length she heard him say, "Well, I have what I need. Good night, Serena." She turned to look at him. He carried his slippers in one hand, and draped over his other arm were a black dressing gown and matching silk neckcloth, and nothing else.

"But, my lord, where is your—ah—that is—" Serena stammered, and felt herself turn crimson again. "Ah— good night, my lord."

His lordship coughed. "Yes, well, good night, Serena. Sleep well." He turned and left the room, closing the door behind him.

Serena stared after him. Where, she wondered, were his nightshirt and his nightcap? And if he didn't sleep with either, then what— She felt that strange warmth again, and quickly ferreted out the last of her things.

Ten minutes later Serena stood in her bare feet with her hair down and perhaps half the buttons of her gown undone. Once again, she stretched both hands around her back and twisted and squirmed in a futile effort to reach more buttons. "Ugh!" she groaned. "I shall never get these damn buttons undone!" After two more minutes, quite panting with the effort, she gave up. She grabbed her hairbrush from the nightstand and yanked it through her thick locks. She now had three choices. She could try ringing again for Hannah, but did not suppose she would have better luck than his lordship. Or she could simply sleep in her gown, but what with two layers of petticoats and the stiff fabric of her dress, that would be decidedly uncomfortable. Resolutely she put down the hairbrush. She marched to the dressing room door, opened it, and marched through. She stood at the door to the sitting room and took a deep breath. Gingerly, she knocked.

She heard footsteps, and then the door opened. He wore his dressing gown, slippers, neckcloth, and very possibly, she recalled, nothing else. She saw the curling black hairs on his chest where the dressing gown gaped open. She swallowed hard.

"Serena? Is anything wrong?"

"N-no, I—ah—" She forced herself to meet his eyes. "No. Forgive me for disturbing you, my lord, but I—I cannot seem to undo these odious buttons. W-would you mind?"

He smiled, a smile that was different from all his others. It made her feel very strange. "Not at all, Serena. But I do think, under the circumstances, that you had ought to call me 'Richard.' "

"Very well, Richard."

"That's better. Turn around."

She complied, and for some reason she felt her heartbeat accelerate as soon as he touched her. And there was that strange warmth again — she remembered a feeling of warmth when he'd helped her with her dress at the beach, but this was very different. She actually felt weak now, as if her legs could not support her, and she could not think why.

"There, I — I think that should do it," he said, his voice a bit hoarse. He put his hands on her bare shoulders and turned her around to face him. She quickly reached behind her to hold the gown together and he dropped his hands to his sides.

"Thank you," was all she managed to say.

"You are welcome. Good night, my dear," he rasped.

She could feel his breath on her face. For some reason she wanted to reach up and touch his face, but she didn't dare. "Good night, Richard," she murmured, and then fled to her room.

Serena slept fitfully but nonetheless woke early, as was her habit. As Hannah slipped her into still another gown with row upon row of ruffles, Serena questioned her about the night before.

"Oh, but my lady, you told me not to wait up, you did," the maid replied. Serena denied having done so, but so mildly insistent was Hannah, so innocent her face, that Serena began to wonder whether perhaps, given all the turmoil of the day, she had after all made such a strange request. She made it clear that she did wish Hannah's services this evening, and tactfully suggested that the dressing room might stand a bit of rearranging. It occurred to Serena, as she dashed down to breakfast, that Hannah had been oddly unruffled by the entire discussion.

Richard slept nary a wink. As he tossed and turned on the lumpy sofa, images of two women vied for place in his mind's eye. He saw Serena as she'd looked tonight, so innocent and disconcertingly attractive as she'd stood before him with her hair down and her gown half undone. She'd been a trump to agree to do without her maid—most women would swoon at the thought. And he imagined it had taken some courage for her to ask his assistance. And then Caroline would overtake his mind, Caroline looking adorable as she'd asked him about the Corn Laws, Caroline with her silky golden hair that he longed to touch again. With Caroline, he thought, he would not be sleeping on this blasted sofa!

He awoke with a wretched backache, and demanded irascibly of Watkins where the hell he'd been last night. Watkins was most contrite and owned that it was blue ruin and not rum what caused such a lapse in duty. Richard grinned and said never mind, but Watkins damn well better do something about that dressing room. It was all at sixes and sevens, and as if a man didn't have enough problems without finding lace pantalettes where he expected silk neckcloths!

His mood did not at all improve when he descended to the breakfast parlor and found Serena already there, sipping her coffee, blithely unaware that ladies were supposed to rise well *past* seven o'clock and then breakfast in their beds. Serena was an early riser and he should not have been surprised, yet he was not at all sure he liked such a habit in a wife. It was well enough at Gateshead, but for a lifetime . . . ?

They greeted each other politely and Richard allowed the footman to fill his plate and then dismissed him. Seating himself, he poured coffee and then eyed the newspaper next his plate longingly. Women, he knew, expected conversation. And so he commented on the weather and Serena replied that yes, it looked to be another warm, sunny day.

For several minutes they each concentrated on their food and then he said, "Serena, I should like very much to show you some of the estates, but I am afraid I shall be rather occupied today. There are a number of matters pending which I must see to in my father's stead. Will you be able to amuse yourself?"

"Oh, yes, my l—Richard. Do not trouble yourself about me. I shall see if your mother needs me. And I can sketch or paint, and I do love to walk. I am persuaded the terrain here is very beautiful."

"It is indeed. Do you ride, Serena?" he asked, realizing once again how little he really knew about her.

"Of course. I am a country girl, after all."

He somehow had the feeling she rode very well, which every country girl most certainly did not. "We shall have to see about finding you a suitable mount, then. If you can wait a day or so, that is," he added, smiling as her eyes lit with delight.

"Oh, thank you, Richard. I should like that very much."

73

Conversation lagged after that, and Richard found his eyes straying to the newspaper several times as he consumed his scrambled eggs and dry toast.

"Oh, do go ahead, Richard. You needn't trouble about me."

He looked abashed. "Oh, no, Serena, it—it's just that at Gateshead there *was* no morning paper and, it being—"

"Richard," she interrupted, setting down her blueberry muffin and eyeing him directly, "you know you are simply itching to open that paper. And besides, I know well that at this hour I am intruding on a man's solitary domain. No, do go ahead. I promise I shan't be in the least offended."

Smiling, Richard capitulated. "Er—would you like a section, my dear?" he asked as he unfolded the newpaper.

"No thank you. I am well content with the view of the gardens. I shall think about what to paint next."

He lifted an eyebrow and she laughed. "You know, Richard, I do find conversation stimulating, yet often I—I love the silence. Do not you?"

Richard cocked his head wonderingly at her. He had never heard of a woman who loved silence. He had thought it a strictly male province.

After breakfast Serena found the duchess in her private sitting room, the housekeeper having just left. Her mother-in-law greeted her with pleasure, but Serena knew she was preoccupied and so kept their interview short. The duchess demurred when Serena volunteered to sit with the duke for a while, but Serena pointed out that when his fever finally broke he would need his wife at least as much as now. The duchess surely would not want to make herself ill with exhaustion, Serena pressed, and so finally her mother-in-law allowed that Serena might stay with the duke at tea time.

Her mission accomplished, Serena took herself off to her own chamber. She had placed her easel permanently in front of the largest window in the room, and now turned it this way and that until the sun hit it at just the right angle. Once they settled in at Wheatfield she would ask Richard if she might set up a painting studio, but she had no desire to discommode anyone here with such a request. And as it was, the window had an eastern aspect and so was quite perfect for morning work. She rolled up her sleeves and began to arrange her paints. She wanted to begin painting the chicks in the nest while the colors were still fresh in her mind.

As always, she became so intent on her work that all else was forgotten. She simply did not hear the luncheon bell and was surprised when a footman appeared to escort her down. She was sorry she'd bothered, however. Richard, it seemed, was out on one of the tenant farms and would not be back for lunch, and the duchess, of course, was with the duke. And so Serena sat down with Livvy and Caroline, who, she could not help thinking, were as rude as they were pretty. Other than a snide remark about a smudge of paint on her cheek, they addressed nary a word to her, treated her, in fact, as if she were not there. Serena would have joined in their conversation anyway, except that they were again discussing fashions. And while Serena knew what she liked and what looked well on her, she had precious little knowledge of the latest styles. Her mother had thought perusing fashion magazines a frivolous activity that led to needless expense.

And so she quietly nibbled her food, thinking that it was much more lonely to be with people who disliked one so than to be alone, when one might enjoy one's own company. As to their dislike, Caroline clearly saw Serena as having stolen her suitor, and Livvy idolized Caroline. She had dressed her hair similarly, and even seemed to be imitating Caroline's gestures and the lilt in her voice.

Well, so be it, Serena thought, and quit the dining room as soon as she reasonably could. The day had fulfilled its sunny promise, and she went up to change into a walking dress. She rolled up her sleeves as soon as she reached the garden, so warm had the day grown. She liked the feel of the sun on her face and was glad she'd left her bonnet behind. She wandered for some time, sketch pad in hand, enjoying the scent of honeysuckle and the sight of the gladiolas and red poppies still in bloom. The house was so large and the gardens so lush that she knew it would take the better part of the afternoon just to negotiate her way around. The surrounding park she would leave for another day. She heard the trickle of water and remembered the fountain at the center of the circular rose garden. It was there that she made her way now, glancing back at the house several times to admire its grandeur. Most of the rear windows were open and a slight breeze ruffled the trees. Serena could hear birds singing overhead and, despite her troubles, she felt happy.

Livvy was bored. She flopped down onto the white lace coverlet of her bed, feeling very fretful indeed. Why was it that everyone else seemed occupied? Her restless thoughts drifted to her mother, sitting hour after hour with her father. Livvy had only been allowed into the sickroom for brief intervals, but she could hardly bear even that. To think of her strong, vital father lying there, so ill . . . .He *had* to get better, Livvy told herself. It just couldn't be his time to die.

Livvy sat up abruptly, clutching one of the pillow shams under her chin. She had never been much good at amusing herself, and it seemed the outside of enough that there was no one about just now. Richard was working, and Caroline had gone to have her afternoon rest. Caroline always said that was a habit that Livvy should cultivate, it being a virtual requirement of any girl who called herself a lady. But somehow Livvy was never tired enough to warrant two hours in her bed of an afternoon.

As to Serena, Livvy had no notion where she was, but that didn't signify, for they could never be friends. Serena had spoiled Richard's chances for happiness with the woman he loved. He and Caroline belonged together. It was not fair that Serena had married Richard. Caroline, who was so beautiful, so sweet, loved Richard and needed him. Serena didn't. And Serena had no consequence whatever. She would never be the sort of duchess Richard deserved.

Livvy jumped off the bed and stalked out of her room and down the hall. *Never*, she vowed, would she do what Richard had done. *Never* would she allow *anyone* to marry her off to a man she did not love!

77

She wandered aimlessly through the main floor saloons for a while, still searching her mind for some diversion, and then an idea came to her. She remembered Caroline telling her that when she was in need of amusement, she would often eavesdrop on servants' conversations. Servants, Caroline said, knew simply *everything* that was going on *everywhere*. And if they didn't, they had a cousin who did. It was not Livvy's habit to eavesdrop, but she *was* terribly bored. And after all, she would not be hurting anyone.

The housekeeper was alone, humming to herself in the linen room, and so Livvy continued on her way. The door to one of the upstairs apartments was open, and she heard two maids chattering inside. She crept closer and realized that they were speaking about the butcher's boy, with whom one of the kitchen maids was stepping out. But everyone knows that already, Livvy thought, and in her distraction bumped into a small table with a vase of flowers on it. The talk inside the room ceased abruptly. Darn! thought Livvy. She clearly was not a master spy.

She had better luck belowstairs. What with so many recesses and dark corners, it was quite easy to contrive not to be noticed. Cook was having tea with Serena's maid in the butler's pantry. Livvy ventured only one glance at them and then pressed herself back against the wall so that she was hidden in the shadows. But for all her trouble, they seemed to have nothing better to talk about than Cook's latest recipe for strawberry tart. Livvy's mind began to wander as she contemplated what to do next, and she nearly took herself off, but then she realized that Hannah's voice had become lower and nearly tremulous. Surely not over strawberry tart!

78

Livvy strained to hear her.

". . . the poor little mite. I tell you it's lonely she is. All alone in that big bed. It just breaks my heart, it does. And I would never tell you this, Mary, excepting you be my very own cousin and I know as you would never breathe a word."

"Of course I wouldn't," Cook replied soothingly. "But are you certain — that is — they must have — well — the first night at least, I'll be bound."

Livvy's body was tensed; she hardly dared draw breath as she cocked her ear and listened. For a moment all she heard was the clatter of tea cups, and then Hannah said, "And how I wish 'twere so, Mary, that I do. But 'taint, and I reckon as I be the one what would know."

"I reckon so, Hannah. But ain't nothin' none of us can do, 'cept hope for the best. And things do have a way — why I remember their graces, onc't upon a time, roarin' and —"

For some reason Livvy thought she ought not to stay to hear such confidences about her parents. She lifted her skirts and tiptoed away as quietly as she had come. It was not until she reached the upstairs corridor that she thought about what she'd overheard. Richard did not share Serena's bed; not even once had he done so. Livvy thought she knew something, though perhaps not a very great deal, about the marriage bed. She had gleaned whatever she could from all the romantical novels she read, and from certain things Caroline had said. (Livvy was never sure how Caroline had come to know of such things, but as always, Caroline spoke with such authority . . .). At all events, Livvy knew enough to realize that things were not at all right between Richard and Serena. And if Richard had not touched his bride, that must mean that despite all, he was still very much in love with Caroline. Livvy's heart soared and her pace quickened on the wood plank floors of the corridor. She would go to Caroline straightaway. Of a certain her friend would not mind having her rest interrupted for the sake of such tidings. The knowledge that Richard still loved her, and probably always would, would be a great comfort to Caroline during her exile in Yorkshire.

"Come in," Richard said in automatic response to the knock on the library door. He did not look up from his work, for he had still a great deal to do this day, and he assumed that the butler or footman would state his business soon enough. He heard the distinct rustle of petticoats, however, and was shocked to look up and see Caroline standing before his desk. "Caroline! What a surprise," he said, rising and trying to sound casual despite the sudden pounding of his heart.

"Hello, Richard," she said, putting her hands on the desk and leaning forward. He could see her breasts straining against the thin fabric of her mint green dress and he forced himself to look up.

"What—ah—what can I do for you, my dear?" he asked, feeling warm despite his proximity to the open window.

"Oh, Richard," she moaned, her lower lip protruding in a pout. "Pray do not be so formal with me. Not when we—" she lowered her voice and moved suddenly, very quickly, to his side of the desk—"not when we have meant so very much to each other."

She stood very close to him, her amber eyes moist and her lips trembling. Richard felt his palms sweating and held his hands rigidly at his sides. "Caroline, I explained all of that to you before my wedding. Things cannot be as they were. Surely you can see that it simply will not do. And besides, it would only make it more — more painful, for both of us. To be so near and not —"

Serena was coming back from the rose garden, ambling along the side of the house, when the voices filtered toward her from an upper window.

"Oh, Richard, my poor Richard, such brave words." Serena froze in her tracks as Caroline's voice rang out. "But I am persuaded *she* cannot care for you as I do. Does she hold you like this, Richard?" The voice had grown softer and Serena felt sick. Despite herself she looked up. At first she could not see Richard, but Caroline's back was to the window, and suddenly Serena saw, through the haze of her tears, Richard's arm encircle Caroline's waist and pull her close. And then his head bent to Caroline's. His hand began to caress her back, and then Serena could take no more. Blindly, she turned back the way she had come. She ran, heedless of the tears spilling onto the sketch pad clutched to her breast, wanting to get as far away from the house as possible.

Somehow Richard found the strength to tear himself away from Caroline. "I — forgive me, Caroline. We mustn't —"

"Oh, Richard, I have missed you so," Caroline breathed softly. "And I know you have missed me." Caroline stood very close, her breasts heaving and her eyelashes fluttering. "Your little wife doesn't give you what I would, were I your wife. I—"

"Caroline, you go too far," he interrupted, suddenly stern. "Matters between a husband and wife are private, and must remain so." He took a step back from her, very uncomfortable with the turn the conversation had taken. How could she possibly know—

"Richard, dearest," she purred, "nothing is private for long in a household such as this. Surely you know that."

Richard kept his face impassive as he admonished Caroline not to listen to idle gossip, especially that which was so obviously without foundation, and then ushered her out of the library with polite formality. But he found it very difficult to work after that, his mind running in all manner of unpleasant directions. He yearned for Caroline, yet he was annoyed with himself for yielding to his desire, even for that one kiss. To offer insult to his wife under his own roof was unthinkable, and besides, it was a kiss that could lead nowhere. A gentleman simply did not dally with unmarried ladies of quality. He did not suppose Caroline realized that kisses often lead to a good deal more. And come to think on 't, she had nearly thrown herself at him. That was not at all like Caroline. Nor was it a part of her sweet, gentle nature to listen to gossip, much less to repeat it. He had not liked her tone at all, and her behavior puzzled him, but then he realized that she must be distraught at seeing him here with his wife.

His wife. Richard sighed. He knew he had got to put Caroline out of his mind and concentrate on Serena. She wasn't at all unattractive, he reflected. In fact, he had found her proximity last night downright unnerving. It was high time, he decided, that he made Serena his wife in fact if not in form. For one thing, if such ugly gossip *was* abroad in the household—though he could not imagine how, for both their personal servants were exceedingly discreet—but if it was so, life would become very uncomfortable here for Serena, more so than for him. And besides, dammit, Serena was his wife and it was time she began acting like one!

Richard was living in limbo and he did not like it one bit, not to mention that blasted sofa! He would put an end to such nonsense this very night, he assured himself. And then he recalled a certain very rash, very ill-advised promise he had made on their wedding night. And he remembered Serena fleeing from the dressing room last night like a startled rabbit. Richard cursed fluently and ran his fingers through his hair. How the hell did a man set about seducing his virgin wife?

Chapter Five

Serena slowed her pace when she reached the out-skirts of the formal gardens, but she continued walking rapidly through the park surrounding Luntsford. She barely noticed the lush greenery around her, and with every step she took a litany sounded in her head. Richard loved Caroline. Richard had never held her the way he'd held Caroline. There was no hope. No hope.

Serena's breath finally gave out, and she collapsed onto a stone bench. No wonder he'd made such a case of wanting to be alone, she thought bitterly. But then she reflected that perhaps it might well have been Caroline's doing. She might have come to him unex-pectedly. But still, Caroline had access to Richard and Serena did not. Serena stood up. She guessed that there lacked several hours until tea time, when she was to sit with the duke. Well, she sighed, she would not go back to the house a moment before she had to. She wandered deeper into the park, until the fine lawns gave way to wooded pathways. She was still on Gower land, of course, and she marveled at its variety and richness. But much as she wished the distraction, she could not concentrate long enough to decide on something to sketch. She would stare at a twisting branch of elderberries, and all she would see was Richard's arm coming around Caroline's back.

The day had grown very hot; she repinned her falling hair and undid the top buttons of her dress. At length she came to a cluster of trees that seemed to cling together to hide an enchanting dell beyond. She penetrated the trees and saw that not only was there a lovely, private retreat, but at its base a gentle winding stream with crystal clear water that seemed to beckon her. Running down the gentle incline to the ground below, she threw down her sketch pad and was barefoot in seconds. Lifting her skirts, she ventured to the grassy bank and tiptoed into the water. It was cool, delicious, and the ground beneath was a soft cushion of earth. She moved several steps in, lifting her skirts even higher. The water came to her knees in no time, and she realized that the stream must be deeper still at its center. Why, she could swim in this, she thought, delighted. She was exceedingly warm, and she knew the water would relax her. She spared only a moment's thought as to the advisability of doing so. There was obviously not a soul around, and she did not suppose there ever was. The dell, indeed, the stream as far as she could see, had a certain untouched quality that she loved. She looked about her. The stream was surrounded by a thick curtain of trees. All was silent save the occasional call of a bird and the ripple of water at her feet. Without further thought she dashed to the grassy bank. Somehow she felt better with every piece of clothing she shed. There was no one here to notice, and, she reflected sadly, no one at the house to notice her absence. When she stood in her chemise she debated a moment. Damn him! she thought. Damn Richard Gower and his damned sense of duty! She threw the chemise off and darted into the water. It felt heavenly, and she knew it was just what she needed. People were just too civilized, she mused, always doing what duty demanded instead of what their hearts told them. And it always led to misery for everyone in the end.

She had no idea how long she splashed about, enjoying the feel of the water and the amazing stillness around her. Several locks of hair came down and she let them fall unheeded.

"You swim like a fish." The sudden, unfamiliar voice rent the silence. Startled, Serena found her footing, for the water was not very deep. She was grateful that the water came to her shoulders and even more that the voice was female.

"Who is there?" she asked tentatively.

"Why, *I* am," came the voice, very sweet, almost musical.

Serena turned in the direction of the voice. At first she could see nothing, for the sun blinded her. She moved forward until the sunlight caught in the trees and then she saw her. Perched on a rock not far from Serena's clothes was a young girl, her knees drawn up to her chest, her bare feet and brown calves visible beneath her multi-colored skirt. Serena moved closer, careful to keep herself covered by the water.

"Who are you?" she asked.

"I am Gaya," the girl replied.

86

"Gaya. Why, you are a Gypsy." Serena had seen gypsies a few times when they were camped near Stoneleigh. But they never stayed long; her father always chased them away.

"I am Rom," the girl said proudly, tossing her head so that her long straight black hair rippled down her back.

"Yes, of course. Ah—Gaya—is anyone else with you?"

"Oh, no. I like to wander the woods alone. And my brother not like that I talk to gorgio woman. But I stay. I like you. You swim like a fish."

"Yes, well, I should like to come out now, Gaya. Would you—ah—turn around for a bit please?

"Turn around?" the girl asked, puzzled. "Oh, yes. I forget. Gorgio have strange customs." And with that, Gaya swiveled about until her back was to Serena.

Serena hurried out of the water and into her clothes, not wanting the girl to leave. She was glad that for once her dress buttoned in front, and when it was done up she moved silently toward Gaya.

Gaya must have sensed her movement, for she swiveled back around. Her large dark eyes widened as she stared at Serena.

"Why, you are rawnie," Gaya said, astounded.

"Rawnie?"

"A lady. You are a lady, with such clothes. I did not think to see a lady in the water."

Serena smiled. "Yes, well, 'tis hot, you know. And I do like to swim."

"You are not like other gorgio women. What is your name?"

Serena hesitated a moment. "My name is Serena."

"Serena," echoed the girl, as if trying it out. She

smiled. Serena thought she was very pretty in an exotic sort of way with her strong nose, high cheekbones, and dark coloring.

"That is a very pretty name. You have no shoes, Serena. You not like other gorgios."

Serena looked down at her bare feet. "You're right. I left my shoes over there. And—" Serena paused and sighed, "I suppose I am *not* like other gorgios."

"You are lonely, Serena," Gaya said simply, and then slithered down her rock and onto the grassy bank with the ease and grace of a lizard. She had a lovely figure and Serena guessed she might be thirteen or fourteen years old. Gaya lifted her skirt and dangled her feet in the water. On impulse Serena sat down and did the same, although with considerably more effort, for her long skirt and petticoats kept trailing in the water.

They were silent for several moments and then Serena said, "Where do you live, Gaya? That is— where is your family camped?"

"Oh, not far from here. My brother says it is where the land of the great house meets the field of the smaller manor to the east."

"Oh! Well—that's my—er—that is—the land is very beautiful there."

Gaya stiffened. "I should not have told you. You be a rawnie of the great house, is not so?"

Serena sighed. She supposed it really didn't signify whether or not Gaya knew who she was. "Yes, I am. But you needn't fear. I shan't tell anyone you are here." Gaya relaxed and Serena went on. "The gypsies never stayed long on my father's land. I should love to visit your camp, Gaya. Do you think I might?"

"I do not know. We do not like the gorgio to visit with

us, but you not like other gorgios. Mayhap I ask my brother."

Serena smiled. "Thank you, Gaya."

"But happen that be difficult to do, seeing how Marco very angry at me now," Gaya added, and pursed her lips in vexation.

"Why is he angry with you?"

Gaya tossed her head back and put her face to the sun. "Because I not want to marry anybody. Marco says—"

"Marry! Why, Gaya, are you not much too young to marry?"

"Too young? Oh, no. I am fourteen," Gaya stated firmly, as if that explained everything.

"Fourteen," repeated Serena doubtfully.

"Yes. Marco says girls should marry at twelve, mayhap thirteen. He reckons I soon be too old. But I love George and cannot marry him," Gaya said tragically, lifting one foot from the water so that droplets fell from her toes.

"Oh? Why is that?"

Gaya sighed. "He's in love with Addie. They are married last year. They have baby now." Gaya submerged her foot again and swung her calves back and forth.

"Oh, I see," Serena said quietly, amused despite herself. She had the distinct feeling that Gaya fully enjoyed her unrequited love.

"You are in love, too, Serena, and you are very sad," Gaya said, staring at the ripples her toes were making in the water.

That was nonsense, Serena thought; she was not in love with anyone. But still it was uncanny the way the girl knew that she was troubled. Having no intention of discussing her ill-fated marriage, however, she searched her mind for a new topic of conversation. Her eyes swept the water and then came to rest on Gaya. An idea came to her. "Gaya, I should very much like to paint you."

"Paint me?" the girl asked, startled.

"Yes. First I shall sketch you, of course, and then later I shall do the painting."

"Oh, you be an artist, is not so?"

"Well," Serena smiled, "let us just say that I love to paint. And I do not usually do people, but I think you would make a very striking subject with your dark coloring and red blouse and beautiful face."

"I think it is a very good idea, Serena," Gaya said, tossing her glossy hair down her back. "You paint me. Go ahead."

Serena laughed. "Very well. I do happen to have my sketch pad with me." Serena swung her feet from the water and stood up. "I should like you to sit on that rock again. With your knees drawn up, just the way you were when I first saw you."

Gaya seemed to move from the water to the rock in one easy motion. Serena went to retrieve her sketch pad from where she'd left it near her shoes. Then she sat down on the grass, a few feet from Gaya. As Serena was used to drawing plants and animals, neither of which could be moved to suit the artist, she was able to capture her subject no matter which way the sunlight fell. And so without preamble Serena began to work, her pencil moving rapidly and her mind intent. She worked silently and Gaya, with what seemed an instinctive understanding of the process, sat quietly and still.

The shadows had begun to lengthen before Serena put her pencil down and looked up. "There. I daresay I have made a very pleasing start," she said, rising and showing Gaya what she thought was a very creditable beginning. The facial details were missing, but she had got the body stance and Gaya's hair and costume very well. She would need one, perhaps two more sittings, and then she could paint.

Gaya uncurled her long legs and stared intently at the sketch. "You are right. I am very good—what is it you say—subject. And you are very good artist, Serena."

Serena's lips twitched. "Thank you, Gaya. Will you sit for me again?"

"Yes, I will come again," Gaya replied. She wriggled from the rock and stood beside Serena.

Serena wanted to ask if they might meet tomorrow, but she knew it was foolish to do so. Gypsies just weren't the sort to make appointments, or keep them. Besides, Serena herself did not know when she might get away again. "Good. Then we shall meet again soon," she said. "And I had better be getting back now. It is nigh onto tea time, I daresay." She did not want to miss her hour with the duke and bade her new friend farewell.

"Goodbye," Gaya said, and then, "you still have no shoes, Serena."

Serena chuckled. "So I don't. But, in truth, I do not care to wear them just now," she replied lightheartedly and, going to collect them, rolled the stockings up and tucked them into the toes. With a smile to Gaya, she set off, her sketch pad in one hand, her shoes swinging in the other. The grass felt smooth and silky underfoot, and even the dirt was warming. She stumbled on pebbles several times, but all in all she thought one's bare feet were a perfectly acceptable means of transport.

It was not until she reached the outskirts of the formal gardens that she recalled the scene that had sent her running into the woods. She sighed. She was not happy to be coming back, but she had had a fine afternoon nonetheless.

When she was within sight of the house, she remembered to pin the several wayward locks of her hair back up. It was so thick that the underside was still wet. But she did not yet don her shoes — she wanted to glide over the lush fine lawns barefoot. There was time enough for shoes once she reached the rose garden.

But as soon as she turned the corner to the rose garden, she knew she was too late. For there, walking in a straight path toward her, were Livvy and Caroline. Serena had no choice but to amble forward, shoes in one hand, bare toes visible beneath her skirts.

"Hello Livvy, Caroline," she said pleasantly, when they came together.

"Hello, Serena," Livvy said coolly.

Caroline merely inclined her head in a nod and then eyed Serena up and down, a smirk on her lips. "Why Serena, your skirt is all muddy, and wet. And your hair is wet also. You might catch a chill. Have you fallen into the fish pond?" Caroline cooed with feigned concern.

"And you have no shoes on!" Livvy exclaimed with unfeigned surprise.

Three pairs of eyes looked down at the bare toes

peeking out from beneath the yellow skirt.

"No, I don't," Serena snapped, looking up and meeting first Caroline's, then Livvy's eyes.

Livvy giggled, but stopped abruptly, her eyes widening as she stared beyond Serena. Caroline's lips spread into a very smug, very unpleasant smile, and, finally hearing footsteps behind her, Serena whirled around.

There, not fifteen feet away and fast approaching, was Richard, the scowl on his face telling her he'd heard the entire exchange. It was quite possible, she knew, since several winding paths lined with hedges led to the rose garden, and he could easily have overheard them without betraying his presence. Serena braced herself and resisted the urge to shove her shoes behind her back. He came up to her in but a moment and stopped in his tracks. "Serena, are you all right?" he asked a bit curtly.

"Yes, Richard," she answered softly. He frowned, then greeted Livvy and Caroline with a brief "Afternoon, ladies," before returning his attention to Serena. His eyes flitted over her, from her hair to the shoes in her hand to her toes. He took a deep breath. "Serena, I would have a word with you," he said with controlled calm.

Well, at the least he would not make the scene public, she thought. "Very well, Richard," she said, holding her head high. And without a word to Caroline and Livvy she followed in his wake.

"Well, Serena," he said abruptly as soon as they'd reached the library, "*did* you meet with some accident?" They stood in front of the leather sofa, just two feet apart.

Serena was glad to answer truthfully. "Oh, no Richard. I am right. You needn't trouble about me," she said lightly.

He did not share her mood. "I didn't think so. Then where were you?"

"Why, I went for a walk, Richard. Did you get all of your work done?"

"Don't shift the subject, Serena! You went for a walk and just happened to get your hair wet? Do not gammon me, dear wife. I know you too well. Now kindly tell me what you've been about."

From the corner of her eye Serena could see his fists clenched and knew he was making a great effort to hold his temper in check. She had got to think fast, for though she knew she had not actually done anything wrong, he mightn't see it that way. And besides, she had no intention of revealing her newfound retreat to anyone. She searched her mind frantically, and Caroline's nasty tongue came to her rescue.

She sighed as if the matter were of no import. "If you must know, Richard, I *was* at the fish pond. I had been out for some time and it was frightfully hot. I bent to rinse my face and neck in the water, and I'm afraid my skirts rather tumbled into the pond." She tried to look sheepish, and sincere. She disliked lying, but then, she reminded herself, he hadn't been truthful with her either. "You must not worry about Caroline," he'd said. "*You* are my wife." Hah! What empty words *they* had been.

His eyes penetrated hers, as if he were deciding whether or not to believe her. "And your shoes, Serena?" he asked sternly. She still held them in her hand.

A gleam of mischief lit her eyes. "Oh, Richard, it is

much too lovely a day to keep one's feet confined in shoes. It was exceedingly delicious to glide across the beautiful lawns with the smooth grass tickling my feet. Truly, you had ought to try it, you know."

For a moment she thought his lips twitched and then the stern mask descended again onto his face. He stared at her hard for a moment and then sighed. "Very well, Serena. We shall say no more about it. You will kindly don your shoes before leaving this room, and in future I will expect you to—"

His tone was beginning to sound a bit too much like her father's and Serena was no longer listening. She was thinking of Gaya, wondering whether the girl even possessed a pair of bloody shoes.

"Serena, are you attending me?" he demanded.

"Ah—why—of course, my l—Richard. You were saying that I must—ah—conduct myself—"

"Serena," Richard interrupted, sighing and taking a step closer to her. Suddenly his tone was gentler and his body did not seem quite so rigid. "You must believe that I do not wish to question your every move." He raised his hand and swept a tendril of hair from her brow. She was oddly moved by the gesture. "It is merely that we have a certain position to uphold, you and I, and we must—well—behave accordingly."

Without thinking she blurted, "Oh, Richard, if you, heir to the dukedom, cannot run barefoot in your own garden, then who can?"

Richard smiled, in spite of himself, she thought. "My dear, not everyone desires above all things to run barefoot through the grass." And then, as if remembering himself, he added stiffly, "Such a thing is simply not done. We are not at Gateshead, nor are you a little girl dashing through your father's wood. Even coming home with muddied skirts is not at all the thing. Appearances *are* important, Serena, whether you will it or no." His tone had softened again at this last, but Serena bristled. You damned hypocrite, she wanted to shout at him. Taking one's shoes off was inappropriate but kissing Caroline Lister was not? But she said nothing, merely stared mutely at him.

"Serena, do you understand what I am saying? I do not wish to argue with you."

"I understand you very well, Richard," she snapped finally. "And I do assure you we are not arguing! It simply isn't done! And now, if you will excuse me—" She dropped a deep curtsy, careful to keep the offending shoes behind her back, and then turned without a word and sashayed from the room.

It was a moment later in the wide upstairs corridor that she encountered the duchess, speaking with the butler.

"But Rivers, I had thought we'd put it about that we were not receiving visitors," the duchess said in some consternation.

"Indeed, your grace, that we have. But I believe, beggin' your grace's pardon, that the Babbingtons have been away. Only just returned, you must know, and mayhap they don't quite know what's what," replied the butler.

"Your grace, may I be of help?" Serena asked, stepping forward.

"Oh, my dear. I only just left the duke with Hudson for a moment, for it is at least an hour until tea time, when you will be—"

"What seems to be the trouble, Mother?" came

Richard's booming voice, and Serena stiffened. She had not yet changed her clothes nor—

"Oh, Mama, it's the vicar and his wife, come to call," chirped Livvy, darting into the corridor from the music room. Caroline followed at a more decorous pace.

Oh Lord, an assembly, Serena thought, and tried to hide her shoes in the folds of her yellow skirt. She could only hope that this time no one would notice her bare feet.

"Such an odd hour, Mama, is it not?" Livvy asked. "Not yet tea time, but—"

"Yes, Livvy, it is," the duchess sighed. "Richard, we cannot very well refuse the vicar, yet I simply do not see how I can entertain—"

"Now, Mother," Richard said soothingly, "we need not invite them to tea. Surely a simple drink will suffice, and it will require only a few minutes to—"

"Excuse me, Richard," Serena interrupted, ignoring her husband's scowl. "But I think your mother needs must attend to the duke. Do not trouble yourself, your grace," she said gently. "I am persuaded that we can see to the visitors. You belong with his grace, until such time as you are relieved, and so I shall make your excuses to the Babbingtons." Somehow Serena did not wish to make known her intention of sitting with the duke, and she was glad when the duchess, after glancing briefly at Richard, merely nodded her assent.

At his mother's grateful smile and murmur of thanks, Richard's scowl subsided. His mother disappeared and Serena turned to the butler. "Rivers, where are they now?"

"In the gray saloon, my lady."

"Very good. Pray conduct them to the drawing

room. Oh, and as it *is* too early for tea, do bring some cakes and sherry and lemonade — that sort of thing," Serena instructed him easily.

The butler bowed and departed, and Richard stared at his wife. He disliked being gainsaid, but she *was*, after all, only thinking of his mother, as she had last night. It was her quiet air of command that amazed him. This despite her muddied skirts and disheveled hair. She glanced at him uncertainly and he smiled and moved to take her arm. Caroline, he noted, looked none too happy, and he frowned, remembering their encounter in the library. Then he looked down and saw Serena's bare feet. Good God, hadn't she put on those damn shoes yet? he cursed inwardly, and hoped no one else would notice.

They had assembled in the drawing room but a moment before the door burst open.

"Oh, my dear Lord Egremont," pronounced Mrs. Babbington effusively, making straight for him, a huge basket of fruit in her plump arms. "So happy to see you. We have only now returned from our visit in Yorkshire, and here we are greeted with such news! And one hardly knows what to say first, does one? Is it felicitations on your marriage — such a surprise! such wonderful news! Or our sympathy upon the illness of your dear father, the duke?"

"Er — ah — thank you, Mrs. Babbington," Richard answered when she finally paused for breath. Then he smiled briefly at the vicar, who bowed and murmured simply "my lord," before his wife plunged ahead.

"And how *is* your dear father, my lord?" she clucked, her round face bobbing up and down around the basket she seemed loath to relinquish.

"He is quite feverish, I'm afraid," Richard replied solemnly.

"Oh dear. And I had so hoped—well—our prayers are with you, are they not, dear Oliver?" she asked her husband, but did not await a reply. "And here I have brought him a basket of fruit—not but what he can use it now. But soon, soon, my dear Lord Egremont, and dear, dear Livvy! My, how overset you must be! And your poor mother—Oh, here my girl, do take this won't you?" she asked, turning abruptly to Serena and nearly dumping the basket in her arms.

Startled, Serena moved to place the over-large offering on a side table. Richard did not much care for his wife's being mistaken for an upstairs maid, muddy skirts or not. Livvy twittered and Caroline smiled sweetly.

"Er, Reverend, Mrs. Babbington," he began, "may I present my wife?"

"Oh, yes, of course, do. We are simply *dying* to meet her, are we not, Oliver?"

"Indeed, my dear," the vicar managed, before Mrs. Babbington went on.

To Richard's astonishment, and before he could stop her, she made straight for Caroline, who stood demurely next to Livvy. "And you must be the new marchioness!" she exclaimed, clapping her hands at her waist. "Such a beauty, you are. Oh, you are a one, Lord Egremont, to capture such a prize. Such hair, like spun gold, do you not agree, dear Oliver?"

The vicar murmured something suitable and Richard cast a sidelong glance at Serena. She stood, one hand on the fruit basket, her body completely rigid, her face still and unreadable. Caroline flashed Mrs.

Babbington a lovely smile and Livvy seemed to be choking. Richard took a deep breath, and stepped into the breach.

"Ah, ahem, Mrs. Babbington, Reverend, may I present my wife, Lady Serena, Marchioness of Egremont," he said quickly, striding to Serena and propelling her forward.

The Reverend Babbington began to cough and his wife whirled around crimson faced. "B-but—I—I thought—" she stopped and suddenly began to giggle, covering her mouth like a schoolroom miss. "Oh, my, I—I have made a muddle of things, haven't I, Oliver?" she asked ruefully.

"Yes, Flora, you certainly have," the vicar replied, but he was smiling fondly. Richard blinked. He had never understood what an otherwise sane man saw in that woman.

Mrs. Babbington dashed to Serena in a flutter of aquamarine silk. "Oh, my dear Lady Egremont," she gushed, assaying a small curtsy, "can you ever forgive me?" Serena smiled ever so slightly and the woman obviously took this for assent, for she continued right on. "But, I mean to say, my dear, well—how was I to know? You are perfectly charming, I am persuaded, but—well—not—not quite in the ordinary way, are you?"

"No, I'm not, Mrs. Babbington," Serena replied politely, her tight smile not reaching her eyes. "And now, why do we not all be seated?"

"Yes, of course, Lady Egremont," concurred the vicar's wife, totally ignoring the request. With a puzzled frown she turned vaguely to Caroline. "But, ah, who—who then is—"

Richard once more found his voice, and quickly made the introductions. The vicar said he was charmed to meet both ladies, and Serena repeated her invitation that they all be seated.

"We should love to, Lady Egremont," Mrs. Babbington replied, "and we shall all have a comfortable cose, I am certain. But—ah—" here Mrs. Babbington paused for breath and lowered her voice—"my dear child, are you—are you aware that you—you are—are wearing *no shoes*?"

After which the vicar succumbed to a paroxysm of coughing, Livvy gave way to uncontrollable giggles, and Rivers promptly entered to announce sherry and rum cakes.

Some fifteen minutes later, Richard paced the floor of his study in high dudgeon. But he was unsure at whom to be more angry—Serena for her unpardonable appearance, the dithering Mrs. Babbington, or Livvy, for taking such delight in it all! And Caroline—he would have expected her to blush with maidenly embarrassment, even to flee in tears, but she had done neither of those. Just stood there and—"

Oh hell! What a disaster it had been! Not but what after the refreshments came, Serena had handled them all rather smoothly, slipping into the role of hostess with remarkable ease. He recalled his mother's comment, weeks ago, about Serena's having been bred to her role, and he tried to be pleased. But then he remembered those bare little toes, peeking out from under the dirty yellow skirt as she served around the rum cakes and biscuits, and his fists clenched. Mrs.

Babbington, kindly soul though she be, was a premier gossip. And by tomorrow half the Kentish countryside would know that Richard Gower was married to a — a — oh, blast! Richard exploded, and wanted to wring Serena's neck. But then he stopped in his pacing and shook his head ruefully, recalling his resolve to make her his wife in truth — this evening if possible. He could not have it both ways and decided he would rather not wring her lovely little neck, after all.

Serena had escaped the drawing room at first opportunity, careful to avoid her husband's eyes. A tumble of emotions had assailed her as she'd maintained her outward calm and played hostess. There had been humiliation, anger, defiance. But now, as she lay on her bed, she felt only an oppressive sadness. As Mrs. Babbington had so unwittingly demonstrated, she was not all a proper marchioness. And she never would be. She would always prefer sketching in the woods to drawing room teas, and her hair would never look like spun gold, or spun anything. No, it was Caroline who fit the bill, and it was Caroline Richard wanted.

Desperately Serena tried to squelch her thoughts, and her tears. In a short while it would be time to sit with the duke, and she needed to rest.

Even though she had mentally prepared herself, Serena found her hour with the duke most perturbing. That a man who had been so vital just days ago could be felled so completely . . . The doctor, Lady Luntsford had said, did not hold with bleeding for a fever.

Thank goodness for that, Serena thought—the duke was weak enough as it was. She bathed his brow and kept him covered when he thrashed about, and listened to the incoherent mutterings of his delirium. Twice he called "Bella," and Serena assured him that his wife would return soon. She doubted he understood, but her voice seemed to soothe him. And in fact, it was soon after that the duchess came back into the sickroom. An hour had not yet passed, but Serena knew better than to cavil.

"Thank you, Serena," the duchess whispered. "I am well rested now." She sat down at the side of the bed and took her husband's hand in hers.

"Bella," Serena heard the duke mumble. It was not the wail she'd heard before, but a soft sound, almost contented.

"I am here, John," the duchess answered, stroking his brow with her free hand. "I was merely gone a moment. I shall always be here, John. You rest now."

Serena felt a sob choke in her throat at the intimacy of the scene she was witnessing. She felt an interloper, just as Richard had. Without a word, and totally unheeded, she turned and tiptoed back to her room. There she threw herself on the huge, lonely bed and indulged in a very long cry. She cried for Bella and John, fighting desperately for life to continue. And she cried for Serena and Richard, who would never know life for what it really was, or could be.

Dinner was much the same as yesterday, Richard thought, his father's empty chair speaking volumes while everyone else said little. Caroline looked very smug, which Richard failed to understand, and he decided that that particular expression was not at all attractive to her.

His mother looked more rested this evening and when he said as much, she smiled gently. "Thank you, Richard. That is Serena's doing, as you must know." Richard looked puzzled. Surely Serena's relieving his mother of the Babbingtons would not have—"Oh, didn't you know, Richard?" the duchess queried. "Serena sat with your father at tea time, rather insisted on doing so, in fact, and I lay down to rest."

Richard responded in pleasant surprise, and smiled appreciatively at his wife. Livvy, he noted, looked a bit perturbed, and he wondered why. Caroline's expression was strangely unreadable, but he could not concern himself with either of them now. He glanced back at Serena, who was concentrating on her poached turbot. He would express his gratitude later, he thought—it would fit in well with his plans for her this evening.

"Richard," said his mother after the stuffed capon was served, "you worked very hard today, I know, but I do think you ought to have a respite tomorrow. Why don't you take Serena on an outing for the day? You might ride out over the estates, and I believe there is a fair in Meadsham."

Richard smiled. "An admirable idea, Mother. Indeed, I had been thinking along the same lines myself." He turned to Serena and was surprised to see only a polite smile on her face. He had expected her to be quite pleased. But before he could address his wife, Livvy spoke.

"Oh, how perfectly splendid! I do so love the village

fairs. Mother, may we go too, Caroline and I? I declare we have not been away from Luntsford this age. Oh, Richard, say we may go!" exclaimed Livvy in a breathless rush of words.

Richard ground his teeth. Why could his mother not have made her suggestion in private? The last thing he wanted was to have his sister and Caroline, of all people, join an outing whose main purpose was to put his wife enough at ease to—

"No, Livvy dear," he realized his mother was saying. "I think Richard and Serena need some time alone together. Their wedding trip was cut short, after all."

You're a trump, Mother, Richard thought, and flashed her a grateful smile. Livvy pouted in disappointment but Richard thought Caroline looked peeved. He was finding it increasingly difficult to understand her.

"Well, then, it's settled," he said, turning to Serena, who sat at his right. "We shall find you a mount and leave early in the morning. We can have a picnic in the woods, if you'd like that."

"Thank you, Richard. That would be lovely," his wife replied with a decided lack of enthusiasm. Richard sighed. It did not augur well for the evening ahead.

As he had last evening, Richard followed Serena into the bedchamber. *Their* bedchamber, he reminded himself as he once more led her to the center of the room, ignoring her puzzled expression. He had placed his hand at her elbow and did not release it as he turned to face her when they stood just before the bed. Instead he grasped the other elbow as well and gently pulled her closer to him.

"Serena, I would like to thank you for staying with my father," he began, his voice low and soft.

"I — I was happy to do it, Richard," she replied hesitantly.

"I sat with him for a bit this morning myself, but my mother chased me away," he continued. "I think you gave her the longest respite she's had yet from the sickroom." Serena seemed stiff, on her guard. Somehow he had to relax her. Even if tonight he didn't succeed in — well, at the least he must make some headway, he told himself. He brought a finger up to graze her cheek. "You are very generous, Serena," he whispered. "And I think there is much I do not know about you."

Her shoulders and neck were bare above her gold taffeta evening dress, and he caught the flutter of her pulse at her throat. He thought she flushed, too, but her words lacked any warmth whatever. "We shall become better acquainted as time passes, I am persuaded," she said in the devastatingly polite tone one might use to dismiss an unwelcome suitor.

Damn! Was she that terrified of him? Somehow, he didn't think so. She just wasn't the simpering, timid type. And he'd seen her staring at him several times, with a certain look . . . He would try once more, this time more suggestively.

He ran his hands up her bare arms and let them rest at her shoulders. "Yes, well, I should like to become better acquainted *before* time passes, Serena."

She swallowed hard and he felt her stiffen. He could not read the expression in her eyes, but he knew it was not fear. It was nothing at all like the look he'd seen that first night. "Richard," she said in a voice he was pleased to note was shaky, "I — I am certain our — ah — outing tomorrow will provide just such an opportunity. Now, do you not think we should see if Hannah and your man are here?" she asked and deftly wriggled from his grasp.

Damn! he thought, and sincerely hoped Watkins had attacked another jug of blue ruin. He hadn't. Both servants were dutifully awaiting them, and Richard had no choice but to bid Serena goodnight and submit to the ministrations of his valet. Serena seemed distinctly relieved to see Hannah and Watkins, and Richard cursed himself repeatedly for the idiotic promise he'd made to her on their wedding night. A little voice at the back of his head reminded him that it had been a threat and not a promise, and so he cursed himself again for his unbelievable arrogance.

But why the hell, he wondered as Watkins shrugged him out of his coat, was she resisting? She was not indifferent to him — he'd seen evidence of that tonight. And why was he making such a muck of it? For all of his twenty-two years, he'd had plenty of women. None of them virgins, of course, but still . . .

Suddenly he remembered about this afternoon and that nonsensical woman — he dashed toward the dressing room in his shirtsleeves, leaving a startled Watkins behind. Serena and her maid were even more taken aback when he unceremoniously burst into the bedchamber.

"Serena, you — you're not still upset about what that hen-witted Babbington woman said this afternoon, are you?" he blurted, then felt himself flush. "Oh, sorry," he muttered, as she gave a start and groped for the back of her gown, which he now realized was gaping partly open. Hannah, who had obviously been working on the myriad buttons, glared at him, but he ignored her. "I do beg your pardon, Serena, but I *must* know," he pleaded.

Serena nodded dismissal to her maid, who scurried out. "No, Richard, I am not upset," Serena said calmly, one hand clutching the back of her dress. But the other hand held tightly to the nightstand, he noted.

"That is good," he said, smiling now, and sauntering toward her. "For truly, she is naught but an addleplated pea-goose. She means no harm."

"No, of course not," she said politely, her body stiff.

"And you must admit,"he went on with a gleam in his eye, hoping to inject some humor, to unbend her a bit, "that with your attire, and — and your very delicate little toes —"

"Will that be all, Richard?" Serena interrupted frostily. Richard cursed himself for a blundering idiot. Was he no better than that birdwitted vicar's wife?

He must try again, he resolved, and stepped close to Serena. Gently he cupped her chin in his large hand. "I was only roasting you, my dear. But as to the rest; well, we have been through this before, but, well, Caroline is a *guest* here, Serena. There is no question of your place in this household. You *do* understand what I am trying to say, do you not?" he asked meaningfully.

"Yes, Richard," she replied, a bit breathlessly, he thought.

"Good," he murmured, emboldened enough to stroke her cheek. "I am glad, Serena. Er — about tonight —"

"Richard, I should like to finish my toilette now. I

108

bid you good night," she interjected, hurriedly retreating several steps back.

Richard sighed. The message was clear, and he was not sure what—oh, hell! There would be other nights, after all.

Serena was shaking when Richard finally said goodnight and departed. What was wrong with her that her body reacted so strangely to his proximity, his slightest touch? She reminded herself that he had, only hours ago, kissed another woman, and she resolutely called for Hannah.

The sofa was distinctly more uncomfortable tonight than last night. Richard tossed and turned and pounded the cushions beneath him. Cushions? Where the devil were the sofa cushions? He sat up and patted the bedding. There was a blanket, a pillow for his head, a sheet and—dammit! There *were* no cushions. He was practically sleeping on upholstery springs!

He rose, pulled his dressing gown on, and stalked to the dressing room. One taper still flickered but even in the dim light he could see no cushions lurking about. Still he checked the corners and the wardrobes. There were no cushions. Blast! he thought, his eyes sweeping the dressing room. They came to rest on the velvet chaise. He walked over and ran his hands over it. It was rather narrow but at the least he would not be poked about by those blasted springs all night.

Less than pleased, he went to the sitting room for his bedding. He arranged it as best he might on the chaise, shrugged off his robe, and snuffed the taper. The chaise, however, while conducive to a lady's afternoon's rest, was not precisely meant for a man's sleep. Its curve allowed one to recline but not to lie flat. With a groan, Richard pulled the blanket up to his chin and turned onto his side.

The door to Serena's room opened several moments later. She stepped hesitantly over the threshold; he could see her clearly in the light from her room, but it seemed she could not see him in his dark corner. He almost gasped when he realized that she carried two large sofa cushions in her arms. What the deuce — But he kept silent, watching her. She wore another high-necked white nightdress, with a dressing gown sashed tightly about her waist. Her thick hair fell loose down her back. She paused before the closed door to the sitting room and knocked tentatively. When no answer came she knocked again, and then whispered his name. Finally, she turned the knob and pushed the door open.

"Richard," she called softly, and then tiptoed into the room.

He smiled in the darkness. This was no simpering, timid little miss, this wife of his. He heard the swoosh of her nightclothes as she circled the room. She would be back in a moment, he knew, and without allowing himself to think clearly, he bounded off the chaise. As quickly and quietly as he could, he pushed the couch until it stood in the middle of the dressing room, right in the path between the two doors. Then he closed the door to her room, so that most of the dressing room was bathed in darkness. He drew his robe back on; he would not want to shock her overmuch. He climbed back onto the chaise, and only then did it occur to him that he was behaving like an idiot. But it was too late —

he heard her approaching the doorway. She had left the cushions behind, and as she stepped over the threshold she conveniently closed the sitting room door behind her. The dressing room was dark now, but his eyes had already adjusted and so he could see her begin to cross the room. Her head was cocked, as if she were perplexed, and she walked absently and slowly. Still it was only a moment before she would reach the side of the couch.

"Ow!" she exclaimed as she collided neatly with the chaise. Her knees buckled and she fell, just as he'd hoped, straight into his lap. He sat up and grabbed her round the waist to steady her.

"Oh! My God, who—who's here?" she shrieked, trying to slap his hands and squirm out of them at the same time.

"Calm down, Serena. It is I, Richard. It's all right," he said soothingly, pulling her a little closer.

"Oh, Richard," she sighed, rather breathless, "thank God it's you. For a moment I thought—I thought—oh, God, I don't know quite what I thought." She turned her head into his shoulder and he realized she was shaking. He hadn't meant to frighten her, but perhaps it wasn't a bad idea after all. He held her close, gently massaging her back with one hand. She felt warm and good, her body pressed against his chest; he resisted the urge to run his hand over her soft curves.

After a moment she lifted her head but did not pull away. "Richard, I don't understand. How did—"

"I'm sorry, my dear. 'Tis my fault, really. The sofa was very uncomfortable, so I decided to sleep in here. I didn't care to sleep in the corner and so moved the chaise."

"But—but on my way in I didn't—"

"I must have been asleep, since I didn't see you, Serena. I suppose you simply didn't walk this way," he lied unabashedly. His hand had moved up first to stroke her hair, and then to caress her neck, and he could feel her whole body begin to relax.

"But of course I did, Richard. I had to—"

"Serena," he interrupted, his voice low as he breathed into her ear, "was there any special reason that you were coming to my room?"

He felt her tense, as if she had just become aware of what he was trying to do. "Oh, yes, Richard, there—there was," she stammered. She tried to inch away from him but he held her fast. "I—I found your sofa cushions in my bed and I thought you would be uncomfortable without them, and so I—"

"Indeed I was," he murmured, pulling her head back down and beginning to nuzzle the side of her neck. She did not offer any resistance. "And you know, my dear, the chaise is not that much better."

He could actually feel a hot flush go through her as his lips touched her throat. Her body swayed to his and he felt a surge of triumph even as the heat surged in his loins. He would move his lips gradually to hers, and then—

"Ah, Richard, I—" she protested feebly, her hand trying, not very hard, to push his arm from her waist.

"Yes, Serena?" he whispered huskily. Thought was becoming increasingly difficult. His hand moved from her neck to caress her back. His lips moved over her throat and encountered the stiff unyielding collar of her neckline. And then he made a tactical error; he unbuttoned the top button of her nightgown.

112

Immediately her body went rigid, as if his action had shocked her. She put her hands to his chest to push him away. One hand found its way between the lapels of the dressing gown, and she gasped when she touched his bare skin. Suddenly she twisted free of him and stood up. Richard followed suit, thinking it just as well he was wearing his dressing gown.

"Richard—I—I must go now," she said, not breathing quite regularly. "I hadn't meant to disturb you."

"You were not disturbing me, Serena," he said smoothly, moving close to her. "I think you know that. As I said, 'tis not very comfortable sleeping on—"

"Richard, I have an idea!" she blurted, taking two steps back. He put his hands in his pockets and waited. "'Tis not fair that you should be so uncomfortable whilst I—"

He moved forward. "I was trying to remedy that very situation, Serena."

"Yes, well, the solution is quite simple, really," she chattered, moving backwards as he advanced. "We shall simply switch off. Tonight I shall sleep on the sofa and you the bed. And then tomorrow I shall take the bed again and you—"

"That is not precisely what I had in mind, Serena," he said silkily, very close to her now.

This time she did not move away, but raised her chin and spoke in a chilly tone he'd never heard from her before. "I think it is the best solution under the circumstances, Richard," she said firmly, standing very still and straight. Her sudden coldness baffled him, for he could swear that moments ago—

But that was neither here nor there. For now, he knew he was vanquished; this was quite the clearest rebuff he'd ever received. He shrugged, reminding himself that tomorrow was another night and that he had, after all, made some headway. He knew of a certain that she was not completely indifferent. He had stirred her, and he could do it again. But as he tossed restlessly on his solitary sofa a while later, he was most disconcerted by the thought that she had stirred him as well.

Chapter Six

Serena had very mixed feelings about today's outing with Richard. She was glad of the opportunity to get away from the house, and she had enjoyed their outings at Gateshead. Indeed, had circumstances been different, she would have looked forward to the day. As it was, she could only assume Richard had agreed to it for his usual reason — to keep up appearances. She knew well that he had rather be with Caroline Lister.

But appearances could not account for his behavior in the dressing room last night, she thought, flushing even now as Hannah helped her don her dark brown riding habit. She did not at all like the strange feelings that he invoked in her — not that they were unpleasant; quite the opposite in fact. But they were dangerous feelings, for, much as she was loath to admit it, she had *wanted* him to touch her, to keep doing what he was doing. But she could not allow it. Not when it was Caroline he was thinking of all the while. And Serena did not understand him. Even with her little knowledge, she knew he had been trying to seduce her last night. How could he do such a thing if he were in love with another woman?

Serena surveyed herself in the looking glass as Hannah put the finishing touches to her toilette. Her riding habit looked well on her, she thought. The rich chocolate brown color matched her hair and brought a sparkle to her deep blue eyes, and the simplicity of the dress suited her. Even Mama could not put flounces all over a riding habit, she mused impishly. The habit was rather form fitting, accentuating her figure in a way that her over-embellished gowns never did. She wondered for a moment if that was precisely *why* Mama insisted on such flounces and furbelows as she did. Well, no matter. Mama would no longer have a say in Serena's dress. And Richard, autocratic though he might be, did not share Mama's dubious taste. But that was neither here nor there, for she had been dictated to long enough and intended to choose her own clothes from now on.

Serena watched Hannah pin her small riding hat to the side of her head. It was nearly hidden by all her hair, which even now, newly brushed and pinned up, had begun to sprout a delicate halo of tendrils. Richard, she knew, would not approve. But that was just too damned bad, she thought rebelliously. She *liked* her hair, and that was all that mattered.

Breakfast was a brief interlude in which Richard spoke hesitantly about several of the tenant farms they would visit, if Serena would not mind a bit of business interspersed with the pleasure of the day. Serena said that of course that would be fine; she wished to meet the people whom Luntsford served. At that Richard smiled that special smile of his, the one that made her knees feel weak. She could not understand herself at all.

"I'm glad, Serena. We'll start with the tenant farms, then," he said, and refilled both of their coffee cups.

Conversation lagged after that, and Serena's eyes caught Richard's wandering to the unopened newspaper next his plate again. Suddenly she giggled. "Do you mean to keep reading the same three paragraphs, Richard, or will you open it to see what's inside?" she asked.

Richard flushed. "You really do not mind, Serena?"

"No, Richard, I do not mind," she said, stifling a grin, and then popping a piece of buttered biscuit into her mouth.

"Would you care to read a portion?" he asked.

She swallowed the biscuit and could not repress a gleam in her eye. "No, Richard, I wouldn't. I shall just gaze out the window and think about—"

"Think about what to paint next. Yes, I know, Serena. And you *have* made your point. And I do not think it all *that* humorous, you know."

She giggled again. "Oh, Richard, I'm sorry. 'Tis just that I had a sudden image of us, many years hence when we are quite in our dotage, sitting at this very table and having this very same conversation."

A curious light came into his eyes. "Did you now, my dear?" he mused, and then a moment later added, "Eat hearty, Serena. We've a full morning ahead of us."

Richard had said, as they departed the breakfast parlor, that he would take a large saddle bag, should she wish to take her sketch pad. And then he'd asked whether he minded if he took his net and pocket box, for one never knew when an interesting specimen might be got. Of course, that would be fine, she'd said, and then skipped off to fetch her pad and riding gloves.

Livvy was blue-devilled. She had risen earlier than usual, too early, she thought, but it could not be helped. She simply could not sleep any more; she'd not slept all that well at first stop. She'd rung for her chocolate and now sat in bed, sipping it without enthusiasm, her lips turned down into a pout.

The summer had been so delightful here. She and Richard and Caroline had gone everywhere together and enjoyed themselves excessively. The Court had been full of laughter and sunshine. And now everything had gone awry. Papa was ill; Mama was with him, of course. And Richard, with whom she had once been so close, had hardly spoken to her in weeks. First he'd been preoccupied with his marriage, and then away on his wedding trip, and now he was preoccupied with business and Serena. And that last did not make sense—it was not as though he really cared for her. Livvy wondered if he'd had any time to be private with Caroline since his return. She couldn't imagine when.

Things just didn't seem right. Serena had somehow contrived to become the center of attention. And it wasn't fair. Livvy had lived here all her life, not Serena. This was *her* family, not Serena's. Not that Serena puffed herself up, nor did she try to lord it over Livvy, or Caroline for that matter. But Mama seemed to have a special smile just for Serena, seemed to be always thinking about Serena's comfort, despite Mama's own trouble just now. And only Serena had been able to supplant Mama in the sickroom, and Mama and Richard had smiled their gratitude all through dinner last night. Livvy knew well that her mother's refusal to allow anyone, her daughter included, to stand guard over Papa had nothing to do with lack of trust. Mama simply could not bear to leave Papa's bedside. Livvy had, of course, volunteered to sit with him, but had been relieved to be refused; she truly could not bear the sickroom. Still, it hurt that Serena had become something of a heroine over it all.

And Livvy could not fail to note the special privileges accorded Serena. She could roam the parkland at will, without troubling about a chaperone. Today she was to have a special outing with Richard, and she would be given a horse, probably one of the beautiful new mounts Durwood had been training. The fact that Livvy was an indifferent rider and was content with her old gelding she chose to ignore.

If Livvy would be fair, which she didn't care to be, she could suppose those were all just the prerogatives of a married woman; they would one day be Livvy's as well. But still, she felt supplanted in her family's affection, and that rankled.

She jumped out of bed, an idea coming to her. She *did* want to help her Mama, and she needed to show that Serena was not the only unselfish person in the household. Serena and Richard would just be preparing to depart, and there might still be time.

Serena left her room, gloves and sketch pad in hand, and was just turning the corner to the main stairwell when Livvy accosted her. The girl was still in her dressing gown and Serena was immediately concerned.

"Is anything wrong, Livvy?"

"No, there's nothing wrong, Serena. 'Tis just — well,

I know you will be tired when you come home today. You shall probably return just before tea time and I—I was wondering if *I* might sit with Papa in your stead."

Serena was puzzled. Surely Livvy could not suddenly be concerned for her? "I shan't be that tired, Livvy. Why do you not ask your mother if you might sit with the duke at another time? That way she will have an added rest."

Livvy pouted. "I *did* ask, but Mama refused all offers of help but yours. 'Tis not that she doesn't trust anyone else, but merely that she will not leave Papa, except for a few brief intervals when she allows Papa's valet to relieve her. And so I thought that perhaps just this once, since you would be away a good part of the day anyway, that—that I might do it."

Livvy sounded almost pleading, very unlike the spiteful girl who'd come to tell her about Caroline Lister, and suddenly Serena understood. Livvy was jealous. Jealous that Serena had won her mother's approval, and had access to the sickroom. And jealous that Serena would be spending the day with Richard, whom Serena suspected Livvy truly adored. Livvy needed some attention and she needed to feel useful.

Serena smiled. "Very well, Livvy, just for today. But be sure to tell your mother."

Livvy's pretty face brightened immediately. Now her mother would see that she, too, could be helpful. *Of course* she would tell her. But not until afterward. She would not want her mother to deny her this chance. And so to Serena she merely said, "Thank you, Serena. Of course, I shall tell her."

Livvy skipped back down the corridor and Serena stood for a moment where she was, lost in thought.

Perhaps, despite all, she ought to have made more of an effort to befriend her sister-in-law. She shrugged and turned toward the stairwell. She did not see the pair of eyes that watched her from behind a slightly opened door, nor did she realize just whose bedchamber stood a mere few feet from where she and Livvy had been talking.

"I thought you might like Lightfoot, Serena. He's a fine horse. Very beautiful, is he not?" asked Richard, patting the smooth gray flanks as he led the horse from his stall.

"He looks very — ah — well cared for, Richard. A bit tame, perhaps?" Serena asked. Richard frowned.

"Ahem," Durwood interjected. "Mayhap my lady would like to put the gelding through his paces, right here in the stable yard, before making her decision, my lord."

Richard scowled at his head groom. What the hell was he trying to do? Durwood knew very well that Richard wanted Serena to have the gelding. He was strong and trustworthy, not perhaps the most exciting of the Gower mounts, but still, Richard could feel at ease if he knew Serena was riding Lightfoot. She might have a good seat, but even so, with some of the other horses. . .

"I should love to trot him 'round, Durwood. Thank you," Serena said, smiling at the groom and then at Richard.

Richard glared at her; he was not accustomed to being ridden roughshod over in such a manner. But Serena blithely ignored him and Durwood's lips twitched as he led Lightfoot out to the stable yard. Richard was not certain whether to be pleased or miffed a few minutes later, however. For it was quite obvious that Serena was, indeed, an excellent rider. She had a good seat and secure command of the gelding as she led him through his paces. She drew back on the reins to halt him before Richard and Durwood.

"He's very friendly," she said, patting the full gray mane. "And very restful. I do think, Richard, that Lightfoot would be fine for someone much younger or *very* much older than I am," she added with a glint in her eye, and then she turned to Durwood. "You *do* have a mount with a bit more spirit, do you not, Durwood?"

Durwood's old craggy face screwed up into a grin, but he said nothing as he helped Serena dismount. Blast the man! Richard thought. Next minute he'd be handing her up onto Firefly, of all things.

"I'm thinkin' that Firefly would be more suited to her ladyship, my lord," Durwood said just moments later as he closed the door to the gelding's stall.

"I think not, Durwood," Richard said repressively, his fists clenched. "That mare has just barely been broken. Hardly suitable for Lady Egremont, I should say."

"Perhaps *I* might be the judge of that, Richard. After all, *I* shall be riding her. And I really shouldn't like a horse whose spirit has been completely broken, should you, Richard?" Serena asked sweetly. Too sweetly, he thought.

He sighed. "Very well, Durwood. Let us have her ladyship put Firefly through her paces."

Durwood helped Serena mount the beautiful chestnut mare, and it was evident from the first that she and Firefly established a firm, secret rapport. Serena had an instinct about animals, it seemed, and about this one in particular, for she rode her with the ease of long familiarity. Richard ground his teeth, telling himself he was pleased to have a wife with such a good seat.

Durwood was trying very hard not to give way to a most unholy guffaw. "Saddle Corinthian for me, you old goat, and I'll have no more of that cheeky grin," Richard ordered, but noted that his words did not discommode Durwood in the least.

Richard had to admit that Serena looked perfect atop the chestnut. The mare's rich color seemed to enhance her own and he thought that Serena looked especially lovely today. Her riding habit hugged her figure and he found himself very much wanting to do the same. A brisk gallop would do him good, he thought ruefully.

Serena enjoyed the ride through the parkland, and it was she who suggested a race over the lush green meadows. Richard demurred at first.

"Oh, come, Richard, whyever not? You cannot tell me 'tis not the thing, for I warrant 'tis *quite* the thing, you know, to race on horseback, through the—"

"Yes, yes Serena, I *know* 'tis done. It's just that you haven't ridden Firefly much above a half an hour and now—"

"To that cluster of trees, Richard," she interrupted. "Now!" And then she was off.

It was exhilarating and she could hear Richard coming up behind her. She did not even mind when he beat her by two yards.

"You ride well, Richard," she said when they were

reined in.

He blinked, seemingly taken aback for a moment. And then he smiled, that special smile that warmed his dark brown eyes and sent strange ripples of sensation down Serena's legs. "As do you, my dear, as do you," he said.

They visited several tenant farms after that, and though Richard apologized each time for allowing business to impinge on their pleasure, Serena replied truthfully that she did not mind a bit.

Farmer Hadley was so overwhelmed and delighted to meet the new Lady Egremont that he stammered and blushed painfully and nearly fell over in making his gallant bow. But there was a friendliness lurking in his eyes that made Serena like him instantly. And she was somehow pleased that he treated Richard not only with the deference due his rank, but with the respect of one man for the abilities of another. Richard began questioning him about the mysterious disappearance of several hens from his chicken coop. Mr. Hadley seemed grateful for the interest, and the two men began discussing possible culprits, human and otherwise. Serena knew very well that this was the sort of thing the estate agent might see to, but Richard obviously did not want to leave it at that. The duke would do the same, she thought. Richard had had a very good teacher.

It was several minutes later that the rotund, pink-cheeked Mrs. Hadley came bustling out of the cottage, all apologies for having been so concerned with the raspberry tarts in the oven that she had nary an inklin' that there be visitors, and such distinguished ones as that. "Ah, newlyweds," she went on, obviously suffering from none of her husband's shyness. "The very idea just makes my eyes mist over. And leave it to you, Lord Egremont, you young rascal, to pick yerself such a beauty. What eyes! And such hair—why, forgive me, Lady Egremont, but I never did see the like. Don't you agree, Mr. Hadley? You know what they say, Gowers have allas married Wexleys, and I can see why. It's a lucky man you are, my lord, but now if you don't mind, I'll just take yer pretty bride inside with me for a spot of tea whilst you men finish this business 'bout the chicken coop. I still say, Mr. Hadley, 'taint no fox been inside that chicken coop. It's Farmer Caffrey what sent one of his boys to crawl under that fence. He's still all het up, yer lordship, 'bout that gate o' his Old Bessie knocked down last June. She be one of our milk cows, don't you know—and—well—I'll leave you men to decide what's to be done."

Mrs Hadley's monologue did not cease when they were seated in the cozy kitchen with its yellow gingham curtains. But Serena enjoyed every minute of her company. She was natural and effusive and friendly. There was no reserve about her at all; she did not govern her every utterance by a set of artificial rules, and Serena found it all most refreshing.

"Well, what do you think, Lady Egremont? Be truthful now. It's a new recipe I be tryin', this raspberry tart, but if you like it—well—I'm thinkin' I'll give it over to your Mary—you know, Cook up t' the Court. Mary used to be a neighbor of my sister's down Surrey way, did you know that, Lady Egremont?" No, Serena hadn't known that, but further explication was prevented by the entrance of the two men into the cottage.

Serena and Richard were off soon after that, and

they stopped again at a neighboring farm. This time Serena remained outside with her husband and Farmer Norton.

"Mrs. Norton's gone to Cornwall, your lordship, Lady Egremont. Gone to be with our daughter for her first—ahem—confinement," the farmer said, blushing to the roots of his blond hair.

Richard deftly switched the conversation to the condition of the soil and the potential harvest this year. Serena listened attentively. It was not that she was so interested in agriculture. It was just that for some reason she enjoyed watching Richard. He seemed to really listen to the farmer, eliciting his opinion on several new farming techniques. Serena tried to imagine her father having a similar conversation with one of his tenants and failed utterly. She couldn't suppose that he even *knew* what a seed drill was, let alone wished to discuss it with a mere farmer. And as to Richard, this was a side of him she'd never seen, and was glad of the opportunity.

They next stopped at a charming two-story cottage with gabled windows and ivy winding its way to the upper story. As soon as they dismounted, a small elderly woman came dashing out of the cottage. Her fine white hair was swept back into a bun, and delicate wrinkles danced on her face.

"Oh, you darling boy, you've come!" she exclaimed, and nearly threw herself into Richard's arms. Much to Serena's shock, Richard hugged her and actually swung her up several inches from the ground before releasing her. Serena stared wide-eyed at her husband. Was this the same proper, upright Marquis of Egremont she knew?

"Serena, I'd like you to meet Nanny Gilbert," Richard said, his arm around the small woman. "And Nanny, this is my wife, Serena, Lady Egremont."

Nanny Gilbert extended her hands. "Lady Egremont, I am so pleased," she said warmly. "Don't know how long I've been sayin' to Mr. Gilbert that this young rapscallion needs a wife to make him happy, and now, here you are. And so lovely, too."

"Thank you, Mrs. Gilbert," Serena said, smiling.

"Oh, pray call me Nanny, Lady Egremont. Near everyone does, even though there hasn't been a babe in the Luntsford nursery since little Livvy." Nanny looked pointedly from Richard to Serena and Serena felt herself blush.

"Very well, Nanny, but then, you must not be so formal with me either," she replied.

"And so I shan't, Lady Serena. Now my lord, you and your bride just come on in for some tea," she said, and ushered them into the cottage and toward a small, sunny dining parlor at the back.

"You'll have to excuse Mr. Gilbert," Nanny said when she had brought the tea things and begun to pour out. "He's up on the roof, trying to fix a very pesky leak."

"That roof *still* giving you trouble, Nanny?" Richard asked, his teacup poised midair. "Why the devil didn't you let me know?"

"Now, my lord, I reckon as how you've enough on your mind just now, what with your charming bride, and now your father—"

Richard frowned and put his cup down. "Nanny, if you start standing on ceremony with me at this late date— Where is he?" he demanded, rising from his chair.

"All right, all right. He's off to the side. Up there. You can see him from this window," Nanny replied, pointing to where a whitehaired man was working on the gentle slope of the roof.

"If you ladies will excuse me, I'll go see just what the trouble is," Richard said, and bowed and took his leave.

Serena turned back to see a fond smile on Nanny's lips. "What's he going to do, Nanny?"

"Oh, I reckon he'll just climb right up alongside my Archie."

"Up? On the roof? Richard's going to climb up on the roof?"

"Oh, do not worry, my lady, he's quite adept at it, believe me. He perfected a method for climbing the highest, most inaccessible rooftops when he was but five years old. I don't reckon he's forgotten." Nanny laughed and sipped her tea.

"But he's not five years old now!" blurted Serena, rising from her chair. "He'll—"

"He'll be fine, child," Nanny said softly, putting a hand over Serena's. "He's strong and agile, and he's done it before, not so long ago. He won't come to harm, I promise you. And he won't take kindly to you runnin' out there tryin' to stop him, you know," she added pointedly.

Serena subsided into her chair, wondering why she should be so concerned.

"No, I don't reckon he *ever* took kindly to anyone tryin' to stop him from doin' anythin' he'd set his mind to. Very set in his ways, he was," Nanny went on.

"He *was?*" Serena could not help asking, and they both giggled.

"Well, now, a man likes to have his way, and that's a fact," Nanny said. "Mayhap Lord Richard more than most. Such a determined little tyke he was, from the very beginning. Why I remember — well — his Mama and Papa mostly called him Diccon, you see, from the time he was born, and so did we all. And then one day, he couldn't ha' been more than two years old, I reckon, well, he stood up on a little chair in the nursery and pounded his chest. 'This Richard!' he declared, and he meant it. And well, he's been Richard ever since."

Serena laughed at the picture of the little boy pounding his chest, but at the same time the image sobered her. Any man determined enough to choose his own name at the age of two . . . She let her eyes drift out the window and gulped as she saw the tall, lean form of her husband in his shirt sleeves and buckskins, walking casually along the slope of the roof to where Mr. Gilbert was crouched over a bucket. Richard bent down to join him and Serena was amazed anew. Richard was such a high stickler and yet — There was a great deal she did not know about Richard, she decided.

Richard, she mused, as Nanny went to refill the teapot. When had she stopped thinking of him as the unapproachable Lord Egremont and begun thinking of him as just — Richard? She had married the Marquis of Egremont, heir to the Dukedom of Luntsford, and he had seemed as formidable as his title and dignities. Had it only been six days since she had become Lady Egremont, his wife? It seemed almost a lifetime ago.

She watched as Richard stood and sauntered back across the roof. And then his broad back was to her as he bent low, grabbed a drain pipe, and shinnied down to the ground with the ease of a little boy. But there was a man's strength in the powerful arms and muscular thighs. Serena felt a ripple of warmth go through her and with it a pang. Had circumstances been different, she might really have deserved the title, Lady Egremont. But as it was, she was not truly a wife to Richard, nor could she be — not when his heart was pledged to another woman.

Richard suggested lunch after their visit to Nanny Gilbert, and Serena followed him at a leisurely pace through the woods. Firefly, though occasionally inclined to follow her own lead, for the most part responded to a firm tug on the reins. If the mare was willful, she was intelligent enough not to plunge herself and her rider into danger, and Serena could not imagine what all the fuss had been about.

They tethered their horses to a sweeping elm tree, and then Richard guided Serena down a winding path that led to a clearing and, just ahead, a grassy knoll fringed by clusters of goldenrod. It presented an enchanting picture, almost as delightful as her own little dell.

"This is lovely, Richard," she said, smiling.

"I thought you might like it," he replied. He stood close to her, his hand grasping her elbow. " 'Tis one of my favorite places. When I was a child I used to scamper to the top and pretend I was a king defending my castle from on high." He grinned, and his eyes crinkled up at the corners. She thought it quite charming and wondered why she had never noticed it before. Perhaps because he spent so much time frowning. "I've always wanted to have a picnic here, you know," he went on.

"And you never have?"

His expression was suddenly very serious. "No, I never have," he said slowly, his eyes a bit too penetrating.

She was uncomfortable under his gaze and shifted her eyes to the knoll. "Well, I declare I am simply famished. Did you have a groom bring the hamper?" she asked, taking a step forward. "Shall we go and—"

"Not just yet, Serena," he interrupted, tightening the grip on her elbow. "Wait a moment."

She looked at him, confused, and then back again at the knoll. She now saw two servants, one on his knees emptying a white wicker hamper, the other carrying a wine cooler. She hadn't noticed them before and wondered from whence they'd come. But they disappeared presently, descending the knoll and vanishing into the nearby bushes.

"Come, my dear, let us dine," Richard said gallantly, and together they moved forward and ascended the little hill.

The "picnic" was more in the nature of a grand banquet feast, Serena thought, as she surveyed the white damask table cloth, crystal goblets, and plates of cold poached salmon, breast of chicken, cheeses and hot-house fruits. Her eyes sought Richard's and he smiled ruefully. "Cook's idea of a light repast," he said.

In truth, she and Richard acquitted themselves quite well, consuming much of the food and several glasses of wine. Serena loved sitting on the grass amidst the goldenrod, the warm sun beating down and a slight breeze ruffling the nearby trees. Conversation was surprisingly light and easy, and Serena most enjoyed the several times a curious insect crept its way across

131

the white tablecloth. For she questioned Richard about the little creatures, and he was more than happy to explain the reasons for a ladybug's spots and the inner workings of an ant colony. Serena found it rather interesting, but it was Richard's enthusiasm that she most enjoyed. When she asked about the orange caterpillar making its way toward the poached salmon, Richard explained that it was the larva of the Red Admiral butterfly.

"Do you collect butterflies, Richard?" she asked.

He smiled. "Among other things, yes. I have a fair collection of specimens and I've done some classification. It's a fascinating endeavor, you know, and butterflies make especially beautiful specimens. The only frustrations are these little fellows," he said, picking up the caterpillar and letting it crawl round his finger. "They don't preserve well, and I should like to do some more correlating of the individual larvae to each type of butterfly."

"Are the larvae that different, Richard?"

"Of course, once you get to know them. Look at this little chap," he replied eagerly, moving close to her and holding up his finger, wrapped in a worm. "He's got an orange body with brown spikes and another might be green with yellow stripes. Here, would you like to hold him, Serena?" he asked.

"Ugh, no Richard. That—that's quite all right," she said, thinking it all very interesting but a worm was a worm and she needn't become *that* well acquainted. But her artist's eye did appreciate the insect with its unique markings.

"Richard, would you like me to sketch him for you? Or—or I could do others. Might that be of some help to you?"

Richard smiled his special smile and put aside the caterpillar. "I should like that very much, Serena. Thank you. But not now. Now I deem it a splendid time to rest after our exertions of the morning. Do you not agree, my dear?" he concluded in a low voice. Somehow, he had nudged himself quite close to her, and she could feel his warm breath in her ear. It made her tingle all over, and she suddenly felt nervous.

"I am persuaded we ought to tidy up first, Richard, shall we?" she asked, and immediately rose up on her knees and proceeded to gather the plates of food.

But Richard joined in, and so it took only a few moments to put everything back in the hamper. Then he rose and extended his hand to Serena. "Time to put the table away, my dear," he said.

They folded up the damask cloth and then Richard sat back down on the blanket beneath it. Serena seated herself, a bit hesitantly, several feet away, though she could not think what made her uneasy. This *was* broad daylight, after all.

She watched as Richard casually shrugged off his riding coat and rolled up his shirt sleeves. She could not help noticing his broad, muscular back and his strong forearms with black curling hair. She swallowed, not certain why she should suddenly begin to feel those strange sensations again.

Richard rolled his coat up and placed it down beside him. Then he lay down and stretched out on his back, hands clasped behind his head. "Ah, this feels good," he said, and then yawned rather loudly. "Mmm, the sun is nice and warm. And I *am* rather sleepy. But come, what about you, my dear?" He turned onto his side, his head propped by his elbow. With his free hand he patted the coat that lay next to his shoulder. "A pillow for my lady. Are you not the least bit sleepy, Serena? What with the sun and the wine—come here. I won't bite, you know," he added softly.

"Richard, I—I do not think—after all, the servants will—"

"The servants will not return for quite some time, Serena. Now come, my dear. I would see you comfortable." His voice was low, but somehow very compelling, and his dark brown eyes held hers.

Slowly she edged closer to him. He smiled lazily. "That's better. Why don't you roll up your sleeves—the sun is a bit warm. And take off that silly hat. It hardly affords much protection from the sun, does it?"

Against her better judgment she complied, and when he patted the "pillow" again, she eased herself down. She wanted to move further away from him but thought she might look foolish. He had not hinted at any intimacy and this *was* broad daylight, she reminded herself. Besides, she *was* rather sleepy. All that wine—

Serena tried unsuccessfully to stifle a yawn and Richard, still propped on his elbow, chuckled. "Go to sleep, Serena," he murmured, and flicked her cheek with his finger.

He turned onto his back again, his head resting on his arms, and stared up at the sky. He seemed perfectly at his ease, which infuriated Serena, for she felt a mixture of tension and unaccountable stirrings in the pit of her stomach. She was also too warm, and wanted very much to unfasten several buttons of her habit. But she didn't dare. It would look—well, she was not quite sure what it would look like but she had no intention of trying.

She too looked up at the sky but after a moment glanced again at Richard. His eyes were closed and there was a faint smile on his face. Insufferable male! How had he maneuvered her into this situation? She tried to concentrate on the sky which, she had to admit, was magnificent — it was a clear blue with only faint wisps of white clouds scattered around. A delicious breeze wafted over her and she gazed at the gently swaying trees in the distance. But her surroundings held her attention only briefly. She still held her body rigidly. She was much too conscious of the man lying beside her, just inches away, of his large size and masculine scent. But he appeared completely oblivious of her, damn him! His breathing seemed even but she could not be sure he slept. She slid one foot up and raised her knee, and without quite realizing it she kicked off her shoes. Much better, she thought, and wished she could roll down her stockings. That was out of the question, but perhaps her buttons —

She turned onto her side, her back to Richard, and undid her top buttons. She thought she heard him chuckle but when she looked back, his eyes were firmly closed, that same dreamy smile on his full, generous lips.

Oh, never mind, she thought. She *was* sleepy and the air was delightful and she might just as well rest. Resolutely she turned her back to Richard and somehow, lost herself to sleep.

She felt as if she had never slept so soundly. There was a mound of blankets close behind her and she snuggled even closer. She felt safe and enveloped in a

135

delicious warmth she'd never felt before. But then a wave of wakefulness drifted over her. Her eyes flickered open and she realized that what enveloped her was Richard's arm, encircling her belly in a firm grasp. And the mound of blankets was Richard's body, molded to hers, his chest pressed close to her back, his thighs— She felt herself flush with embarrassment and some other emotion she could not precisely define. She must get, up she told herself, but instead she sighed deeply and found herself cuddling even closer to Richard. She could hear his deep, even breathing and feel his breath on the back of her neck. She'd get up in a minute, she told herself. Besides, Richard was fast asleep and would be none the wiser. . .

When she next awoke she felt the same flush of embarrassment, and this time she tried to inch forward, to push herself free of Richard's arm. But asleep or no, Richard's grip was like iron and she could not budge. She clasped his forearm in her hand and tried to lift it.

"Where are you going, Serena?" he murmured in her ear. "There's no hurry, you know." His voice was low and husky and very compelling. But my God, she thought, he was awake, and here she was—

"Ah, Richard, I think we had ought—"

"Relax, my dear," he whispered, and pulled her even closer. She could not relax, but she could not bring herself to move either. And then suddenly the iron grip slackened and his large hand came up to her cheek. He began stroking it, softly, rhythmically, and then tracing the curve of her ear with his fingertip. It was a simple gesture, his hand on her face, devoid of meaning, she was certain. And yet, it felt so intimate, so—so caring.

She felt all the tension seep out of her, and all will to pull away. Mmm, she thought, how delicious it would be to sleep like this always. But that could never be, she reminded herself. Yet still she did not move.

It was Richard who moved first. His hand suddenly stopped its sensuous motion and he gently pulled away from her, then sat up. She was stunned at how cold, even bereft she felt. "Come my dear, I think 'tis time we were on our way." He rose and extended a hand to her. She gazed at him perplexed as she stood up, but he merely smiled enigmatically. "We're off to Meadsham, Serena. Surely you remember the fair," he said nonchalantly and began rolling down his sleeves.

"Ah, yes, of course, the fair," she responded vaguely and then turned from him to do up her buttons and hide her terrible confusion.

Chapter Seven

Richard thought the brisk ride to Meadsham would help Serena regain her composure, and so it seemed to do. For when they slowed their horses at the outskirts of the village, she seemed much herself again. Richard smiled, and they continued down the path at a slow trot. He knew very well that he had discomposed Serena back there atop the knoll, and all in all, he was quite pleased with his little picnic. He was making headway with his virgin bride, slow but very definite headway.

He led the way to the Blue Boar Inn, just around the bend from the village green. When they had dismounted, he tossed the reins to an ostler. These he followed by a shiny gold coin and the admonition to see to the horses until her ladyship and he returned. The lad eagerly clutched the coin, nearly scraping the ground with his bow, and assured his lordship that he'd give the horses a fine rubdown, he would.

They could hear the colorful sounds of the fair before they could see it. Richard guided Serena down the dirt road, and, in answer to her questions, explained that although Meadsham was certainly not the largest village in the parish of Luntsford, was in fact one of the smallest, yet its fairs were among the most popular. That was partly, he supposed, because Meadsham boasted a rather expansive green bordered by charming Fifteenth Century timber framed cottages. And in fact, the Meadsham green had been host to fairs since before that. Of course, Richard explained, once upon a time a village fair was a market place, an economic necessity, whereas today, although some merchants did set up stalls, the fair was more an entertainment than anything.

"That much I know, Richard. We do have village fairs in Surrey, you know," she chided gently and Richard chuckled.

"Ah, then you are an old hand at this, are you? And here I had thought to show you something new," he said in mock disappointment.

Suddenly she was serious. "No, actually I'm not. Father never permitted me near the fairs. He said they were frequented by all manner of unsavory persons."

"Well, then, you must stay very close to me, so none will accost you," he whispered, pulling her closer and tucking her arm through his.

It was thus that they approached the village green, and Serena's eyes widened as they beheld the scene before them. There were marionette shows, a skittle alley, a dancing fiddler, vendors hawking chicken pies and every manner of sweet. There were also a few merchants' stalls, selling pots and iron trivets and perfumes purported to be from the mysterious East.

"Oh, Richard, this is wonderful!" Serena exclaimed,

and dashed forward. Richard let her go, but just for a moment. Then he caught up and took her hand.

"Serena, I was quite serious. You are to stay very close," he said soberly. He saw her begin to bristle and added, "Look around at the people. Farmers and their families, laborers, stable boys, a few merchants, and just a smattering of gentry. A marchioness rather stands out in this crowd, I fear. And it *can* get a bit rough you know."

To his relief a smile touched the corners of her mouth. "Why did you bring me here, Richard? I should not have expected — that is — it is not the kind of thing —"

"I thought you would like it, Serena. So did my mother. You are not the sort to content herself with brides' visits and church works, are you?"

"No, Richard, I'm not," she said quietly.

"Well, here we are then," Richard declared and indeed, they had arrived in the thick of it.

Serena laughed heartily at the antics of the dancing fiddler, and Richard marvelled that she seemed not the least discommoded by the jostling crowds nor the cacophony of sound in the air.

As they ambled along, hand in hand, Richard noted several multi-colored gypsy wagons as well as a scattering of Romany children running barefoot in the grass. He wondered fleetingly where the gypsies were camped, but his attention was claimed by Serena, who began pulling him by the hand toward the shooting gallery.

She insisted he try his luck, to which he agreed, but not before he was recognized by several farmers who joined Serena in encouraging him. He introduced

Serena to the men, tenants of his, who managed to doff their caps respectfully, despite having, Richard suspected, dipped too deeply into the kegs of ale this day. He then turned his attention to the shooting, and Serena jumped up and down with glee when he won. As his prize he chose the best of the offerings, a large muslin scarf in a rainbow of colors. He thought it a bit gaudy but Serena was delighted when he presented it to her and quickly wrapped it round her neck. Somehow, she looked quite lovely in it—it gave her sober riding habit a certain flair.

Next Richard bought a huge messy cherry tart which they shared, much to the detriment of their clothes. Serena giggled all the while, and Richard thought she looked adorable with cherry juice dribbling down her chin. He wiped it with his handkerchief, and then she brushed the flakes of crust from his coat.

As they made their way around the green, Richard began to notice people pointing surreptitiously at them and whispering in groups as they passed. Our presence has been duly noted, he thought ruefully, and knew that by dinner time every household for miles around would know that Lord and Lady Egremont had graced the village fair.

A small brown boy with curly black hair tugged at Serena's skirts, pulling her toward a nearby wagon. "Oh come, Richard, do let's go," she said, and it struck him that Caroline would have shrugged the little gypsy boy off with a *moué* of distaste. Caroline. Strange, he mused, but he hadn't thought of her all day.

They followed the boy to the colorful gypsy wagon and watched as the woman inside cajoled three people into buying her special home-brewed remedy for the gout.

"Well, Serena, do you wish a miracle cure for your gout?" he asked genially.

"No, Richard. But I do marvel at her skill. She holds them spellbound, and they part willingly with their coins."

"My lord," said the gypsy woman suddenly to Richard. "Now, how can I help you? I think you do not suffer from the gout, eh? Oh, no. But a trinket, perhaps, for your beautiful lady. Yes, I have the very thing!" she exclaimed, and proceeded to display a case of earrings—large hoops with rings and small coins dangling inside them. "Gold, my lord," the woman said, and Richard knew the only thing gold about them was their color. But one look at Serena told him she was enchanted, and on impulse he selected a pair for her.

She put them on and pirouetted for him. "No, wait," she said, "I must do this right." She pulled the scarf from her neck and somehow wound it round her head, over her hat and all that hair. "There, how's that?" she asked.

Richard smiled despite himself. He pictured her with her hair down, with those earrings and the scarf. She would be barefoot, of course, and he decided that she very much looked the part. Acted it too, what with her artistic nature and penchant for running barefoot through fields, even her way with animals. "Little gypsy," he murmured softly, and drew her arm through his.

Sometime later the same little boy tugged at Serena's skirts. This time he led them to a tent, atop of which were the words: Madame Sibella, Teller of Fortunes. "Oh, Richard, do let us have our fortunes read!" Serena exclaimed.

"Now, Serena, I really don't think—" he began, but Serena was already pulling him inside.

The tent was much larger on the inside than it had appeared outside. There was a small anteroom and then a flap which hid an inner chamber. It took a moment for Richard to realize that the little boy had followed them in and to see why. His hand outstretched, a smile on his face, he drove a very hard bargain for the price of two fortunes. Business completed, the boy disappeared behind the flap, then returned and beckoned Richard.

"Madame will see my lord first," he said.

Richard looked doubtfully at Serena, not wanting to leave her. But she merely smiled. "Go ahead Richard. I shall be fine."

What a ridiculous waste of time, Richard thought as he stepped past the flap to the inner chamber. The room was dark, draped in folds of gold fabric. Madame Sibella was seated before a skirted table, her bejeweled hand idly fingering a large crystal ball.

She looked up as he entered. "So, you have come, my lord," she said in a soft guttural voice that had a foreign sound to it. She sat back and regarded Richard with an expression in her dark brown eyes that was not at all unfriendly. Richard had the uncanny feeling that she knew exactly who he was and, stranger still, had been expecting him. For a moment he stared at the wrinkled face, framed by graying fringes of hair that protruded from a red and gold silk scarf.

"Sit down, Lord Egremont," she said at last, gesturing with her hand. Her earrings, larger, more intricate versions of Serena's, flashed in the darkened tent as she spoke.

Richard was jarred by her use of his name, although he'd half expected it. He sat down warily, reminding himself that this was all a bit of fustian and that the boy had undoubtedly heard his name bandied about outside. But yet. . . .

Madame Sibella closed her hands over the crystal ball and gazed into it. Then abruptly she looked up and stared at Richard's face. He was not accustomed to such scrutiny and did not much like it. He was about to tell the old woman so when she raised her hand to silence him. Then, as if to herself, she said, "No, it is not in the crystal, this one. It is in the face." Richard watched fascinated as she clutched the table with her hands, lifted her head, and gazed at him through narrowed eyes. There was absolute silence in the tent, and Richard suddenly felt uneasy, very uneasy.

Marco dropped down on a wooden barrel just outside the rear flap of Sibella's tent. Damn that girl! he thought again, his hand clenched tightly around a mug of ale. He should have beaten Gaya for such disobedience, that he should have. But he hadn't. He was much too angry at the ungrateful wench. No tellin' what he might do when he was in such a takin'. And well—'twas better just to leave camp. And so he had, and come to the fair for a bit of amusement.

Damn her! Still she would not wed. 'Tweren't natural. Nor safe neither, to have such a one as she walkin' freely about the camp, temptin' all the men, even she

144

not know it. And always roamin' the woods by herself. A husband it was she needed, to bed her and teach her what was what. Let her husband worry about where she be all the time and should he beat her when she deserved it. Marco was tired of lookin' after that sister of his, tired of arguin' about marriage. Time he was thinkin' of his own marriage, what with his wife gone these two years now. And today, Gaya be askin' could some gorgio woman come to camp! He told her to stay away from the gorgios! But that was Gaya—allas talkin' to anyone she pleased. She'd not wanted to tell him who the woman was, but he'd got out of her that she was of the great house. A rawnie she was! Damn that girl! She'd have them all in the suds yet.

Sibella's voice drifted through the flap toward Marco. "It is in the face," he heard her say. He felt a chill, as he allas did, when Sibella spoke. Some other Rom women maybe—well—fanciful when they read fortunes, maybe tell a clanker or two, but not Sibella. She didn't have to. She *knew*. Marco didn't like to listen too closely; it made him nervous. But her voice was very clear, and he couldn't help himself.

Richard watched as Sibella's eyes closed tightly and she opened her mouth to speak. "There is a hidden jewel in the great house of Gower," she said slowly, her guttural voice very strong. Richard's eyes widened but he didn't move a muscle as she continued. " 'Tis a fortune in sapphires. Everyone can see it, but no one knows 'tis there." She took a breath and opened her eyes. She leaned forward and stared piercingly into Richard's eyes. "You will find it, my lord, but—you

145

will know a woman's deceit before you do." Richard felt himself stiffen at this last, but she bowed her head and waved him away with a hand.

Richard rose unsteadily, telling himself sternly that this was all a bag of moonshine. There were no hidden jewels, and as for deceit—Serena would never—why, she wouldn't even know what—oh, hell! It was time they were going on home at all events. But Serena was quite adamant that she too would have her fortune read, and so Richard was left stewing in the anteroom, concentrating on forgetting his ridiculous fortune, while Serena disappeared inside.

Sibella's words had mesmerized Marco. "A hidden jewel, that everyone can see." By God, could they use a fortune in sapphires just now! Coffers were low and they needed new horses, and several new caravans. Some of the men had begun questioning Marco's leadership—said a man who couldn't control his own sister . . . But this would quiet them all! Mayhap not such a bad idea havin' the rawnie visit camp. It were a start, at all events. Marco jumped up. Best get back to Gaya afore she took herself off into the woods again.

"Come in, my dear," the old woman said gently.

Serena came forward a bit hesitantly. Richard had looked like the very devil a moment ago—she could not imagine what the gypsy woman might have said to put him all out of countenance. She would expect Richard to discount it all as so much fiddle-faddle at all events.

Serena sat down and watched expectantly as Madame Sibella fingered the crystal ball. She'd never had her fortune told, and the tent, the gypsy woman— everything was just as she'd imagined it would be.

"I see fire, my child," Madame Sibella said in her soft, throaty voice. She was frowning as she gazed into the crystal. Her words came slowly now, as if they were wrenched out of her "Fire and—drums, and—violence." The last word was almost a whisper, and Serena shivered, for she felt that Mme. Sibella had not wanted to say it. "But—but in the end, there is the sunshine," the old woman concluded, and then she bowed her head in dismissal.

Serena could hardly look Richard in the face as they emerged from the tent. She did not wish to repeat what the gypsy had said. It frightened her; she needed time to think about it. But Richard seemed no more inclined to speak of it than she.

"Well, a great farrago of nonsense, is it not, Serena?" he said as they walked across the green. His voice was casual but his body seemed rigid and his face was unsmiling.

"Yes," she hastened to agree. "A grand bit of fustian."

He looked at her searchingly for a moment but said only, "I believe it time to head back, Serena."

A grand bit of fustian, she reminded herself. But she thought of Gaya and her uncanny sense and was not so sure at all.

"Oh my God! Caroline! 'Tis past tea time. Oh, how did I allow myself to become so distracted? Not but what I didn't enjoy myself immensely, ferreting through those ancient things in your attic! I did so love

147

going back to your house. It was a capital idea of yours. But I had wanted to be back by tea time," Livvy fairly wailed as the two girls hurried through the park toward the Court.

"Do not trouble yourself, Livvy, dear," Caroline said. "I am persuaded we have not yet been missed. If we hurry we shall have just enough time to dress for dinner and join everyone for sherry."

Oh God, Livvy thought. If Caroline only knew what it was that Livvy had forgotten. But she was too ashamed to tell her, and she did not know how she would face the family now.

Livvy heard the words even before she and Caroline rounded the corner to the Gold Salon, where Rivers was pouring out the sherry.

"I would not have minded at all, Serena, had you told me you were fatigued," her mama was saying. "But simply not to go to him, when you know how very ill he is—why, I—I just do not know what to say."

Serena's anguished eyes flew to the doorway as Caroline and Livvy entered the room. How could Livvy do this to her? But one look at Livvy's stricken face told Serena that Livvy was horrified by her dereliction. Livvy's eyes met Serena's and there was pleading in them. But Caroline looked—my God, thought Serena, Caroline looked positively smug. So it was she, Serena thought, who had distracted Livvy enough so— And was Caroline so sure Serena would not blurt the truth? Serena glanced quickly at all the faces staring expectantly at hers. Richard was seething; the duchess looked so disappointed in her. Yet how could Serena throw the blame on to Livvy, allow Livvy, who so needed their affection now, to suffer their anger? Besides, Serena should never have put aside her responsibility at first stop. And she could not even know whether Richard and the duchess would believe her. It would sound so like one child telling tales on another. And then Caroline might join the fray. It was all too degrading. No, she could not do it, and Caroline had known she couldn't.

Serena met Richard's eyes and sighed inwardly. Richard would always find some reason to be out of charity with her. As for the duchess, she could not look her in the eye. "I—I am truly sorry, your grace," she said at last. "I have no excuse, save that I was exhausted after our excursion today and I quite forgot. It won't—that is—I care deeply that the duke recover. He—he is no worse, I pray?"

"No, he is no worse. But he was alone for the hour and it might well have been—but never mind. Let us go in to dinner," the duchess said regally, and swept from the room.

As Serena turned to follow her, her eyes met Livvy's. They were moist, brimming with relief and gratitude and—Serena smiled ever so slightly at her sister-in-law. Well, she thought, she had at least one friend in the house.

Richard found dinner unbearable. He wanted to thrash Serena for her neglect of his father. But he did not understand it—it was not like her at all. And there was Caroline looking like the cat that swallowed the canary. What the devil was she so smug about? Livvy was unusually quiet, and Richard thought she looked pale. His mother said nary a word, ate even less, and Richard wished to hell the meal would end. He wanted to get Serena upstairs, to talk to her and—he had plans for her this evening. He might well want to thrash her, but that did not change the fact that he still wanted to make love to her. He'd waited long enough, dammit!

But Caroline was not content with the silence that seemed to please everyone else very well, and she began asking questions about the outing today. It was not long before Livvy joined in.

"Did you play any games at the fair? Was there a skittle alley? Did you win anything?" Livvy asked as soon as the saddle of lamb and ham mousse with cucumbers were served.

Richard was silent and after a moment Serena said, "Richard is a very good shot, Livvy, as you must know. Of course he won, in the shooting gallery."

Livvy was not content until she had ascertained the exact nature of the prize Richard had won. "Oh, I should love to see your scarf, Serena," Livvy said, chewing on a piece of lamb.

Richard wondered at his sister's unexpectedly friendly tone toward Serena. Then he glanced at Caroline, but her lip was curled unpleasantly and she murmured, "How quaint."

Richard frowned slightly, but Livvy had jumped to another topic. "Did you have your fortunes told? I am persuaded every fair has a fortune teller's booth."

This time Serena did not answer, but looked to Richard. She seemed uncomfortable and he wondered why. What could the gypsy have told her? He certainly did not wish to discuss what Madame Sibella had told *him*, but he knew Livvy would not easily be put off.

"Yes, Livvy, we did have our fortunes read. An old gypsy woman with her crystal ball. Such a great farrago of nonsense, as you must know. And, I confess,

I was gulled. Her little accomplice drove a hard bargain, I must say," he said, but Livvy was not deterred.

She downed a mouthful of the ham mousse and then asked eagerly, "What is your fortune, Serena? What did the gypsy say?" Richard noted that Caroline and even his mother were looking at Serena expectantly.

Serena took a sip of wine. "Well—it is as Richard said—a great bit of fustian about—fire and drums. Really, it was quite provoking not to have understood her. I declare the woman quite spoke in riddles!" Serena concluded blithely. Good girl, Richard thought, but he wondered what the devil the woman *had* said. Fire and drums and what else?

Serena's answer seemed to satisfy the company, and now all eyes turned to Richard. What the hell, he thought. Why not tell them, at least about the "hidden jewel"? Perhaps contemplating it would occupy Livvy and Caroline for a bit. "Madame Sibella said that— well—'tis quite absurd, you must know, but she said there is a hidden jewel in the House of Gower. A fortune in sapphires, she said. And she claimed that everyone can see it, but no one knows it's there."

"How curious," his mother murmured.

"Oh, Richard, how exciting!" Livvy exclaimed, predictably.

Richard looked at Caroline and was disconcerted at the expression in her eyes. He could not quite define it, but they glittered with a strange kind of excitement. It made him rather uncomfortable, but Serena's words disconcerted him even more.

"She knew who we were, Richard, didn't she?" Serena whispered.

"Yes, Serena, she did," he replied.

Richard escorted Serena to her room, as always. He was still angry with her and felt he had got to say something about his father. But he did not wish to dwell on it—it was bad enough Serena's humiliation had been so public. Nor, he realized, now he had her alone, had he the slightest wish to thrash her. He thought instead of the fire Watkins would have laid in the sitting room, the love seat drawn up close, the warming glasses of brandy awaiting them.

Serena was looking at him with uncertain eyes, and he thought she looked lovely, despite a rather ridiculous green dress with rows of ruffles completely obscuring her bosom. His mind drifted to how she would look in her night clothes, her hair down . . . .

But first he must deal with the unpleasant matter of this afternoon. He was her husband, after all. "Serena, about my father," he began, "I—well—devil take it, Serena what did happen this afternoon? 'Tis not at all like you to be so negligent. Are you not feeling quite the thing?"

She stiffened and held herself ramrod straight. "It is as I explained to your mother, Richard. I have no wish to discuss it further, save to say it shall not happen again."

Had she cried, had she asked for his forgiveness, Richard knew he would have been happy to end the discussion. But this cold haughtiness infuriated him.

"I am afraid you shall *have* to discuss it, Serena," he said sternly. "Do you realize what could have happened in that hour? Do you, Serena?" he demanded.

He saw her eyes become moist and knew he had gone too far. "Yes, Richard," she said at length. "I do. May I — may I go now, please?"

Damn! This was not at all what he had planned for tonight. He took a deep breath to quell his anger. "Very well, Serena, we shall speak no more of this, and I shall send your maid to you presently. I should like it if you would come to my room afterwards, for a drink. We can sit by the fire."

"Very well, Richard, thank you," she said formally, coldly, her face devoid of expression. Damn, Richard thought, wondering if the fire and the brandy could even begin to thaw her out.

He went into the dressing room and sent Hannah to Serena, then opened the door to the sitting room. And then all thoughts of seduction flew from his mind, for a gust of smoke blasted his face. When he managed to clear his eyes he walked into the room, but the smoke became thicker. The room stank something awful and he couldn't see two feet in front of him. Then he heard a cough.

"That you, my lord?" called Watkins from near the fireplace, Richard guessed. "Don't know what all happened, my lord. I was sure the flue was open, I truly was."

"Oh, for pity sakes, Watkins! It's very obvious — oh, never mind! I presume you've opened all the windows, haven't you?"

"Oh, now that's a right good idea, my lord, I declare it is. I'll see to it straight away, I will."

Richard muttered a most unseemly epithet under his breath. What the bloody hell was wrong with Watkins tonight? The man's wits seemed to have gone abegging.

A few minutes later, they stood in the dressing room, Watkins helping Richard out of his clothes, which now stank as badly as his room.

"Well, it's obvious I cannot sleep in there," Richard said.

"No, my lord. As you say," concurred Watkins.

"Well then, make up the chaise for me here, will you, Watkins."

"Yes, my lord, of course. But er, beggin' your pardon, but the chaise, well, it ain't exactly here, you see."

"What do you mean, 'it ain't exactly here?' " Richard demanded, whirling around to the corner where the chaise *should* have been. "Where the devil is the chaise, Watkins?"

"Well, ahem, I don't rightly know, my lord, 'cept that two footmen come by for it this afternoon. Housekeeper's orders they said. Needs to be cleaned and aired or somethin' like."

"Cleaned and—now? It had to be cleaned now? Today?" Richard fairly bellowed.

"I—I'm sorry, my lord. Might I suggest that you—"

"No, Watkins, you may not! I am perfectly capable of—oh, never mind! You may take yourself off, and see you keep mum belowstairs!"

Blast it all! Richard paced the floor of the dressing room once Watkins had gone. What the hell was he to say to Serena now? He stopped short and shook his head ruefully. How ironic that he would have quite welcomed this state of affairs had he and Serena not had words just moments ago. As it was, how would she take all this? Would she even believe him that his room

154

and the chaise just happened to be unavailable at the same time? His eyes narrowed. He was not sure he believed it himself, but he would deal with that later.

He rapped gently on the door and entered the bedchamber at the sound of her muffled, "Come in." She was standing near the window, facing the door. Her hair fell in luxurious waves, and she wore a rather full, flowing dressing gown that had twice as much fabric as necessary. Her night clothes would be the first items in her wardrobe to go, he thought wryly. She looked utterly desirable, nevertheless, and he fervently wished he might have the opportunity to remove the absurd garment before the night was out. Her implacable expression did not augur well, however.

He walked purposefully to where she stood. "Serena, I—I don't quite know how to say this. My room is— there has been some mishap. Watkins—oh—come— you'd better see for yourself." On impulse he took her hand and pulled her after him to the door of his room.

"Richard, what in heaven's name happened?" she asked, coughing and waving the smoke away from her face.

He explained briefly and then pulled her back into the dressing room, closing the door. "And so I thought I would sleep in here, but, as you see, the chaise has been removed. On this week's cleaning list it seems."

"So what you are saying is that—that you will have to sleep in my room," Serena said.

He tried to look distressed. "Yes, yes, I suppose I am, Serena."

"I see," she said and then led the way into the bedchamber. "Well, Richard, as you can see, the chairs are far too delicate for you to be comfortable, even should you put two together. No, it simply won't answer. *You* must take the bed, and I shall make do with the chairs."

"Chairs?" Richard asked, moving close to her. "Ah, but Serena, is that really necessary? I thought perhaps—that is—"

"*What* did you think, Richard?" she asked frostily, her head high and lips pursed.

"Never mind, Serena," he growled and sighed inwardly. She seemed about as approachable as an iceberg and suddenly he felt devoid of desire himself. "And *I* shall take the chairs. I have no wish to discommode you."

"Oh, but—"

"Don't argue with me, dammit! I say I shall sleep on the chairs, and there is an end to it, Serena!" Richard barked.

Neither of them spoke as he stormed into the dressing room for bedclothes, then returned to drag two delicately carved chairs together. He brushed off her offer of help and threw the pillows and blankets together into a semblance of order.

"Go to sleep, Serena," he muttered as he negotiated himself between the arms of the chairs and somehow heaved himself, dressing gown and all, down onto quite the most uncomfortable bed he had ever occupied.

He heard her climb into bed. "Good night, Richard," she whispered at length.

"Good night, Serena," he grumbled, trying to figure out how to keep his knee from bumping the arm of the chair.

It was *not* a good night. Long after he heard Serena's even breathing, Richard stared into the black night.

He could not even toss and turn—there was not enough room!

He could not say what time it was that he heard the scream. It was a woman's cry, and then he heard several voices, then a loud scuffling. He was up in a moment, toppling a chair in the process.

"What—what is it, Richard? I heard a scream," Serena mumbled, rising and hurriedly donning her dressing gown.

"I don't know, Serena, but I mean to find out," Richard replied, trying to sound calmer than he felt. The scream had come from the direction of his parents' suite and he felt his heart pound in his chest as he raced down the corridor, Serena at his heels.

The door to his parents' sitting room was open and they darted in. "Mrs. Grayson!" Richard blurted at the sight of the housekeeper. "Whatever—what's happened?"

"Oh, praised be, my lord! It be his grace. The fever's broke!" she exclaimed, clasping her hands together.

"Thank God," Richard breathed, and instinctively turned to Serena.

"Oh, Richard, I am so happy," she whispered, and somehow, their hands met and clung together. They moved, as one unit, toward the door of the ducal bedchamber, but stopped when his father's valet emerged.

"Hudson, how is he?" Richard asked.

Hudson grinned. "He's right fine my lord, my lady. Sweatin' something awful and orderin' me around to boot. Wantin' food in the middle of the night, if that don't beat all! Well now, I suppose you'll want to see him. Just hold a minute, why don't you." Hudson disappeared for a moment and then returned to usher them into the bedchamber.

They advanced slowly to the large, partially curtained bed. His father was sitting up, propped by several pillows. In the dim candlelight Richard could see that his eyes were lowered, a soft smile on his face. Then he saw his mother. She sat at the bedside, her body bent so that her head rested on the bed.

"I'm sorry, my love; I gave you quite a scare, I know," the duke murmured, stroking his wife's hair.

The duchess did not answer, and Richard realized that she was quietly weeping. A muffled sob broke from Serena's throat, and Richard tightened his grip on her hand.

"Father," Richard said unsteadily when they reached the foot of the bed. The duke slowly raised his eyes. "I am so happy to see you well again."

"And I am happy to be among the living again, my son. And Serena, it is good to see you, my dear. You look lovely."

"Oh, your grace, I—I—we were all so—so worried and—" Serena's voice broke and she covered her mouth with her hand.

"Well, Richard," his father said with a gleam in his eye. "It seems we are both saddled with dewy-eyed women tonight. Take your wife back to bed. There is time enough for talk tomorrow."

Richard led Serena away and once inside their own room she turned to him and he very naturally took her into his arms. She clutched at him as loud, wrenching sobs broke from her. He held her tightly and felt her small body tremble against his. "Oh, R-Richard," she said at length. "I—I am so h-happy."

"I know, Serena. I know."

"I — life — life is so short, Richard" she whispered, sniffling. "It — it scares me so."

For answer he stroked her hair and kissed her brow and then her eyes, salty with tears. "Come to bed, little gypsy," he murmured. "Do you think — well, the chairs are excessively uncomfortable, you must know. Do you think we might both — ah — sleep on the bed?"

She stiffened in his arms. "Richard, I —"

"Serena. It is very late. I wish only to sleep, I do assure you."

He felt her relax against him again. "Well, I — I am persuaded the chairs *are* frightful. Perhaps, well — but just for . . . I — that is —"

"No more talk, Serena. As my father said, there is time enough tomorrow."

And so for the first time, Richard spent the night, or what was left of it, in bed with his wife. And if she slept some four feet away from him, her back turned resolutely toward him, well, at the least, he told himself, he was getting closer.

Chapter Eight

Serena awoke with the sun and wondered what she was doing curled on her side at the very edge of the bed. She stretched leisurely and allowed herself a long, pleasant yawn that came to an abrupt end when her foot encountered a strange, warm object in her bed. She tapped at it gingerly. My God! It was a foot! Someone *else's* foot! She whirled around and gasped. Richard! She scrambled out of bed and yanked on her dressing gown.

"You needn't act like the house is afire, Serena. Good morning," he said with a crooked smile.

"Richard, what are you doing in my—that is—oh, I remember now," she concluded lamely.

"Just so, my dear," he murmured, and then he too rose from the bed.

She realized that he had slept in his dressing gown and was about to comment when she recalled his singular lack of a garment to sleep in. She felt herself flush. Had they really spent the night in bed together? She did not recall him touching her, but still he might think—

"Richard, I—I realize that—that circumstances last night were exceptional, but—but I would not want you to think—that is—nothing has changed, Richard."

She saw the brief flash of anger in his eyes before the impassive mask descended onto his face. "Yes, that is quite obvious," he said repressively.

Damn him! What right did he have to be angry? Did he expect her to welcome him into her bed, knowing all the while it was another woman he was thinking of?

The silence at breakfast was not companionable. Serena picked at her food; Richard did not attempt more than a cup of coffee and a piece of dry toast. At length he said, "Serena, I am afraid I must attend to business today. If I don't, I fear my father will take the corkbrained notion that *he* ought to do so. I trust you will be all right."

"Of course, Richard. I can always amuse myself. And I shall see if your mother would like some help."

"Very good, Serena," he replied. "And this time I trust that you will take your respon—"

"Richard," Serena interrupted, snapping her fork down and glaring at him.

"Good morning, Richard, Serena." The duchess' voice startled them both, and Serena turned to see her mother-in-law glide into the room. Serena was immediately alarmed, for though the duchess wore a charming morning gown of seafoam green, it was obvious that she had not yet completed her toilette. Her hair was in a state of disarray, and no attempt had been

161

made to soften the redness in her eyes. Besides, it was highly unusual for the duchess to present herself at such an early hour.

"Mother, is something wrong?" Richard asked, rising abruptly and guiding the duchess to her seat.

"Your father is quite weak, but he is on the mend, thank God," the duchess replied, but her eyes were fixed on Serena.

A footman poured his mother coffee and Richard waved the man away. Serena felt acutely uncomfortable in the silence, felt she ought to say something, but then the duchess suddenly leaned forward and clasped her hand.

"Livvy came to see me at first light," the duchess said softly. Serena's eyes widened. "I don't think she slept all night for all her remorse. You are—you are very good, Serena, to have taken all that on yourself. You needn't have, you know."

From the corner of her eyes Serena could see Richard's perplexed frown. She ignored him. "I—I couldn't let Livvy—that is—the responsibility was mine at first stop."

"That is not the point, my dear, as you must know. You have a good heart. I'm not at all sure we deserve you." The duchess rose and stared pointedly at Richard; Serena lowered her eyes. "Well now, children," her mother-in-law added bracingly, "I shall retire for a good long rest. Come see me late this afternoon, Serena, why don't you? The duke will not need you, but it's time you and I had a nice comfortable cose, I should think."

And with a speaking glance to Richard, she was

gone.

"Would you mind telling me what that was all about?" Richard demanded, his dark eyes intent and his strong jawline particularly rigid.

Serena looked her husband full in the eye. She was tired of being the object of his frowning countenance. "Yes, Richard, I *would* mind," she said and blithely rose to take her leave. She ignored the very ungentlemanly epithet that he muttered a bit too loudly as she skirted the doorway and glided away.

Serena donned a walking dress, her new scarf and earrings and, sketch book in hand, set out across the fine lawns of Luntsford. Once out of sight of the house, she removed her shoes and revelled in the feel of the soft grass underfoot. The house was confining—Richard's censure always seemed to pervade it. But out here she felt alive and free—almost, she thought impishly, like a gypsy. Strange, she mused now, that Richard had called her 'little gypsy' yesterday, twice in fact. He deplored all those tendencies in her that might be attributable to gypsies. Serena shrugged. And then reluctantly, she let her mind drift to the earlier scene in the breakfast room. She could not help but be grateful that Livvy had confessed, for Serena very much wanted the duchess' good opinion. But as to Richard, well—he was so damned autocratic all the time, just looking for reasons to ring a peel over her. And so she hadn't bothered to tell him the truth.

It was still early and she did not expect to see Gaya in the dell yet. If the girl came at all, it would be this afternoon. Serena sat down on the grass near Gaya's rock and pulled off her stockings. She stretched her legs luxuriously and stared at the quiet, pristine stream wending its way along the thick curtain of trees. Later, when the sun was a bit higher, she would swim. Serena patted the bulge in her walking dress contentedly. Not wishing to arouse curiosity as to her plans for the day, she had not made any special foray to the kitchens. Instead she'd gone back to the breakfast room and pilfered whatever she could from the ample board. She knew she'd be quite adequately nourished for the afternoon. Now she drew forth a biscuit and munched it while she flipped open her sketch pad. The drawing of Gaya still pleased her, and she looked forward to working on it further. But she would wait for her friend.

She flipped to a fresh page. She held her pencil idly in her hand and let her eyes slowly meander about her. A woodthrush came to perch momentarily on the rock, but was gone before Serena could pick up the pencil. She smiled to herself and let her gaze wander over the water again. It was a beautiful scene, and she thought perhaps she ought to sketch a sweeping vista of the dell, but truly she preferred to do smaller objects, closeup.

The sun was beginning to lull her into a pleasant lethargy, and so she almost missed the little green and yellow creature that inched its slow and steady way across the grass and came to rest on a bent twig not two feet from Serena. At the sight of the caterpillar Serena became immediately alert. This, she knew, was what she'd been waiting for. She would sketch the little fellow as a surprise for Richard. Not that he deserved it, she reminded herself, but still . . .

The sun was beating down rather fiercely by the time Serena put down her pencil. She had moved from her sitting position to her belly and back again in an effort to capture the colorful creature in all his striped and fuzzy glory, and she was quite pleased with the result.

Only now did she realize how very hot it was. She could feel beads of sweat on her lip and brow, and her dress clung to her. She stood up, glanced briefly around, and with no further ado shrugged off her clothes. She waded into the water, reveling in its coolness against her skin, reveling in the solitude and peace of her little dell.

Caroline had paced the floor of her bedchamber after breakfast, occasionally gazing out the windows at the rear gardens. She'd seen Serena set out across the lawn wearing a dreadful brown walking dress and her ridiculous scarf. Caroline gave a delicate shudder and turned away.

She needed to think. The duke was on the mend and Richard would be gone soon if Caroline did not act quickly. She had to find a foolproof way to discredit Serena, to make — she idly glanced out of the window again. Serena was nearly out of sight of the house, but Caroline could see her bend down and remove her shoes. Where the devil was the chit going, barefoot and wearing that tawdry gypsy scarf? Where did she go *every* day?

And then Caroline pummelled her head in annoyance at her own stupidity. The answer to her problem had just passed right under her nose. She would go after Serena, follow her and see what she was up to. If Caroline read Serena right, it was something of which her staid marquis of a husband would disapprove. And if it wasn't quite scandalous enough, well, Caroline could always embellish the truth. At all events, it was a start.

Without ringing for a maid, Caroline hurriedly donned the oldest dress she had with her, a once pretty mint green affair that was now a bit skimpy, and a pair of boots she no longer cared for. She had no intention of spoiling good clothes on a trek through the woods. She was not particularly fond of walking, and even less of the woods, what with all the dirt and brambles and insects, but there was no help for it.

Caroline took the most direct path away from the gardens, one that was happily well trod and clear of pesky underbrush and rocks. As to where she would go after that, she hadn't the faintest notion. But when the path diverged and the time for a decision came, Caroline remembered how wet and bedraggled Serena had looked the other day on her return home. Caroline had accused her of falling into the fishpond, but perhaps it was something else. There was a stream that ran through the eastern part of the duke's land. She had only seen portions of it, had never followed its course, but still . . . On impulse, Caroline turned eastward.

Whatever did Serena see in these long walks of hers? Caroline wondered in disgust as she disentangled her

166

gown from yet another bramble bush and pricked her finger in the effort. Caroline hated the country and always had. She had been to London once, as a child, and ever since had dreamed of living there. The balls, the beautiful gowns, the gossip. She had always plied her brother for the latest *on dits,* and he was happy to indulge her, though his brotherly affection never went so far as to make the slightest sacrifice so that Caroline too might enjoy the pleasures of town. Caroline had resented it, and had railed at Martin for being the most selfish of creatures, until one day when he had smiled that very unpleasant smile of his. "And so I am, Caro dear," he'd said, "but then, you would do the same in my place, wouldn't you?"

That had effectively silenced her, but it had further stirred her resentment. London was where she belonged, she thought now, for the hundredth time. She should be driving down Rotten Row in the smartest new barouche, not hiking through some bramble infested wood, and someone else's wood at that. And this summer, she had thought she'd come close to her dream at last.

Richard Gower was wealthy and one day he would be fabulously wealthy. And, even better, he was heir to a dukedom. Not that the estate of marquis was anything to look down one's nose upon, but the thought of herself as a duchess filled Caroline with a deep sense of triumph. She thought of all the girls at school who had pitied and even ridiculed her for her dissolute father and profligate brother. She would show them, she'd thought! She'd caught herself a future duke, and hadn't even needed a Season to bring him up to scratch! And if Richard was a bit too dark, too—well—rugged looking for Caroline's taste, and if he was too passionate, too emotional, well, none of that really mattered.

It had been such a simple matter to befriend Livvy and then flutter her eyelashes at her big brother. Caroline had watched Richard fall in love with her with a secret amusement, and when he had proclaimed his undying love she'd had no compunction about echoing his sentiment. Not that she understood what love had to do with marriage, but if that was what Richard needed to hear . . . And he wasn't getting such a bad bargain, either. She knew she was beautiful, with just the right cool, patrician countenance a duchess ought to have. She would be a marvelous hostess, and she would do her duty and provide him with an heir.

By the end of July Caroline had been certain that Richard was about to formally declare himself. And then his parents had called him in one day and told him about the Gowers and the Wexleys and all those countless generations of tradition, and it had all ended. Neither tears nor pressing her body close to his and plying Richard with kisses had made the slightest difference.

And then the humiliation of seeing Richard married to that—that raggedy looking hoyden! Caroline was near despair until she'd conceived the idea of insinuating herself into the Gower household. She had begun to wonder if she could cajole Livvy into asking the duchess to bring them out together. But then the duke had taken ill and Richard had come home. And then had come the stunning news that his marriage had not been consummated. Livvy, the little fool, hardly understood what that meant, but Caroline knew very well. And most important of all, she knew that such a sham of a marriage could be annulled.

And so Caroline had felt a surge of hope for the first time in weeks. She'd gone to Richard immediately and had seen that his feelings hadn't changed, but still she did not know if she'd made any headway that day in the library. In fact, he'd seemed almost annoyed with her. Caroline kept telling herself that she had nothing to fear from Serena; the chit was hardly a worthy rival. She wasn't warming Richard's bed, and Caroline knew she had to get Richard alone to stoke the fires until she deemed the time ripe to suggest an annullment.

But Caroline had begun to feel uneasy some time after that brief interlude in the library. She was not quite sure what it was, but there was something in the air between Richard and Serena that Caroline didn't like. She had quickly decided more drastic measures were needed. She would have to discredit Serena, make it plain as pikestaff to Richard, if he didn't know already, that Serena was not a suitable wife for him. Distracting Livvy yesterday had been child's play, and it had worked like a charm. Caroline was certain Richard had given Serena a rare dressing down for her negligence. But that wasn't enough, and Livvy might be fool enough to confess the whole at all events.

Caroline yanked aside the branch of a yew hedge and continued on her way. She ought to come to the stream soon. She would find Serena, but even if she didn't — well — she would think of something; she always did.

And then her mind wandered and her eyes lit up as she recalled the other possibility. Richard didn't credit what the old gypsy hag had told him, but Caroline remembered her grandmother's tales of the Romany sight. She wouldn't be fool enough to ignore the gypsy's fortune. And since no one else in the household would bother to look for the sapphires, Caroline would have a clear field. She would prefer to marry Richard; the Gower wealth of a certain exceeded what could be got for any number of sapphires, and there was the title. But still, if Richard refused an annullment, Caroline might yet come out of this a rich woman. Caroline tramped further into the woods. What, she pondered, could Serena do, or seem to do, that was so odious that Richard would send her away? And where in the world could those sapphires be?

Caroline ducked under the branches of another yew hedge, meaning to step through to the other side. "Oh!" she exclaimed as she collided with a wall. But it wasn't a cold stone wall. It was the warm, lean, hard body of a man.

He grasped her by the arms and pulled her through the hedge.

"Steady, wench," the deep voice said, "and right pretty you be, even you be a gorgio." He wore buckskins and a white linen shirt, full in the sleeves and open at the neck. Neither laborer nor gentleman, he.

"I am *not* a wench and I demand that you unhand me, sir!" Caroline commanded.

But the man only laughed. "So, you talk like a rawnie. But I reckon you not. You have no clothes of a rawnie. Stop squirming, wench. I let you go when I am

170

ready. Have no fear," he drawled, looking her up and down suggestively.

More angry at the man's audacity than afraid, Caroline looked up at her tall slim captor. His face was dark, his eyes black, his hawklike nose and firm chin giving him an unyielding air. He reminded her a little of Richard, but this man was darker, more intense. She did not like him. "You are a gypsy," she said at length. He still held her by the arms. "I might have known. You lack manners, sir, and I wish to be on my way."

"Who be your mistress, wench? Which rawnie do you serve?"

"I am my own mistress, sir," Caroline answered haughtily, trying unsuccessfully to jerk herself from his grasp. "I am a guest at Luntsford Court, and I suggest you release me immediately, or it shall be the worse for you."

The gypsy's eyes flickered. "You are guest in the great house? Hmm. You do speak like a rawnie, I think."

"What the devil is a 'rawnie'?"

"A lady. Mayhap you not speak like one after all."

"Of course I am a lady! My family owns Briar Manor, just to the east."

"So. You are rawnie," the gypsy said, releasing her. "At the great house." Then he paused and ran one hand up to her hair. "But your hair—it is golden, not dark." He lifted her left hand. "You not wear ring. You not Gaya's rawnie."

Caroline had had enough of his insolent scrutiny. "Look, I haven't the least notion what you are talking about, nor do I care a fig. Step aside, and I shall be on

171

my way."

"Serena, that be her name. You are not Serena?"

"Serena? How do you know Serena?" Caroline's eyes widened.

"She is friend to my sister. I do not like that Gaya have this friend, Serena. She comes today to visit camp. She is rawnie of the great house, yes?"

Serena in a gypsy camp? How very—interesting. Richard would find it so, she was sure. "Yes. She is the new bride of Lord Egremont, the duke's heir," she said, a certain disdain in her voice.

"Ah. I think you do not like Serena. But the rai, the duke's heir, mayhap you like him very well."

Caroline was taken aback by his perceptiveness, enough so that she spoke more candidly than she ever would have to a stranger, and a gypsy at that. "Richard would have married me if it hadn't been for Serena. It was an arranged match; he had no choice."

"I see. But now you all be at the great house, is not so?"

"Yes," Caroline replied vaguely, her mind churning with possibilities. She had set out to follow Serena, and instead had come upon this man, who was himself about to meet Serena. He was a gypsy, which made him quite disreputable, and he had a lecherous eye. It might simply help her cause to tell Richard that Serena had befriended the gypsies, was visiting their camp. But surely this man's sudden appearance was an opportunity Caroline could not pass up. There must be some way he could help her.

She fluttered her eyelashes and stepped close to him. "I think we should introduce ourselves. I am Miss

Caroline Lister."

He cocked an eyebrow and she caught the glimmer of a smile. "I am Marco. I am Rom." He ran a hand up her arms and then lifted her chin with his finger. "I think, Caroleen Leester, that you be wantin' something from me. What is it?"

Caroline did not like this annoying habit he seemed to have of reading her mind. Nor did she particularly like his hands on her, but she would have to hold out some lure, she knew. She pressed her body close to him.

"How perceptive you are, Marco. You are right—it did occur to me that perhaps you could help me."

"Did it now? And how might that be?" Marco slid his arms around her and curled his lip.

"Well," she pouted prettily, her mind whirling, "I should have been the new Lady Egremont, I truly should, if it hadn't been for Serena. And—" she let her hands come up to rest on his chest—"and Richard is not very happy with her. In fact, I—" she lowered her eyes, "I know that theirs is a marriage in name only, and I—well—if I could discredit Serena he might send her away and have the marriage annulled."

The gypsy traced the line of her lips with his finger. She did not like his touch. He was far too intense and dark. She noted the thick black curling hair visible on his chest and repressed a shudder. "Still you do not tell Marco how he help you, Caroleen."

"Well, it just occurred to me that—especially if Serena is to visit your camp—that you might—well—there are certain things you might do so that Richard might think that you and she—well, I mean to say—"

173

Marco stopped her by pulling her close and pressing his lips to hers. The kiss was brief but she felt a certain urgency in him and she could not repress the shudder this time.

Marco pulled away from the gorgio with a frown. She was cold, this wench, even with a body like that. And suddenly he was angry, very angry. Press her ripe breasts against him, she would, and let him kiss her, even touch her, just so she get her way. But she would never give herself to him. She was too cold, and besides, she wanted this rai of the great house. And Marco knew the rai would want a virgin wife. And this blond wench, she know it too. She was worse than a whore, he thought disgustedly. Willin' to tease a man, use him like that. And did she think her body, or the promise of it, was enough to make him agree to her schemes? Why should Marco get involved in gorgio business? It very bad thing to do, unless there be something in it for Marco. And then he remembered. Of course, there was. He smiled down at her.

"I will help you, Caroleen. But we make business deal—Caroleen and Marco. You want to be wife of the great lord. I want the jewel."

"Jewel? What jewel?"

He gripped her shoulders and spoke harshly. "Do not play with me, Caroleen. You know what jewel. The sapphires."

His eyes blazed and for the first time Caroline was frightened. But she could not turn back now. She would not run away. "How do you know about the sapphires?"

A menacing chuckle escaped his lips. "How do I

174

know, Caroleen? Hah! I am Rom. I know."

"I—I see."

"Good. Now we make business together. You find me jewel and I make trouble for your Serena."

"She's not *my* Serena. And I have no idea where the jewel is."

"You will find it. I will help you, from afar," he said confidently.

Caroline bit her lip, her mind spinning. She knew she needed help if she were to really discredit Serena. There was something about this man—his intense masculinity perhaps—that made her certain that if Richard were to see Serena and Marco together . . . Yes, that would work like a charm. That and the fact that Caroline would be there, ever faithful, ever waiting with open arms.

As to the jewel, well, what would mere sapphires mean to Caroline, Lady Egremont? But if for some reason her plan did not work, they would be her ticket from obscurity into the blazing lights of London. She had no intention of handing over such a fortune to some gypsy, just because he compromised a silly chit who wandered too far from home. Gypsies probably did that all the time, merely for amusement. No, she would never give him the jewel, nor could she agree too readily to his terms, lest he become suspicious.

She licked her lips and fluttered her eyelashes. "I do need your help, Marco. But you know, that is a very large fortune we are talking about. And I will be taking all the risks—snooping about the Court looking for the sapphires. I think—" she heaved a sigh so that her breasts rose and fell quite visibly, "well, I think we had

175

ought to share the profits. Fifty-fifty. I am certain that will set us both up admirably for some time to come."

Marco's grip tightened on her shoulders and she winced. Then he relaxed. "It's a hard bargain you drive, Caroleen, for a gorgio. I think mayhap we do very well, you and Marco, that we do. And now, you come here, sit down. We must plan."

Caroline tried to keep the glow of triumph from her eyes. Together, she and this gypsy couldn't fail. Either way, she would be a very wealthy woman, very soon.

Serena had emerged from the water and was already dressed and shaking out her hair when she heard the lilting voice behind her. "You did not come yesterday. I knew you come today," Gaya said simply.

Serena whirled around and smiled. "I'm sorry. I was occupied all day with my—well, never mind. I am very happy to see you, Gaya."

"You already swim. Now you ready to draw Gaya, no?"

Serena laughed and watched as Gaya, clad again in her red blouse and multi-colored skirt, lifted herself with perfect ease onto her rock. Gaya drew her knees up and tossed back her hair, and Serena reached for her sketch pad.

"Yesterday Marco say, 'No, the gorgio cannot come to camp. Gaya not be friend to gorgio,' " Gaya said quite suddenly, a while later.

"Oh, Gaya, that's quite all right. I didn't really expect—"

"But, very strange. Today, Marco say 'is good.' He

176

say, 'You bring Serena, your friend, to camp.'"

"He did?"

"Oh, yes. You come today — when drawing is finished. Yes?"

Serena chuckled. "Very well, Gaya, I shall come today," she said, and though she would have preferred a third sitting, she judged it wise to fill in as many details today as possible. One never knew about tomorrow, after all.

"You are wife of young lord, is not so?" Gaya asked.

Serena put down her pencil. "Yes, Gaya, I am." She would simply have to trust that her secret was safe.

"He is very foolish, I think. And the duke, he is better now, yes?"

"Ah — yes," Serena mumbled and quickly lowered her eyes to her work, lest Gaya see her expression. How in the world — oh — it was useless to speculate.

Sometime later Serena shared her cache of food, cheese, cold sausage and biscuits, with Gaya and then resumed her drawing. And then quite suddenly, mid-afternoon, Gaya slid down from her perch. "I think my drawing almost done, yes, Serena?"

"Ah — yes, Gaya." Serena cocked her head and eyed the sketch critically. Yes, it was almost done, and it would transfer nicely to canvas. She closed her pad and stood up. Her hair was still down and on impulse she decided to leave it that way, merely securing the scarf about her head. Gaya turned and began climbing out of the dell, and Serena made to follow.

"You forgot your shoes, Serena," Gaya called over her shoulder, without looking back.

With a rueful smile Serena bent to retrieve her

wayward shoes, and together they trod the woods to the gypsy camp.

The Romanies had chosen their location well. The brightly colored caravans, some with intricately carved horses, dragons and flowers, and all with border designs that sometimes extended even to the axles, were scattered inside a clearing bordered by a thick row of trees. There were several tents as well and Serena noticed that horses, chickens and people roamed freely. Gaya smiled at several children scampering barefoot amongst the trees, and she greeted a woman who was hanging linens on a line strung between two wagons. They passed an open pit, over which large heavy pots and the obvious remains of lunch were suspended. In the center of the camp was a rough hewn platform fashioned of wood.

"What is that?" Serena asked.

"Oh, that is for the dancing. At night," Gaya said, and then walked on, as if it were not a subject she was prepared to discuss. They passed a wagon laden with pots, and Serena saw a man sitting on a stool beside it, but he did not look up from the kettle he was mending.

Gaya did not stop till they had reached the furthest end of the camp. This caravan was perhaps the largest, with a barrel top crowned by brilliantly colored mouldings and beautiful etchings in the glass windows. And then the rear door opened and a man emerged. Marco, Serena thought. He resembled Gaya only faintly, for his features were sharper, more rugged. He could not be accounted handsome, but he was certainly striking looking.

Marco stepped down and gazed at the rawnie. What

eyes, he thought, such a deep blue as he had never seen. And what hair! There was fire in this gorgio, that there was. She not cold, like the blond, Caroleen. Marco smiled to himself. He was going to like doing his part of the bargain, very much.

As Gaya made the introductions, Serena found herself tongue-tied. There was a certain — well — magnetism about him that rather disconcerted Serena, and his eyes swept over her in a manner that was even more disconcerting.

"So, this is the rawnie, Serena," he said smoothly, and then raised her hand to his lips in the most gallant English manner. Serena felt her heart pound quite strangely.

"You are most welcome at our camp, Serena," he added with what she thought was a hint of mockery. Or had she just imagined it? She wondered at his familiarity. He reminded her of Richard. She was not sure why — they were alike in stature and coloring, but Marco was darker. Richard was by far the more handsome, and Marco's dark eyes were devoid of humor, which Richard's, she had lately begun to realize, were definitely not.

"Thank you, Marco," she remembered to say, despite her surreptitious scrutiny of his person. He wore buckskins and a white shirt open at the collar. Why did his nearness seem to discompose her so?

"Gaya, you take Serena around camp. I see, Serena, you like our dancing stage. Every night we dance. Mayhap you come and see?"

Serena heard Gaya's intake of breath and realized immediately that such an invitation was not often

179

granted to a gorgio. She did not wish to pass up such an opportunity, nor did she wish to offend, but of course it was not to be.

"I — I should like it above all things, Marco. But — but I think it would be very difficult — nary impossible — for me to come at night."

Marco shrugged. "We shall see. Meantime, Gaya show you the dance. Gaya the best, the very best. I am best, too," he said simply, and meant it.

Gaya and Serena wandered the camp for a while, Gaya introducing her only, it seemed, to select people.

"You like this vardo," Gaya said at length, pointing to a caravan that was smaller but no less brilliantly decorated than that of Marco and Gaya. The jolly faced, vastly overweight woman who emerged when Gaya knocked was introduced as Aunt Violet, and she invited them in to her vardo. Serena was surprised at how comfortable the bed seemed, with its plush down comforter and myriad pillows, and at the amount of cupboard space the wagon accommodated. Opposite the cupboards was a small stove with a chimney cut right through the roof of the caravan. A woman of few words, Aunt Violet put up a kettle without asking and a few minutes later handed Gaya and Serena each a cup of tea. Serena blanched inwardly at its red color and the unusual green bits and pieces floating about. But she followed Gaya's lead and bravely took a sip, finding, to her delight, that it was quite delicious. She prudently decided not to ask what was in it.

When they took their leave of Aunt Violet, Serena asked Gaya if she truly would dance for her.

"I dance for you, Serena. But you not listen to

180

Marco. You not come at night. You make the young lord very angry you do that," Gaya said, walking alongside Serena toward the entrance to the camp.

Serena stopped and turned to her friend. "I know, Gaya. I cannot come," she said soberly, and then her eyes crinkled with mirth, "much as I would love to. Would you teach me your dance, Romany dance?"

Gaya cocked her head. "Where you get diklo?" she asked, fingering Serena's scarf. "And earrings?"

"From—from the young lord," Serena said, wondering at the flush she felt rise to her cheeks.

Gaya nodded knowingly. "I teach you, Serena. I think you dance very well. But not here. Not today. We meet again in the dell, yes?"

With that Serena had to be content, and she imagined that, for a gypsy, that was quite a commitment.

Chapter Nine

No one had missed Serena at lunch, Richard having been attending to business and the duchess to the duke. She was relieved to have such freedom but found it rather lowering at the same time.

Serena made her way to her mother-in-law's chambers just before tea time, as the duchess had requested, but was stopped in the corridor by Livvy.

"Oh, Serena, I—I looked for you at luncheon." So, Serena thought, she had been missed after all.

"Livvy, I—I admire you greatly for telling the duchess the truth. You did not have to, you know."

"Oh, but I did. I—I was such a coward last night in the Gold Salon, but I—I couldn't sleep—and—and—you do understand why I had to tell her, don't you? Even though—" here Livvy's eyes and voice lowered simultaneously, "even though I had to suffer a rare scold for it."

"Did you? Well, I am persuaded your mother has

forgotten all about it by now. I appreciate your telling her, and of course I understand why you did so, my dear."

"You do? I am so glad, for Caroline did not comprehend at all. Said I was a 'silly little fool' and should have 'let the dust fall where it might.' She simply did not understand."

"Didn't she? How very curious," Serena murmured, and deciding that was enough said, patted Livvy's hands and went on her way.

She found the duchess at a gold-leafed escritoire in her sitting room.

"Ah, Serena, do come in, my dear," she said, rising and extending her hands. "I thought we might take tea here together. Come and sit down and I shall ring."

They seated themselves in the sunny bay window on a delicate but surprisingly comfortable camel back sofa. They talked of pleasantries and the duke's health until tea was brought.

The duchess poured out and recommended that Serena try one of the watercress and cucumber sandwiches. Then she said, "Are you happy here, Serena?"

Serena quickly sipped her tea, her eyes lowered, as she tried to compose her thoughts. "Yes, of course I am happy, your grace. Luntsford is beautiful. I—I love to roam the grounds and—and I have my painting."

The duchess regarded her speculatively. "Yes, your painting. Richard tells me you are very talented. He said you were working on some interesting watercolors at Gateshead." Serena could not help the widening of her eyes. She hadn't known Richard had even *seen* those paintings, let alone held them in any esteem. She thought fleetingly that she must keep him from seeing

Gaya's portrait. That would not do at all. "You do have a marvelous ability to amuse yourself, Serena," the duchess was saying, "something I wish Livvy might learn. But that is not precisely what I meant. Are you—are you happy with Richard?"

Serena blinked and nearly choked on a wedge of cucumber. How could she answer a question like that? The duchess' kind eyes were too penetrating for Serena to attempt to gammon her, and yet she couldn't very well tell her mother-in-law about the true state of her marriage.

"I—that is—I think—what I mean to say is that we need time to get to know one another better." That, at least, was true, Serena thought. "I—I am afraid I am not quite as docile a wife as Richard would like," she added, not knowing why. But she could not keep a twinkle from her eye and upon reflection decided that was a very diplomatic way of telling the duchess what an autocratic son she had.

Her mother-in-law's lips twitched. "I see, Serena. Yes, I do see. 'Tis a great pity your time at Gateshead was cut short. Perhaps in a few days, when the duke is on his feet, you may return there. And then you shall set up at Wheatfield. I do believe an establishment of one's own is a great boon to a marriage. It cannot be easy for you here," she added pointedly.

"Yes, your grace," Serena murmured, not knowing where to look. How much did she know about Caroline?

"Is there anything that you want or need, Serena? Is there anything I can do for you while you are here?"

"Oh, your grace. It is *I* who should be doing for you. This is an enormous house and—"

"Oh, piffle, my child. The house runs itself—what with Rivers and Mrs. Grayson. No, we are speaking of you."

Serena took refuge in her tea, and then decided to plunge on. She could never ask this of Richard, but his mother was so much easier to talk to.

"Well—I—I do not wish to inconvenience you in the slightest. But there *is* something. I would not wish you to think I mean to be extravagant but I—" Serena paused and smiled ruefully. "Well, the very crux of the matter is that my mother chose all my gowns—" Serena fingered the several rows of yellow ruffles at the neck and bodice of her afternoon dress— "and in truth I do not think they are at all becoming to me." She saw her mother-in-law stifle a grin and was emboldened to say, "If truth be told, your grace, my gowns are rather hideous. And I do not mean to spend a great deal of Richard's money, but I should love to replace several dresses, and he *has* indicated that he would not be averse to my doing so. 'Tis merely that I do not wish to ask him just now," she concluded softly.

"Yes," murmured the duchess, "I can see that you mightn't. But—" she continued bracingly, "you mustn't worry about Richard's money. I do assure you he has more than enough. And if you do not mind my being frank, my dear, I think perhaps we might replace more than just one or two." The duchess' mouth crinkled with suppressed mirth and suddenly Serena burst out laughing.

"Oh, yes, your grace," she said when she was able, "I would like that very well. In truth, I should like to burn the whole lot of them—every muddy green and yellow gown, every bit of ruffle and flounce and—oh, ma'am—my trousseau is hopeless is it not?" The duchess's control finally gave way and she joined Serena in a delicious peal of laughter.

"I should like nothing better than to buy you a new wardrobe, my dear," the duchess said as Serena wiped the moisture from her eyes. "And, in fact, I do have a creditable modiste right here in Kent. She cannot equal my London dressmaker, of course, but we can of a certain make a start. Sometime before the Season I should like to spend a fortnight with you in London on a mad shopping spree. How does that sound?"

"Oh, your grace, I should like it above all things!"

"Excellent. I shall send word to Mrs. Chalmers for Monday, then." The duchess reached for a flaky scone and began to layer it with butter. "Oh, and Serena, I should like it if you would cease using my title. It's so very formal within the family, you must know. Do you think, well, would it be very presumptuous of me to ask that you call me—'mother'? I should be very honored."

Serena stared at her mother-in-law and felt her eyes well up. There was such kindness in this woman—

"It is I who am honored, M-Mother," she said at length, and took refuge again in her teacup.

The duchess squeezed her hand. "So, we shall begin on your wardrobe straight away. Now, is there anything else, my dear?"

"Ah, well, there is one thing more. Your hair is so smooth and lovely and mine—well—I love it, really, love to feel it long and flowing down my back. But when I wish to look—elegant and—" Serena smiled impishly—"and respectable—well, I fear it is quite hopeless, as you can see."

The duchess cocked her head, a knowing twinkle in her eye. Then she put her cup and saucer down on the silver tea tray. "Take your hair down, Serena. Let us have a look."

Serena complied, shaking her dark locks out till they fell about her face and shoulders. Her mother-in-law fingered her hair gently. "It is truly lovely, Serena. I should not imagine you would wish to cut it."

"Oh, no! I really enjoy it, when I can leave it down. And Richard likes — well — that is, I must put it up every day and it is not very neat."

The duchess regarded her shrewdly. "No, I daresay 'tisn't. But you don't particularly care, do you?"

Serena could not keep the gleam from her eye. "Do you know, I should like to have more becoming dresses, but my hair — well — it's a part of me, don't you see. Most times I don't care a rush if it looks a bit like a bird's nest. But then sometimes I —" Serena lowered her eyes — "I do want to look more elegant you see and —"

"Serena, has my son called this glorious head of hair a 'bird's nest'?"

"Oh, no, your gr — ah, Mother. B-But he has thought it, many times, I am persuaded."

The duchess chuckled. "Well then, my dear, I think a compromise is called for. Perhaps, if we cut the front just a bit, just where your hair frames your face, we might give you a lovely fringe of curls, and the rest would stay just as it is. Angelique, my dresser, is simply a genius with a scissors. But there, I do not wish to push you. You must think on it, and when you are ready —"

"Oh, but it sounds a capital idea. I am ready now."

187

"Are you? Well then, come to my dressing room and I shall ring for Angelique."

A full day's work had made Richard long for a brisk ride over the countryside. He would have enjoyed Serena's company but knew that she would be with his mother now. He smiled ruefully as he recalled his conversation with the duchess today about Serena. The little imp! Why hadn't she told him the truth about Livvy? He supposed it was a measure of her pique at his dressing her down. Well, he would make amends tonight. Yes, and he knew just what sort of amends he wanted to make.

Richard entered the sitting room of their suite and walked toward the open door of the dressing room. Voices from within halted him in his tracks.

"Damned if you ain't in the right of it, Hannah, though what all is takin' them so dang blasted long is more'n I can say." Richard's eyes widened. Since when had the two servants become so very chummy? And just who were they talking about?

"Well, as to that, I couldn't say, Watkins. But then we are agreed what's to do for tonight, are we?"

"As you say, Hannah, I'll be havin' the footmen to take out the green sofa. It be in sore need of a cleanin', don't you know." Richard thought he could hear the suppressed mirth in his valet's voice and frowned in bewilderment. Watkins' next words made everything all too clear, however. "And o'course, the chaise still ain't ready, is it? Well, and I sure do hope this turns the trick, Hannah, because I declare I'm plumb out of ideas. I can't go smokin' up the place again, now can I?

Besides, we've got them just where they ought to be. I reckon the rest is up to them."

"I reckon so, Watkins. You can lead a horse to water, after all."

Richard nearly choked on his rage and took several angry steps forward, but then he checked himself. They were, after all, doing exactly what he wanted to do — get himself into Serena's bed. His mind raced back to their first night here — the servants had disappeared and the clothes were in complete disarray in the dressing room. Then there had been the mixup with the sofa pillows, and then the smoke filled room. Crude tactics, of course, but rather effective. He had, after all, slept with Serena last night, albeit four feet apart. It was a bit lowering to think he needed the help of his valet and a damned lady's maid for God sakes, to seduce his wife, but there it was. And, of course, he didn't actually *need* their help; it was just faster this way.

But he certainly wouldn't let them know he was privy to their machinations. Then he would have to demand the restoration of the various pieces of furniture, and there was no sense to that, now was there? And so Richard Gower, Marquis of Egremont, tiptoed out of his room and decided to forego his riding habit, and his ride, after all.

When Serena came into the Gold Salon with his mother before dinner, Richard's eyes widened and his mouth quite unabashedly gaped open. Serena wore a pink crepe round dress that he thought he'd seen before, but it seemed to have lost some of its overabundance of roses. It looked exceedingly lovely on her and it struck him that for such a little thing she had a remarkably well-proportioned figure. Not willowy like Caroline, but slender, yet rounded just where it ought to be. He itched to touch her. But in truth it was not her gown that caused his mouth to behave so rudely. It was her face.

He found his tongue at last. "Serena, you, you look beautiful," he breathed, and meant it. "Your face — it's — something is different. It's your hair, isn't it? You've cut it." He strode to her and took her hand and brought it to his lips. She smiled shyly.

"Good of you to notice, Richard," his mother said. "We just cut a little, at the front. She looks enchanting, doesn't she?"

"Yes," he said simply, and kept staring at her. He had come to think of his wife as attractive, but he had never before realized that she was actually beautiful. Tiny dark brown curls framed her face delightfully. Her deep blue eyes looked larger than usual, and they shone in the candlelight. He had never noticed how high her cheekbones were, and her lips looked very inviting indeed. And then Livvy and Caroline came bursting in, and Richard thought it was just as well. This was not the time to contemplate those lips.

Dinner was more relaxed than it had been since he and Serena had returned home. The duchess was more herself and Livvy and Serena seemed quite in charity with each other. Conversation flowed freely and in fact, the only one who was curiously silent throughout was Caroline. Richard's efforts to draw her out were to no avail, nor were his effusive and truthful compliments on the lovely mauve chiffon gown she wore.

For Richard the most interesting point of the meal

came when Serena replied to the duchess' query about the comfort of their bedchamber. "Oh, do not tease yourself about it, Mother. I assure you we are right. I had the furniture shifted about a bit, as you suggested, and the room is quite delightful now. Do you not agree, Richard?"

It took Richard several moments to answer, for his attention was arrested by Serena's manner of address toward his mother. Her tone had been matter of fact, and, as his eyes flew from his wife's face to his mother's, he saw that neither seemed to consider it exceptional. Well, well, so Serena had decided to join the family after all. Very promising indeed, he mused, and tried not to be miffed that his mother was making more headway than he was. He stole a glance at Caroline. Her face was unreadable, and he decided that was just as well.

After dinner he elected, as he had for several days, to forego his port, and so escorted the ladies to the family drawing room for coffee. It was in the corridor that Caroline tripped. She was next to Livvy, and as it was rather dark, Richard was not sure what it was she stumbled on. But she cried out in pain and her knees buckled. She clutched Livvy and would have fallen had Richard not darted forward to catch her.

"Oh, Richard, I do not know what happened," she whimpered. "It's my ankle. I twisted it, I fear."

The other women clucked their sympathy and Richard began to carry her toward the drawing room. He shifted her in his arms and she winced in pain.

"It's all right; I'll have you on the sofa in a moment and we'll have a look at it. Just bear up, my dear," he murmured. Caroline leaned her head against his shoulder and he could feel her warm breasts pressed against him. He took a deep breath and hurried to the drawing room.

He laid her gently on the sofa, and though she gasped when he probed the ankle, he could find no evidence of swelling. He ordered brandy when Rivers appeared with the coffee, and held Caroline's hand till it came. The suffering was written on her beautiful face and it was almost more than he could bear. He handed Caroline the brandy and as she gingerly sipped it, he happened to glance up at Serena. He was shocked, for she was glaring at him and then at Caroline. Glaring most fiercely. It was not like Serena to be so unsympathetic unless—unless she were jealous. But that was impossible. Or was it? Hmm. It might be very interesting to find out.

He was very pleased when his mother quite deliberately drew everyone's attention away from Caroline. She insisted they all be seated and furnished each with a cup of coffee.

"Now," she said, obviously searching for some innocuous topic of discussion, "tomorrow is Sunday. Are we to go to church without the duke or not?"

It was agreed upon that, as no one cared to repeat ad nauseum the exact state of the duke's health, they had best stay home on the morrow. His mother murmured something about the servants' grapevine doing a better job of reporting at all events, and Richard thought he would very much like to sleep late tomorrow, and definitely not alone.

To that end, he prudently summoned a footman to convey Caroline abovestairs, rather than attempting it himself. He instructed her to stay completely off the injured foot and said he would summon the doctor in the morning should it prove necessary. He thought he caught a flash of annoyance in her eyes and chose to ignore it.

The annoyance in Serena's eyes was more than a flash, however, and that he could not ignore. She seemed more of an iceberg this night than last as Richard escorted her upstairs and turned her over to her maid. He had ordered a fire and brandy in his room again, but he wondered if they would be sufficiently warming. It was some small comfort to know he would not be assailed by smoke as he opened his door.

Sometime later, garbed in a burgundy satin dressing gown, Richard tapped on Serena's door. *Their* door, he reminded himself. He invited her to take a drink with him, and she agreed with a decided lack of enthusiasm. The love seat had been drawn up to the hearth, as per instructions, and the fire blazed. He seated Serena and poured the brandy.

"Oh, thank you, but I don't drink brandy," she said when he handed her a glass.

"Ah, but there's a first time for everything," he murmured as he slipped down beside her. He sat only a few inches from her and he could sense her whole body stiffen.

She refused to look at him and concentrated on her drink. Richard concentrated on Serena. Once again she wore a high-necked nightgown and that voluminous dressing gown. He thought it amusing that all her nightwear seemed to be white and wondered if Lady Stoneleigh were trying to tell him something. Serena's hair was down and despite her new coiffeur it still fell as wildly as ever down her back. He was glad; he liked it that way.

Serena took a sip of the brandy and immediately began to splutter and cough. Richard patted her on the back until she subsided and then his hand began to gently massage that same very nice back.

"Thank you, Richard," she said coolly. "I am recovered now."

He removed his hand and urged her to try the brandy again, "It's really quite good, once you get used to it, Serena. It'll warm you up."

"I am not cold, Richard."

Oh, yes you are, he wanted to say, but refrained. Serena took a tentative sip of the brandy, and then another, and another. They talked of inconsequentials and gazed at the flames dancing in the grate. Richard was careful not to touch her, but still he could feel her body relax beside him.

At length he rose, set the glasses aside and extended his hand to Serena. "Come, my dear. 'Tis time for bed."

"Mmm, I *am* rather tired, I must say," she said, allowing him to pull her up.

He drew her close and wound his fingers through her hair. "Little gypsy," he whispered, "I love your hair."

"Thank you, Richard," she replied, a little breathlessly, he thought.

And then he didn't want to think any more, or talk. He bent his head and his lips claimed hers. At first the kiss was gentle, undemanding. Then he wound his arms around her and she swayed toward him. He pressed her closer; she did not resist. His kiss deepened and then finally, tentatively, her lips parted under his and she returned the kiss. He felt the quickening of her heartbeat even as his desire mounted, and he let his

194

hand slide down her back to her hips. He thought of the woman, the stranger, who had felt like a stone wall on their wedding night. This was no stranger; this was Serena, his wife, and there was nothing cold about her.

And then, abruptly, she pulled away. Her face was flushed and her breathing irregular. "Richard, I—I don't understand. I—I—"

"Don't you, Serena? Come back, and I'll explain," he said huskily.

"N-no, Richard. I think I'd best go to bed now. G-goodnight." She turned from him and took several steps, then whirled back around. "Richard, where is the green sofa?"

Ah, he thought. The infamous green sofa. It was as well she hadn't noticed before. He sighed. "I'm afraid it's gone the way of the chaise, Serena."

"Oh, dear. And the chaise is still—not here, is it?"

"No, it isn't." He moved slowly toward her.

"And so you have no place to sleep, once again."

"Oh, I wouldn't say that." He stood very close but didn't touch her.

Serena drew herself up. "I shall sleep on the chairs."

"No, Serena," he said firmly. "I think not." His fingers lightly traced the line of her jaw. "Little gypsy. You know, on our first night together, I—I said some things that were very harsh and rather foolish. I apologize for that. And, well—I am still waiting for that invitation."

Serena swallowed hard and took a step back, willing her heart to stop pounding so. How could he do this to her, kiss her, make her feel this way, when only minutes ago he was gazing at Caroline so adoringly? She felt tears prick at the back of her eyes and blinked them

195

back.

"Good night, Richard," she said as coldly as she could, and fled from the room.

"Damn!" Richard muttered. She was more skittish than a filly. How much more patient could he be? This was *already* the longest seduction in history!

He followed her into the bedchamber and found her dragging two chairs together. He tried to keep his voice matter of fact. "No, Serena, I'll not chase you out of your bed. Look, last night we slept in the same bed and nothing — that is — could we not do the same again?"

She looked at him doubtfully. "Serena," he said gruffly, not bothering to hide his annoyance, "I do assure you that you will be safe. I have no intention of ravishing you."

She had the grace to flush. "Very well, Richard, I suppose, under the circumstances . . ."

The circumstances, Richard reflected some time later as he stared up at the ceiling from the exile of his side of the big bed, were absurd. Just how much more of this could a normal, healthy man take?

When Serena awoke early Sunday morning, she knew very well what she was doing curled up on the very edge of the bed. She rose slowly and noiselessly, relieved that this time Richard did not stir. She dressed hurriedly, not paying much heed to her toilette, merely wishing to be away from the house. She gathered her sketch book and painting materials, including her easel. She would catch the early morning light in the garden, she decided.

She worked diligently on Gaya's portrait, transferring it to the canvas, and then decided to put it aside until later to add the finishing touches, and then begin painting. In the meantime she would work on the caterpillar. She assembled her watercolors and closed her eyes to conjure up the colors of the fuzzy little creature she'd encountered yesterday. And then she put brush to paper and, as usual, quite lost track of time.

"Serena!" Richard's voice broke her concentration and Serena looked up to see him leaning out of the breakfast room window. "Come have some breakfast," he said cheerfully.

She smiled and waved, somehow pleased that he had called to her. "I shall be up in a trice," she called back. She had done quite a bit on her fuzzy friend and thought this a good time to stop. She was also glad she'd had the presence to place the easel so that it could not be seen from the house. She wanted her caterpillar to be a surprise. Perhaps, she thought a bit wistfully, the "right time" to give it to him would come.

Breakfast was very pleasant, and Serena was grateful that Richard did not mention last night, nor her precipitate departure this morning. But the meal came to a less than satisfactory close when a footman came to inform Richard that Caroline asked him to wait upon her in her chamber to have a look at her ankle.

"I'm sorry, Serena. I suppose I shall have to go, though I don't expect the pain is too bad if she's waited till now to call."

"No, I don't suppose it is," Serena drawled, and Richard looked at her curiously before departing.

As it was, Caroline's foot seemed fine, not the least bit swollen and, although she said it pained her to walk on it, she most definitely did not wish the doctor called

197

in. She implored Richard to help her try to walk around the room a bit. He did it reluctantly, for somehow he felt uncomfortable with her leaning close against him, the folds of her dressing gown gaping open. And why the hell could she not have gotten dressed before summoning him? She wobbled unsteadily on the foot and he advised her to stay off it for at least the day, though the injury did not seem all that serious. Caroline pouted about being quite lonely all by herself in her bedchamber, and asked Richard if he would wrap her ankle.

"Caroline, I really have no experience in such matters. If you think it needs to be wrapped, then perhaps we had ought to have the doctor."

To which reasonable statement Caroline pursed her lips in vexation and replied that Richard was being singularly unaccommodating. Richard left Caroline's chamber feeling no small amount of exasperation with Caroline, and women in general. Whatever did the creatures want?

Serena spent the morning painting, in her room this time. Livvy darted in at one point, and Serena hastily covered the portrait of Gaya, which she'd been working on.

"Oh, dear, I'm interrupting you," Livvy said. "Well then, I shan't stay long. Mama said that you're to have your fittings tomorrow morning and I thought perhaps — this afternoon maybe — you might like to have a look at my latest issue of *La Belle Assemblee*."

"Oh, Livvy, how kind of you! I should enjoy that very much," Serena replied, wiping the paint from her fingers with a cloth. "And this afternoon would be fine."

Livvy departed soon thereafter, somehow contriving to address Serena as "my dearest new sister" twice before she did so. Serena smiled to herself and resumed working.

She was pleased to see that Caroline had come down to luncheon. Not that Serena wished her company, but at least this way she knew Caroline had given up trying to get Richard to come to her bedchamber. Really, how Richard did not see through such a transparent ploy was beyond anything!

Serena was surprised when, toward the end of the meal, Richard invited her to accompany him to his study, as he wished to show her something. She had never been invited into that male sanctum before and flushed with pleasure. She was even more surprised, however, at the look Caroline trained on her at Richard's words. She had always known Caroline disliked her, but she was not prepared for the pure and utter hatred she saw glittering in the girl's eyes. Serena resolved to stay quite clear of Caroline Lister, and she was relieved when Richard escorted her out of the dining room to his study.

Though Richard had of late been working in his father's library, his own study stood several doors down, and it was here that he brought Serena. He loved this room, with its smell of old leather and its rows and rows of books. Best of all there were the glass enclosed cabinets which held his specimen cases. He would transfer it all the Wheatfield, where he would have much more room to display them.

"I thought," Richard began tentatively, "well, you have expressed interest in my study of insects, and so I thought you might like to see some of my specimens."

"Oh, thank you, Richard. I should like it above all things!" Serena replied enthusiastically, and he knew she meant it.

They spent a most agreeable hour, poring over rows of colorful specimens, neatly pinned and labeled on a black background inside the boxes. And if Richard had to lean very close to Serena to point out special markings on the wings of an orange tip butterfly or a sphinx moth, well, he didn't mind at all. In fact, he liked it very well. She smelled of roses and he liked that very well, too.

She appeared most fascinated by his collections, which pleased him enormously. His parents only murmured politely whenever he showed them something new, and Livvy had lost all interest since she'd become a "young lady." Caroline, he was not pleased to recall, had been quite bored with the whole idea, and so he had never brought her here.

"I think I've exhausted the possibilities for classifications of butterflies hereabouts," he said at length. "At present I am studying dragonflies. Did you know they spend more of their lives in the water than airborne?"

"Ah, no. I didn't know."

"Oh yes. It's quite interesting. I'm working on a paper about the life cycle of several species that I've found here. But what I'd really like to do is travel. I found the most beautiful *Argynniss pandora* in Italy on my Grand Tour, you must know." Serena cocked an eyebrow at him and he added ruefully, "A butterfly. I'm afraid I was quite the despair of my parents on that tour. Not that I didn't attend all the right balls and see the Coliseum and the Sistine Chapel."

Serena giggled. "Oh, Richard, you do not have to explain to *me*. I have never been out of England, you know, but I should think it perfectly splendid to be able to travel. Why, to go to a land so different as Italy, where the sun shines all year! Why, think of the flowers, and the birds, and the insects, too, I am persuaded. I should want to spend all my time in the gardens. Who wouldn't?"

"Who indeed?" he murmured, and smiled fondly at his wife.

He was none too pleased, a moment later, when Rivers came in to announce a visitor.

"Richard, old fellow!" came a booming voice he knew very well. "What mean you by getting riveted when I was nowhere about?"

"Charlie, you rogue!" exclaimed Richard, and the two men embraced heartily. "I wrote you several letters up there at that ancient Scottish manor you seem bent on rehabilitating. Didn't you get them?"

"No, blast it all! Haven't had a letter in ages. Must be that pie-eyed butler. Not but what he blends with the surroundings, as decrepit as the very walls of the— oh!" he exclaimed, turning red as he noticed Serena for the first time.

Richard flushed slightly, having forgotten her momentarily, himself.

"Beg your pardon, ma'am," Charlie said. "Not at all the language one—"

"Er, Serena, my dear," Richard interrupted, grinning, and taking her hand to lead her forward, "may I present my oldest friend, Charles Ruckley, Viscount Atwater. Charlie, my wife, Serena, Lady Egremont," he said and then awaited her reaction.

To his relief, she smiled and extended her hand to his tall chestnut-haired friend. "I am so pleased to meet you, my lord."

"The pleasure is *mine*, Lady Egremont," Charlie replied, taking her hand briefly. "But pray call me Charlie—near everyone does—er, that is, if Richard will give consent."

Richard nodded and Serena responded that Charlie must agree to be informal with her as well. When they were all seated in the comfortable leather chairs, Charlie and Richard with brandy in hand and Serena with sherry, Richard asked, "When did you arrive home?"

"This morning, of course. And was greeted with all manner of news," Charlie replied. "So sorry about the duke's illness. I trust he is improving."

"Yes, thank God. He gave us all a scare, I must say."

"And then your marriage! I had no inkling—would have come down had I known." Charlie cast a questioning glance toward his friend and Richard felt uncomfortable. He was certain Charlie must have heard of the arranged nature of his marriage and now he wondered just what *was* being said about it throughout the countryside. Thank goodness very few people knew about Caroline, but nonetheless he imagined there would be much speculation as to the state of the Gower marriage. He hoped Charlie would not ask him anything, now or in private, for, in truth, he had no idea what he would answer.

The silence lengthened and Richard said, "Yes, well, it all happened rather fast, did it not, Serena?"

She nodded and Charlie amazed him by saying, "And one can certainly see why, Richard. You are indeed fortunate in your bride." You're a trump, Charlie, Richard thought, but then caught the admiring glance Charlie gave Serena and realized he was sincere. She *did* look rather lovely, he thought, with her new hairstyle and the midnight blue dress that made her eyes sparkle so. He suddenly realized that he felt proud of her—not only of her appearance, but of the way she'd handled Charlie's ramshackle entrance with such aplomb. Not all women would have.

Serena, he noted, was blushing under all this scrutiny. But finally she said questioningly, "I collect your family seat is nearby, Charlie?"

"Yes, Richard and I grew up together. Tumbled from one scrape to another, as I recall," he answered with a chuckle, crossing his long legs comfortably. "Lord, Richard, do you remember that basket of tarts, meant for the vicarage, that we devoured? Still in short-coats we were, but I remember the hiding very well."

Richard laughed wholeheartedly. "God, yes, but that wasn't half so bad as what happened that time we decided to take your father's new Arabian out for a ride!"

Richard noted Serena's raised eyebrow and thought ruefully that this conversation was not helping his consequence any. He wished he could stop Charlie from further embarrassing disclosures, but his friend was in high gig, and recounted numerous best forgotten larks.

"And your tutor," Charlie was saying, sipping the brandy Richard had just refilled, "remember the chamber pot we—oh, beg pardon, Serena," Charlie blurted, and Serena tried to stifle her gasps of laughter.

"Now, Serena, you mustn't think your husband was always such a scamp," Charlie amended.

"Oh, no, of course not," she managed, between giggling hiccoughs.

"No. No such thing. There is a very serious side to our Richard. Don't know what I should have done without his support when m' father died. And then there was the time he saved my life. Didn't tell you about that, did he?" Charlie inquired, leaning forward.

"No," said Serena, who had sobered immediately.

"Really, Charlie," Richard began, a warning note in his voice.

"It was about four years ago," Charlie recounted, ignoring Richard's glare. "We were out riding when a thunderstorm struck. My horse bolted and Richard galloped after me, practically straddled both horses trying to slow my half-mad stallion. Which he finally did, but nearly got himself trampled to death in the bargain. I'll never forget it. My horse was wild—would have thrown me to kingdom come had Richard not stopped him."

Richard could feel his face flush as Serena turned to him, her eyes wide with a strange look he'd never seen before. Charlie sank back into the leather chair and regarded them both rather speculatively. In the ensuing silence Richard cleared his throat. "Ah, Charlie, how goes the Scottish manor?"

After a moment Charlie groaned. "Worse than all my imaginings. The ivy was so thick over the front door that I had to use the service door, and the butler such a drunken sot that for three days he refused me entrance!"

Richard grinned. "I should explain, Serena, that

Charlie inherited, from a great uncle, an ancient manor house and run-down estate in the Highlands. And he seems bent on bringing it into the Nineteenth Century. Why, Charlie? Why spend months there?"

Charlie colored up but replied readily enough. "A challenge, I suppose. And if I ever succeed in making the house habitable, there is the land. The neglect has been shocking, and the tenants have suffered for it. Or call it a hobby. You have your fragile winged friends to occupy you, after all, have you not, Richard?" Richard nodded, aware of the quick change of subject, and wondered what else— "Has he been boring you with descriptions of the magpie moth and suchlike, Serena?"

"Oh, but I am not the least bored, Charlie!" she cried rather vehemently. "I find it all most fascinating!"

"Indeed?" Charlie mused, that speculative gleam in his eye once more.

"Serena has an artist's eye, you see, Charlie," Richard found himself saying, "and many of the specimens are quite beautiful."

"Ah, yes, of course," Charlie murmured, and Richard wondered what the devil he found so amusing.

Richard decided to shift the subject. "I expect I shall be doing some refurbishing myself before long." Serena and Charlie both looked questioningly at him and he went on. "We shall be taking up residence at Wheatfield Hall, you must know, and while it has not suffered such terrible neglect, still it will need—"

"You mean you shan't be living here at Luntsford?" Charlie asked.

"No. My parents suggested that we might wish to set up on our own. That is to say—well—they feel it is always wise for a young couple to—ah—"

Richard stammered, and Charlie came to his rescue. "Ah, yes. The voice of experience, no doubt. I do remember your grandmother, Richard. I cannot imagine that those years were easy."

Serena stared at Richard in wonder. So that was why he wished to leave Luntsford. And she had thought he did not want her here. There was much she did not know about this husband of hers, it seemed.

Richard was saved the need to elaborate on this rather ticklish train of conversation, for the door flew open and Livvy burst in. "I thought it was you!" she exclaimed, and rushed headlong into Charlie's arms, just as she had done since her earliest childhood.

Richard was about to reprimand her when he realized that Charlie was treating her like the big brother he always had, and Richard knew that was just as well. Livvy, seventeen or no, was very much a babe. Far more so than Serena had been a year ago, he guessed. And then Caroline came in at a more sedate pace, and fluttered her eyelashes beguilingly as Richard stiffly made the introductions. She looked breathtaking in a pale lavender muslin dress, but Charlie seemed strangely unmoved. Richard could not understand why, for Caroline's beauty was classical in its perfection. But Charlie actually seemed more taken with Serena.

They exchanged pleasantries for several minutes and then somehow, deftly, Charlie dismissed Caroline and Livvy. Neither looked too pleased, but they went, nonetheless.

"I did not wish to forget part of the reason for my visit, Richard," Charlie said. "And I could not ask with Livvy here, should you wish to refuse." At Richard's raised brow he continued, "I cannot imagine trying to deny her a treat and—well—my mother is intent on giving a ball in honor of my return."

"A ball? For pity sakes, Charlie, you've only been gone some three months! And hardly off to the wars," Richard said archly.

"My mother is not so sure. She regards the Highlands as quite wild and untamed, you must know. I believe she is most relieved to see me in Kent again."

A certain glint in Charlie's eyes prompted Richard to ask, "And will you stay, Charlie? Or is there—er—something compelling about that untamed part of the country?"

Charlie's lips twitched and he said briefly, "I shall return there shortly. I left much—ah—unfinished business."

I'll bet, Richard thought, suppressing a grin and wondering what color hair this unfinished and untamed business had. But this was obviously not the time to ask, not with his wife sitting here. A glance at Serena alarmed him, for she was gazing at Charlie with a certain bemused comprehension that he would not have expected.

But then, with supreme tact, she shifted the subject back. "Tell us about the ball, Charlie."

"Ah, yes, well, my mother seems to feel the need of a celebration." Then he went on, the familiar twinkle in his blue eyes. "Actually, I think I am just an excuse. My mother is an inveterate party giver, you must know, Serena. I believe it is some sort of disease," he concluded dryly, and Serena laughed.

"When is it to be, Charlie?" Richard asked, taking a sip of brandy.

"On Tuesday night."

"Tuesday! Why that's only two days from now!" Serena exclaimed, placing her sherry on the side table. "How can she possibly—"

"It is clear you are not acquainted with the Viscountess of Atwater," Richard interrupted amiably.

"Actually, Serena," Charlie added, "I am most thankful it's in two days. That will only give her the opportunity to assemble some eighty of our closest friends. A small little do, you must know."

"I should say," Richard countered. "I recall her last rout in London. There were four hundred people at the least!"

"Oh, my! I cannot imagine such a crush!" Serena exclaimed.

Richard frowned and in the momentary silence that followed, Charlie asked softly, "Have you not had a Season, Serena?"

Her face sobered, and she stammered a reply. "No, I—that is—I have only just turned eighteen, and with our marriage and—"

"We'll be there soon, Charlie, for the Little Season," Richard interjected quickly. He did not like the penetrating look Charlie trained on the two of them. Charlie might be his best friend, but there were certain things he was not prepared to discuss. For the first time Richard wondered if Serena had minded not having a proper Season. But why should that be, for wasn't finding a husband the main reason for—

"Well," Charlie broke into his thoughts, "I am persuaded she will enjoy London, what with the parties and all the sights. And as to my mother's ball— Richard, I know that your father is ill, and I cautioned my mother that this was not an opportune time. But she thought that as he is, most thankfully, on the mend, you and Serena might consent to honor us. We would not expect the duchess, but Livvy might come. I know she's young, not out and all that, but 'tis only a country ball, after all. Oh, and of course her friend is welcome as well," he added.

"I don't know, Charlie. Father *is* recovering, but still—"

"I know, Richard. And so I told my mother. You must do what you think best. Although," Charlie grinned, "I do wish you'd come. 'Tis like to be devilish dull if you don't. And by the by, it would give Serena a chance to meet much of the neighborhood." At this Serena's face tensed, and Richard saw that Charlie too had noted it. "Well, perhaps not, after all," Charlie amended, "as it's to be a masquerade."

Serena's face brightened and Richard asked, "What think you, Serena? Shall we go?"

"I should very much enjoy a masquerade, Richard, but I am persuaded that we needs must ask the duchess."

"Serena's right, Charlie. Although now I think on 't, I believe my mother will encourage us to go. Livvy and Caroline, especially, could use the diversion."

"Excellent. Then we shall expect you all, unless I hear otherwise. And there's one thing more. My mother is getting up something of a houseparty, you must know, and there is to be a hunt Tuesday morning. Will you join us?"

"Yes, of course," Richard replied readily, "though probably not Livvy. She is quite an indifferent rider, you may recall. But the rest of us—"

"Ah, Charlie," Serena chimed in, a frown on her brow, "I hope you will excuse me if I do not join the hunt."

"Of course, Serena," Charlie answered. "I would—"

"Whyever not, Serena?" Richard blurted. "You ride superbly."

"Thank you, Richard, but I do not care for the hunt."

"Not care for the hunt?" Richard echoed, incredulously. How could an Englishwoman, a good horsewoman, and his *wife*, for heavens sakes, not enjoy the hunt?

"No, I don't, but I do like masquerades," Serena said sweetly but with a firmness that Richard did not like at all. Then she rose and extended her hand to Charlie, who immediately stood as well. Richard followed suit after a moment, but he could not keep the frown from his face. "It's been a pleasure to meet you, Charlie. I hope to see you Tuesday night, and I look forward to making the viscountess' acquaintance."

"Thank you, Serena," his friend said, smiling with suppressed mirth, which infuriated Richard. "The pleasure has been all mine, I assure you."

Serena smiled, cocked her head at Richard and blithely ignored his obvious annoyance. "Well, now I shall leave you two gentlemen alone. I know you have much catching up to do. And I am persuaded Richard is simply dying to hear all about the—ah—Highlands, untamed as they are. But beautiful, I hear tell," Serena said with a gleam in her eye. Now Richard was furious. How dare she be so forward with Charlie, if indeed she was presuming what he thought she was!

But Charlie did not seem to mind in the least, rather

threw back his head and laughed. "That they are, my dear Serena. Very, very bonny. Someday I shall tell you all about it." And then with a wink, he let go her hand.

She turned to Richard, smiled in the face of his scowl, and bid him good day.

He and Charlie sat back in their chairs and he took a long gulp of his brandy, trying not to notice how pensively Charlie regarded him.

"She's charming, Richard," his friend said at length.

"Hmmn," Richard grunted, then, remembering himself, said "Thank you."

Charlie leaned forward, his voice low. "Richard, I know this may be out of line, but, well—don't know any of the details—no one does and I'm not asking, but I *do* know it all happened very fast and that—" Richard glowered at him and Charlie paused and took a swig of his own drink. "Ah, hell, Richard, it's none of my business, but you're my oldest friend, and I just wanted to say, well, give it a chance, Richard. You're a very lucky man."

Reluctantly Richard smiled. "Thanks, Charlie. I—it has been rather sudden, for both of us." And then, again recalling himself, Richard said, "Now tell me about the wild and bonny—er—Highlands, Charlie. Serena was right. I am most curious."

Charlie laughed and proceeded to enlighten him about a certain redheaded innkeeper's daughter, who had assured him that, if a gentleman knew what he was about, the Highlands needn't be all that cold in winter at all.

Richard grinned and guffawed throughout the delicious tale, but when it was over his eyes narrowed. "Don't you *dare* tell any of this to my wife, Charlie!" he admonished.

"Why I wouldn't dream of it, Richard," Charlie replied genially. "Not until she's a grandmother, at least."

After which comment Richard felt himself flush unaccountably, and quickly changed the subject.

Serena had difficulty concentrating on her work that afternoon, her mind awhirl. She had liked Richard's friend, Charlie, a great deal, and had learned some very interesting, and pleasing, things about her husband. The time spent with Richard's specimens had been most enjoyable, as well, and in fact, she and Richard had seemed very much in charity with each other until Charlie had mentioned the hunt. Serena sighed, remembering Richard's frown of displeasure. She supposed she ought to have been more diplomatic, languidly claiming that she could not possibly exert herself on horseback in the morning and then attend a ball in the evening. But she could never have uttered such a farrago of nonsense with a straight face. She knew it was positively *un*English not to like the hunt, especially when she rode as well as she did, but she could not help it. Nor could she explain to Richard that she had much rather be painting a fox than watching it be torn to shreds by the hounds. He might praise her artist's eye to all and sundry, but the hunt was sacred. Putting her palette down and shaking her head, she knew she'd not heard the last of this.

Serena contrived, as she'd promised, to spend some

time with Livvy in the late afternoon. She did not mention the ball, not yet knowing whether they would in fact be attending, but instead they pored through *La Belle Assemblee* and several other fashion magazines. They giggled over drawings of the more outrageous hats that were about to descend on London for the Season. But their pleasant cose was interrupted by a servant conveying the duke's wish that Serena wait upon him at her earliest convenience. Surprised, Serena took her leave of Livvy and followed the servant to the ducal chambers.

She was gratified to see the duke sitting in a large comfortable chair in his sitting room. He wore a black dressing gown with a silver grey silk cravat at his neck. He put aside his book as she entered and made as if to rise.

"Oh, please don't, your grace. You'll tire yourself. She hastily took a seat across from him and added, "You're looking very well, you know. How are you feeling?"

"Thank you, my dear. I still tire easily, and I suppose I shall retain this wretched cough for weeks, but I am, as my dear Bella is fond of saying, 'on the mend'."

Serena laughed. "We're all so glad. But then, you know that."

He smiled, and she thought how handsome he was, like his son. "Serena, I want to thank you for relieving my wife of her martyr's vigil for a spell."

"Oh, come now, your grace, there is nothing of the martyr in the duchess, and well you know it."

The duke's brown eyes twinkled. "Well, at all events, you have been most helpful and I appreciate it."

"I did little enough, your grace. I should have liked

213

to have been of more use."

"Fustian! You have done more in this household than you know. But enough of that. I must apologize, my dear, for cutting short your wedding trip. Tell me, Serena, how are you getting along here? Are you happy?"

Serena had the distinct memory of being asked the same thing just yesterday and wondered if her parents-in-law were in league together.

"Oh, of course, your grace. The Court is beautiful. I love the gardens and the woods and—"

"That is not what I meant, Serena. How are you and Richard getting along?"

"Oh, we go on fine together, your grace," she said lightly, but her voice sounded brittle in her own ears.

The duke sighed and shook his dead. "Damn shame you two had to leave Gateshead. A young couple needs privacy, a place of their own. Perhaps you can go back there before week's end. You need to get to know each other better, 'tis all."

"Yes, of course," Serena whispered, a forced smile on her lips.

"You know, Serena," he mused, "I am persuaded that you and Richard are very well-suited. Perhaps you simply need more time."

It might have been the kindness in his voice that prompted her to murmur, much too candidly, "There are more than just the two of us, your grace."

"Ah, so we come to crux of it." He paused and gazed intently at her. "She is no threat to you, Serena. You must believe that."

Serena's eyes filled with moisture and she found that she couldn't speak for the lump in her throat. She

214

shook her head and dashed away a wayward tear.

"I know my son, Serena. Trust me in this," he said softly, his hand reaching across to grasp hers for a moment.

"Thank you, your grace, for being so kind to me," Serena said, but her heart was heavy. The duke didn't know his son very well at all.

"Serena, might I ask you not to be so formal with me? I should prefer a more—familial term of address."

Serena smiled. "Like 'Father', for instance?" she asked. Now she was certain they were in cahoots.

"Yes, my dear daughter. I should like that very well," he replied with a smug grin.

Serena chuckled and as she took her leave, kissed her new father on the cheek. And she thought, as she made her way down the corridor, that though she mightn't truly have a husband, she did at last have a family, a real family.

Richard escorted Serena to the Gold Salon before dinner and, as they were early, he was surprised to see Caroline already there. She appeared to be examining, rather closely, one of the two antique jewel-encrusted Italian vases on the mantel.

"Caroline, what on earth are you doing?" Richard blurted. He had never known Caroline to be interested in antiques.

"Oh, you startled me, Richard dear," she said, whirling around. "I was looking for my pearl earring." She came toward them and laughed, a bit strangely, he thought. Whatever was wrong with her? "I seem to have misplaced it last night."

"Well, we'll all help you look for it, won't we Serena?" Richard said gallantly.

"Oh, of course," Serena answered very sweetly, and marveled that Richard, ever besotted, hadn't noticed that Caroline had forgotten to limp.

Serena found dinner difficult, as she'd known it would be. Richard announced that they would be attending the Atwater ball, which pronouncement filled Livvy with glee and Caroline with a strange excitement. Serena pictured Caroline dancing in Richard's arms and had to force her own smile of delight. Livvy begged to be allowed to go into the village on the morrow to shop for materials for the costumes. But the duchess shook her head, saying the attics were full of all manner of garments, hats, and fripperies dating back at least three-quarters of a century. Surely enough could be found there to bedeck everyone satisfactorily. Livvy and Caroline chattered enthusiastically about it all, right through the oxtail soup and broiled sole, but Serena heard nary a word.

And then, inevitably, Richard mentioned the hunt. Livvy declined, which no one questioned, but when Serena did the same, she felt all eyes on her.

"But why not, Serena? Richard tells me you are an accomplished horsewoman," her mother-in-law asked in a kindly tone. "Is it simply that you feel it would be too much activity for one day?"

Serena hesitated, then said softly. "No, no it isn't that. 'Tis merely that I do not wish to go."

Someone coughed and the duchess' eyes widened. "But—" she began.

"Serena does not *care* for the hunt," Richard interjected bluntly, his eyes piercing hers. Serena lifted her

216

chin a trifle.

"Oh, I see," the duchess said, as if she saw nothing at all.

"How very — singular," Caroline drawled. "I myself *adore* the hunt. I should *love* to accompany you, Richard."

Richard turned to her and smiled. "Thank you, Caroline," he said, and Serena's heart sank.

Richard found himself in something of a quandary as he and Serena ascended the stairs after dinner. He had not meant to be annoyed with Serena, but she had embarrassed him twice already over the ridiculous matter of the Atwater hunt. And now he would have to escort Caroline, when he had much rather be taking Serena. She had a much better seat, and besides, she was his wife, dammit!

And *that* was the crux of the matter, for if he now brought up the hunt, they would surely have words. And then what chance would there be to make her his wife in truth this night? But he had to say something. He escorted her into the bedchamber, and with a glance toward the massive bed, decided to be conciliatory.

"Serena, I realize you do not wish to hunt. I will not press you further about it, but will you not tell me why?" he asked gently.

She blinked, as if his tone had disarmed her. "Richard, please, I really cannot — "she paused, and he knew she was about to dissemble. His gaze held hers firmly and at last she relented. "Oh, 'tis just that I cannot bear to see the poor creature t-torn to shreds in such a manner."

"What poor creature? The fox?" Richard asked in amazement, and at her nod tried to keep his countenance sober. "Oh, my dear, in the first place, you are not supposed to watch that part of it. 'Tis the chase that's the thing. And in the second — well — your sympathy is quite misplaced, you know. The fox is a crafty fellow, quite the bane of every farmer in the country."

"Th-that may well be, Richard, b-but I — I still have no wish to be part of it," she mumbled.

He frowned, not understanding her attitude, nor liking it, but he thought of the big carved bed and raised a hand to graze her cheek. "Very well, little gypsy. I do not understand, but I shall say no more. You do not have to go if you do not wish to. 'Tis merely that I should like your company."

She smiled gratefully, "Th-thank you, Richard."

He drew closer, softly cupping her face in his hands. "You are quite welcome, Serena," he murmured, and she swallowed hard. "And now, my dear," he whispered, "we —"

"And — and now, R-Richard I believe Hannah awaits me," she stuttered, spinning away from him toward the dressing room.

Both servants awaited, blast them, and Richard wondered what machinations they'd planned for tonight. He accompanied Watkins through the dressing room to the sitting room beyond, and noted that the chaise had returned, as had the green sofa. But he was having neither, he vowed. Richard willed himself to calm down as Watkins divested him of his clothes and helped him into his black dressing gown. He dismissed the valet as soon as he could and waited for the sounds of Serena's maid retreating. He glanced carefully around the sitting room. Nothing else untoward seemed to be afoot, and he realized that Watkins and Hannah had finally left him to his own devices. Or had run out of ideas. Well, he had in intention of disappointing them.

He brought the glasses of brandy with him into the bedchamber this time. Serena, already sitting up in bed with a book, was surprised to see him. "Richard, haven't they brought back the—"

"I've brought us a drink, Serena," he interrupted smoothly and without so much as a by-your-leave sat down on the edge of the bed right next to her. She inched away.

"Richard, I don't think—"

"A toast, Serena. To my father's health." He tossed her book aside. "Come now, you really must drink, you know." Serena drank.

After a few minutes he put the glasses on the bedside table. Then he moved closer to her, taking her hands in his. "Serena, we have been wed for more than a se'ennight," he said softly, his eyes gazing into hers. "It really is time that we became—man and wife." He lifted a finger to lightly trace the curve of her lips. Her breath came unevenly and he wasn't too sure about his own breathing either. "I think you will find it a rather—pleasant experience, you know."

"Richard," she said hoarsely, "I—I am not—ready."

Dammit! What would it take for her to be ready? Richard willed himself to remain calm, willed the heat already rising in his body to stay at bay. "All brides are hesitant, Serena. You will see that—"

"No, Richard. It is not like that," she rasped, and he

saw the tears in her eyes before she looked away.

He took her chin gently in his hand and turned her to face him. "What is it, little gypsy?" he asked quietly.

But she shook her head and tried to scamper away. His hand clamped over her wrist and held her fast. "I shall sleep on the chairs, Richard. It is best."

"No, dammit!" he nearly shouted. His body was rigid as he tried to maintain his control. "We'll neither of us sleep curled up like caterpillars on a bent twig. Just go to sleep, Serena. I shall stay on my side of the bed."

"But Richard—"

"You may trust me, Serena. I am a man of my word," he said coldly.

And suddenly Serena felt a chill go through her, for she realized that for the first time, it was not Richard whom she didn't trust. Oh, God, she thought as she burrowed under the covers. Whatever was happening to her?

Chapter Ten

Serena had expected that she and the duchess would journey to the dressmaker's establishment on Monday morning. But in this she was mistaken, for Mrs. Chalmers was announced after breakfast. The duchess ushered Serena upstairs and they were followed into Serena's bedchamber by the little gray-haired modiste, two assistants carrying fashion sketchbooks, and several footmen staggering under the weight of countless swatches and even full bolts of fabric.

Serena cast an incredulous look at her mother-in-law, who whispered in her ear, "One of the prerogatives of being a duchess, my dear." Then she gave Serena's hand an encouraging squeeze and they set to work.

The next two hours passed in a whirl of activity. The duchess's idea of a "few dresses to start" turned out to be half a trousseau. There were innumerable decisions to be made — how many each of morning dresses, walking dresses, evening gowns . . . Should the carriage dress be done in midnight blue bombazine or the lavender silk? The second evening gown in primrose pink taffeta or the delicate seafoam muslin? Should the rose be on the right or left shoulder?

Serena was a bit breathless when all was said and done, and quite exhausted from standing still and having bolts of fabric draped about her, not to mention pins stuck in the most inconvenient places. But she enjoyed herself excessively, nonetheless, for it was a completely new experience for her. No decision was made without her approval. In fact, she realized, *she* made nearly all the decisions, the duchess and Mrs. Chalmers offering suggestions and sharing ideas. It seemed that they all laughed a good deal together, even giggled. Remarkable, she thought; Mama *never* giggled.

Livvy came in for a while, saying that she and Caroline were about to explore the attics for costume materials and would Serena like to come. But Serena was much too happily occupied; she would design her costume later. She and the duchess did, however, elicit Livvy's opinion on various lace and satin trims, which would be used quite sparingly. Livvy departed in high spirits, and Serena and the duchess continued on.

Toward the end of the session, Richard entered the room. He looked around bemused, and then bent to pick up an untouched bolt of pink coral crepe lisse. "Have you used this?" he asked.

The duchess shook her head and, without a word, Richard walked to Serena and draped the fabric over her shoulder and under her chin. Serena looked at herself in the glass and then smiled. Amazing that none of them had picked up the pink coral, for the color made her skin look almost radiant, her cheeks a soft, glowing pink.

"A ball gown," Richard announced in a tone that brooked no argument. "For our first ball at Wheatfield." Then he smiled at her and at his mother and abruptly departed.

Serena and the duchess wasted only a moment exchanging looks of incredulity, and then devoted themselves to the design of her new ball gown.

Caroline had spent the early morning with Marco; they had plans to make. She thought it a great shame that Marco could not attend the Atwater ball — the possibilities for discrediting Serena there were endless. But no matter; Caroline would contrive something else.

When she and Livvy went up to the attics in the mid-morning, Caroline sneezed from all the dust. But Livvy was delighted, just as she had been that day Caroline had, for her own purposes, dragged Livvy through the damp attics of her own home. As Livvy opened several old hatboxes and exclaimed over the trunks crammed with gowns of the last century, Caroline glanced around sharply. The jewel, she thought. Why not? The gypsy's fortune had said "that everyone could see it, but no one knows it's there." So it wouldn't be in the bottom of a trunk, but why not in plain sight in the attic? Heaven knew Caroline had nearly exhausted the possibilities of the main rooms of the house and even some of the bedchambers. And so while Livvy pulled shawls and gowns and feather boas from one trunk and another, Caroline circled the huge, musty attic room, and several smaller ones leading out from it. She scanned every shelf, floorboard, and table top she could, and finally muttered a curse when she knew it was hopeless.

"What do you think, Caroline? The pink or the lavender?" Livvy was asking, and Caroline went back to the larger room. "I shall go as a shepherdess, and see, there are two costumes! And here is the proper wig—all high and puffy from simply *ages* ago! And even a staff and mask!" Livvy exclaimed with glee.

Caroline refrained from telling her that every second woman at any masquerade always came as a shepherdess. Livvy tugged the white wig onto her head and Caroline suggested she try the pink gown, which the girl promptly held up to herself and then danced before the cracked, filthy mirror that sat atop an old bureau.

Caroline had had quite enough, but Livvy insisted she choose her own costume, which of course, she must. Caroline stared at the tumble of gowns now strewn on the floor and two old Jacobean chairs. She wanted to look so beautiful tomorrow night that Richard could not resist her. She must wear something that would stir his blood, but at the same time not appear too immodest. She decided against an ancient looking, gold encrusted gown worn with the wide paniers of the last century. No man could get near her in that. And she rejected a man's fencing outfit out of hand, but her eyes lighted on a pair of very sheer harem pants— undoubtedly brought back from a trip east once upon a time. But she knew that was a bit too much for the staid Marquis of Egremont.

At last she found what she wanted. A flimsy, simple

and flowing white gown in the Grecian mode. It dated back some twenty years, at least, to the beginning of the classical style. It was sheer enough to attract men like bees to honey, but no one could call it indiscreet. And, of course, it was all rather clever. Caroline would go as Helen of Troy, the most beautiful woman of all time, the woman over whom two nations fought a war. For she was clearly declaring war on Serena, supposed Marchioness of Egremont.

After luncheon Richard took himself off to his account books, and Serena took her sketch pad and headed for the dell. She found it difficult to sit still and sketch. Her mind kept drifting to Richard and the pink coral crepe lisse. Amazing that he'd known . . . that he'd cared enough to . . . And then she could not help thinking of last night, and the night before, for that matter. Richard was arousing sensations in her that were best off left hidden. And, come to think on 't, Marco had made her feel strange as well, albeit in a different way. Oh, damn! she thought, slamming shut her sketch book. Such rumination was useless. All she knew was that she had to maintain her distance from Richard. Anything else was dangerous.

Feeling restless and more than a bit warm, Serena jumped up and with a brief glance to insure her privacy, quickly stripped and darted into the water.

She swam and paddled and lazed about in the stream, delighting, as always, in the sheer freedom of it. She wondered after a time whether Gaya would come today, or whether she would have to wait another day for her dance lesson. Well, no matter, she thought. Gaya knew where to find her. In the meantime, she decided to swim to the opposite bank and back.

When she'd had her fill of the water, she scampered up onto the bank and bent to retrieve her clothes from behind Gaya's rock, where she'd left them. That was strange, she thought. Her sketch book was here but — she could have sworn that she'd left her clothes here as well. Her eyes darted anxiously over the grass, but her yellow dress was quite obviously not there. Apprehension mounting, for she was, after all, wearing absolutely nothing, Serena looked back at the rock. Maybe on the other side . . .

"Huh!" she gasped, for, indeed, on the other side of the rock lay a pile of clothes, but they were definitely not hers. Gingerly she picked them up — a pair of black breeches and a fine white lawn shirt. Who in the — Serena decided to don the garments first and ask questions later. She was surprised that they fit so well. They were small, almost as though they belonged to a young boy. Only when she was tucking the shirt tails in did she venture another look around, and then she called out, "Who is here?"

There was silence, utter stillness, in the dell. She peered through the trees and up the little hill. There was no one. She shrugged and tried to tuck some of her hair back up. She still wore her scarf and was glad it hadn't been taken. As to the yellow dress, it was not a great loss. Still, it was very disconcerting to think that her little dell had been invaded and that someone had been watching her and seen who knows what. It was a very naughty prank, indeed. Probably a young lad, she thought, and a gentleman's son, judging by the quality of the clothes. But it was rather odd, now she thought on 't. She could understand his swiping her clothes — but leaving his own? She laughed, wondering how he looked in her dress, or had he something else to wear? Pensive, she went to retrieve her sketch pad and took one last look around. She sighed. In future she would have to be more careful, and she supposed she'd have to swim in her chemise from now on.

The afternoon was lengthening and she surmised that Gaya would not come today. And then she chuckled. Gaya would have been most amused by this little episode. She would probably have told Serena she looked very handsome in breeches, and of course reminded her that she had no shoes on. But her shoes, along with everything else, were gone.

Serena climbed the hill and started back. With any luck, she thought, Richard would still be at his books and everyone else would be resting. She would enter through the back door and hope to reach the refuge of her room before anyone saw her and started asking unpleasant questions.

Caroline sat at the window of her chamber, staring out at the gardens. She ought to come any time now, Caroline thought. And as soon as she rounded the bend, Caroline would go to Richard — they would have to catch Serena before she escaped to her room. The clothes of a young boy, Marco had said. For Serena must not for one moment suspect Marco. Not if the rest of their plan were to work. Caroline could barely contain her excitement. Of course it would work! How could it not?

"I am so sorry to disturb you, Richard."

"Yes, Caroline, what is it?" Richard really did not care to be disturbed just now.

"Well, 'tis—'tis just that Serena has returned home and—and—"

"Is something wrong, Caroline?"

"Oh, I truly hope not, Richard. 'Tis just that—well—Serena is wearing a most singular costume."

Richard stood abruptly. "Where is she?"

They found her in the rear hallway, headed for the back stairs. "Serena!" Richard's eyes bulged at the sight of her. In a man's clothes of all things! Her hair down, her feet bare, and those breeches hugging her hips in that way! My God! Whatever could have . . . "Serena, what the devil has happened?"

Serena whirled around. She looked at them both and raised her chin. "Richard, I think we might best discuss this upstairs."

"Yes, do let's," he said gruffly, fear and a growing suspicion in his mind. Had she been hurt or was she up to some mischief? With a mere nod to Caroline he took Serena's hand and led her up the stairs.

He hurried along the corridor and pulled her into their bedchamber, shutting the door with more force than he'd intended. Serena walked slowly to the center of the room.

"Are you all right, Serena? Have you been hurt?"

"Oh, no, Richard. I am right," she said lightly,

228

but her eyes were wary.

He recalled a similar conversation just days ago, when she'd come home with muddied skirts and wet hair. He hadn't been exactly satisfied with her explanation and he had the feeling he was going to like today's even less. And her appearance now was no end of scandalous. Why, the way her thighs and hips were outlined—he felt himself grow warm, even as his temper rose.

"Well, then, Serena would you kindly explain yourself? What cause have you for parading about in such a manner?" He tried to keep his voice calm, and clenched his fists in the effort.

"I was not 'parading about,' Richard. I was walking home."

"That has nothing to say to the matter, Serena. What happened to your clothes?" Richard growled, slowly moving toward her.

Serena smiled slightly. "Well, the truth is, Richard, that I am not quite sure *what* happened. I was—er—swimming, you must know—oh, in a very private place, I do assure you, and—"

"Swimming! You were swimming? Can I have heard you aright?" he demanded, stalking closer to her.

She backed up. "Er—well—yes, Richard, but you see—"

"Swimming? Without your clothes on?" he bellowed, his temples beginning to throb.

"Well, of course without my clothes, Richard. I—"

"How could you, Serena? How could you behave so scandalously?" he railed, striding to her and grabbing her by the shoulders. "And how dare you?" He shook her, harder and harder, his fury mounting with each word. "Have you no care at all for your consequence? And if not for your own then for mine? I am your husband, dammit! How dare you disobey me!" he thundered.

"R-Richard, please, you are hurting me," she implored, but he was too enraged to let her go. He stopped shaking her but his fingers bit into the soft flesh of her upper arms. Either that or he knew he would strike her.

"And this is not the first time, is it? That Banbury tale you told me about the fish pond—you'd been swimming that day, hadn't you? Hadn't you?" he demanded.

"Yes, Richard," she admitted, almost sullenly, as she tried to twist from his grasp.

"You lied to me! You are my wife and I will not have you deceive me, Serena!" he shouted.

Suddenly, fiercely, Serena wrenched herself from his grasp. "You damned hypocrite!" she railed back at him, much to his amazement. "You'll not have *me* deceive *you* ? Why, *you've* been deceiving *me* since the day we were married!"

"What in blazes are you talking about? How have I—"

"With Caroline. Do you think I do not notice the two of you making sheep's eyes at each other? And you—you're so—so bewitched that you haven't even noticed that dear Caroline has forgotten to limp today. Such a speedy recovery from her injury!" she spat sarcastically.

"Serena! You don't know what you're saying!" He put his hands to her shoulders again, more gently this

230

time.

"Oh, don't I, Richard? I *saw* you," she said, her voice low. "I saw you with *her*. In the library. You were kissing her. You kissed *her* when you had never even . . . never . . ."

"I had never even what, Serena?" he interrupted quietly. He had never seen her angry, not truly angry, not like this. Her blue eyes flashed and her cheeks were flushed. And what exactly was she so furious about? Was it possible that she was jealous? Suddenly he wanted her, very much. He pulled her close. "I'd never done *what* to you, Serena?" he asked again, softly.

Her eyes looked uncertain and she took several short, unsteady breaths, then swallowed hard. "Nothing," she said curtly, after a moment. "Is this interview finished?"

By God, she knew how to raise the hackles in a man! He dropped his hands and took a step back. "No, dammit! You haven't yet told me what happened." He ran his hands through his hair. "How did you contrive to lose your clothes?"

Serena took a deep breath. Or was it a sigh? "I left my clothes beside a large rock when I went into the water, you see. And when I emerged, all my things were gone. All except my sketch book."

"Good God! And you — you're not even wearing your chemise," he said, sweeping his eyes over her. "You removed that too, Serena, didn't you?"

"Well it *is* more comfortable to swim without—"

"Comfortable? I don't give a damn about your comfort!" he stormed, pacing the floor. "Do you realize that some man was watching you swim? Have you no

231

shame? No sense of decency?" He came to stand before her, his eyes piercing hers. She met his gaze unwaveringly. "Why, even now you have no remorse. You act like a—like a—"

"Like a what, Richard?"

"Never mind! Did you see anyone? Hear anything?"

"No, Richard. I own it is most curious. I *was* on Gower land after all."

"Curious? It's a damn sight worse than that, Gower land or no. It's shameful—and dangerous. Don't you know there are always poachers about, not to mention our own gamekeepers, and God knows who else?"

"These are not the clothes of a poacher, Richard."

"No, they aren't, are they, Serena? They are the clothes of a gentleman. A man who stood there and watched you and—"

"He would not have seen much, I assure you. I was in the middle of the water, submerged up to my neck at least."

"Then he would have used his imagination!" he shouted, grabbing her again. "And he might well have waited, on the not too illogical assumption that you were no lady. Do you know what would have happened then? Do you Serena?" he roared, shaking her again, the blood pounding at his temples at the thought of another man watching, waiting . . . "Answer me, dammit! You can't be that naive as not to know—"

"R-Richard, stop it. I can't talk while you shake me!" His hands stilled themselves immediately. Had he really been shaking her? She went on in a more matter of fact tone. "Of course had I known that a man would be there I should not have gone swimming. But—"

232

"That is much beside the point, Serena! The chap ain't about to send round his calling card to announce himself. The point is that—"

"The point is that he did *not* stay. Whoever it was merely exchanged our clothes. I am persuaded it was no more than the prank of an exuberant lad with a flair for mischief. Why, look how small the clothes are. Truly Richard, you refine too much upon it."

"Refine too much!" spluttered Richard. "It was *not* a child's prank, I assure you. Oh, God, Serena, don't you understand anything about men and women?"

"I understand the important things, Richard," she flung back, and stalked to the window. Richard stood rooted to his spot and felt himself actually shaking with a mass of emotions—rage, fear for her, and shock at his own violence. Never in his life had his temper been aroused so. Why, he had wanted to strike her, to beat her. And hold her close at the same time.

"I suggest you take tea here, Serena, and not come down until dinner," he said between clenched teeth when he had got his voice under control. He deliberately did not move toward her. Instead he strode from the room, slamming the door behind him.

Damn! Damn! Damn! Serena stamped her foot and began pacing the floor. How dare he treat her so! To shake her like that, and then confine her to her room like a wayward child! For pity sakes, it wasn't *her* fault that some muttonheaded nodcock had decided to abscond with her clothes! Why, in all the years at Stoneleigh no one had *ever* disturbed her privacy. Oh damn! She didn't want to be at odds with her husband. They mightn't be—that is—their relationship might be somewhat irregular, but still, she wished they could be friends.

Serena felt tears prick at the back of her eyes and brushed them away. Oh, it was all such a coil!

She walked to her easel and uncovered the portrait of Gaya. The light was not the best now, but she would work, nonetheless. It was a long time until dinner. But despite her concentration, she could not quite keep the tears from spilling onto her cheeks.

The duke came down to dinner for the first time that evening. Richard, however, was still smoldering inside and was afraid he was very poor company. Serena, he noted, was as silent as he. At one point he caught his parents exchanging a look that told him they were well aware that something was amiss, and Richard groaned inwardly. He made an effort to address several remarks to his father, but then allowed Livvy and Caroline to take over the conversation with their prattle about their costumes and the upcoming ball. Caroline looked unaccountably smug throughout the meal, and there was a certain glint in her eye that Richard could not like.

Livvy tried several times to bring Serena into the conversation. Perhaps the girl is growing up, he thought, and was pleased she and Serena were getting on better. He reflected grimly that the only person in his family that his wife did not get on with was her husband.

"Have you chosen your costume yet, Serena?" Livvy asked. "Have you been to the attics? Caroline and I

234

had such fun! Mama was right — there is ever so much up there!"

Serena quickly took a sip of her wine. She had hardly been attending to the conversation thus far, and now she realized she had to answer Livvy. The truth was that with all the unpleasantness of this afternoon, she had completely forgotten about her costume. She would just have to contrive something in the morning. But she was not about to announce that — especially not with Caroline looking like the cat who'd just had the canary. Instead she made an attempt to smile and said, "Why, of course, I've chosen it, Livvy. But I wish it to be a surprise, you must know."

Livvy giggled conspiratorially and thought that a marvelous idea, but Richard was not sure he liked it at all. And then Caroline smiled very sweetly and said, "I am persuaded Serena is most clever with costumes and that we shall all be pleasantly surprised. Why, only this afternoon she wore the most striking and — unusual — garments."

Richard nearly choked on a slice of roast pheasant. How could she say such a thing? He quickly scanned the table. Livvy's eyes were wide, Serena had gone red and taken refuge in her wine, and his parents looked mystified. He glared at Caroline but she returned his gaze with such a look of guileless innocence that Richard's expression softened. She must not have realized what she was saying. How could she know, after all, that the incident had caused such a tiff between Serena and himself? Still, it was an ill-advised remark, and he was uneasy.

His mother mercifully changed the subject and

dinner came to a close. His father retired immediately thereafter, and the duchess suggested a game of whist for everyone else. Richard quickly demurred, and the four women had no choice but to sit down without him, however taken aback they were. He further surprised them by excusing himself unaccustomedly early, but he was beyond caring.

Watkins was waiting for him and Richard was silent as the valet went through his nightly ministrations. It was not long after Watkins departed that Richard heard voices in the dressing room, and he knew Serena was there. Then Hannah seemed to retreat, leaving Serena alone. Richard sighed. There would be no shared brandy tonight, no warming fire. And it would be the green sofa once again, he knew. One could not expect to seduce a woman just hours after a terrible row such as they'd had today. And yet, he did not relish the thought of sleeping alone, not after he'd made such headway. Not to mention the lumpy discomfort of the sofa. Perhaps he had ought to try to talk to her, make her understand the danger of what she had done. He wondered if they could contrive to have such a conversation without waking the entire household. He doubted it.

Richard poured himself a solitary glass of brandy and sipped it, standing at the hearth and staring at the empty grate. For some reason he thought of Caroline. She had been acting very strangely of late. That remark tonight still puzzled him. Was it an innocent observation, or had she deliberately meant to be provoking? It did not seem possible. He knew Caroline had been hurt by his marriage, but still he could not believe she would — Suddenly he recalled Serena's words about Caroline's injured foot. Could Caroline really be capable of such pretense? Richard could hardly credit it, but he supposed he ought to have a talk with her. He sighed, knowing that could wait. Matters between his wife and himself could not, however.

At that thought his eyes shifted to the connecting door. Serena had claimed to understand the important things about men and women. But he knew that in one respect at least her education was sorely lacking. Well, he would be the one to teach her, and the sooner, the better. Tonight was not, perhaps, the most propitious time, but he had, at the least, to try.

He entered the bedchamber to find Serena sitting up in bed, book in hand. She raised a brow, but otherwise did not stir. "You might at the least knock," she said after a moment.

He strolled toward the bed, gazing intently at her white-clad form. Her billowing nightgown was absurd, but, oh, God, that hair! "I believe this is *my* chamber as well, Serena, as you may recall," he countered.

She shrugged indifferently. "As you wish," she said woodenly, and went back to her book.

He did not make the mistake of sitting on the bed. Instead he pulled a chair up close. "Serena, I think we should talk."

She looked up at that, but her dark blue eyes were icy. "I believe you said quite enough this afternoon, Richard," she said in the coldest tone he'd ever heard her use. "And now, if you do not mind, I should like to be alone."

"But I *do* mind, Serena. You must realize that—"

"Richard," she interrupted, sliding to the opposite side of the bed and standing up. "What I realize is that the sofa is uncomfortable," she continued in a frigid, remote voice, "and I would not think of putting you out of *your* bed. I shall go to the sitting room."

Her chin was thrust up defiantly and Richard's eyes blazed. Damn her! Didn't she know that as her husband he had the right to—Oh, hell! He didn't want her that way. And it seemed that he would not get her any other way either.

He stood up and matched her chill tone. "There is no need to play the martyr, Serena," he drawled. "You are welcome to your solitary bed." And with fists clenched he turned and stalked from the room.

Chapter Eleven

Serena awoke early the next morning, her recollection of yesterday's events all too vivid: that dreadful quarrel with Richard in the afternoon, and the cold and bitter encounter last night. Matters between them seemed to be getting worse instead of better. She imagined he would already have gone to the hunt and she felt relieved; she did not wish to see him. But as Hannah came to help her dress, Serena forced herself to think rationally of what had transpired. Perhaps, she had to admit, it was not just Richard's concern for propriety that had overset him when she appeared wearing a man's clothes. Perhaps there *had* been just the merest bit of danger in what she'd done. Maybe, she thought with a sigh, she *had* ought not to swim alone. At least, she amended, not at Luntsford.

Her toilette was accomplished quickly and after eating a light breakfast, she set herself to the task of devising a costume for this evening. In point of fact, she could muster little enthusiasm for the ball, though she was glad it was a masquerade; none of her new gowns would be ready for a se'ennight. Still, she did not care to scrounge through the attics, and instead threw open the doors to the large wardrobe in the dressing room, seeking inspiration. None came, however, and she sank down onto the chaise in exasperation. She had no desire to go to the ball all trussed up in stays and a wig, as Livvy meant to do. Nor did she care to exhibit her body in the way she suspected Caroline's gown would. Contrary to what Richard seemed determined to believe, Serena was not an immodest woman; she merely liked to be comfortable.

And then the idea came to her. She quickly rummaged through her drawers and then rang for Hannah. They set to work, and a little while later Serena left Hannah to ply her needle.

It was a fine day, and Serena took her sketch book and set off to her favorite spot. But she changed her direction midway, uncomfortable with the thought that someone might be there again, watching. Instead she meandered through the woods until she found herself in a small copse with a rise of green moss at its center. She ensconced herself on the rise, where sunlight was able to beam upon her through the break in the trees. She removed her shoes and looked about her. She saw no living creature, neither winged nor earthbound, and instead set to drawing a thicket of purple wildflowers that stood at the base of the rise.

"You not at hunt," came a familiar voice, piercing the morning stillness.

Serena laughed and put down her pencil, motioning for Gaya to sit beside her. She hadn't seen her friend in days and was glad of her company.

240

"No, I'm not. "How—how did you find me, Gaya?"

Gaya shrugged, tossing her beautiful black mane of hair behind her. "I am Rom," she said simply.

"Oh," replied Serena, as if that explained it. Did it?

"Why you not join hunt?"

Serena smiled and did not bother to ask how Gaya knew about the hunt. "I'm afraid I am very *un*English when it comes to the hunt," she said. "I have too much sympathy for the fox, you see."

Gaya frowned. "I think the young lord—he not like that."

Serena lowered her eyes. It was useless to dissemble. "Er—well, no, he doesn't," she murmured and then looked up to see a twinkle in Gaya's dark eyes.

"You not like other gorgios," Gaya declared.

Serena laughed ruefully. "No, I'm not. Actually, I would love to *draw* a fox, but I've never been able to get close enough."

Gaya stood up. "You wait," she said, and literally disappeared. She was back in minutes, cradling a red and furry bundle. Serena's eyes widened as Gaya came and sat down again. For there, in her arms, nestled a beautiful pointed-nosed fox. Gaya was murmuring a soft chant in Romany, and amazingly, the fox seemed perfectly calm and content. At one with nature, Serena mused, as she watched Gaya stroke the fox's ear and throat. "You draw him, Serena," she said, and Serena obediently picked up her pencil.

She loved the way the animal's fur swirled this way and that, and the way his nose rested so trustingly on Gaya's knee. Gaya made no sound as she worked intently.

241

"Gaya! Gaya, where you be?" a male voice shouted from the near distance, and Gaya started.

"Marco," she whispered. "I must go. Here. You take fox."

"B-but he'll never stay with me. He'll—"

"He stay. You not like other gorgios, Serena," Gaya said, and whispered her magical Romany chant again. Then she deftly transferred the little bundle into Serena's lap. And then, as quickly as she had come, Gaya vanished into the woods.

He did stay. Serena stroked his short wiry fur with one hand, just as Gaya had done. And with her right hand she sketched, the pad resting on her knee. At one point the fox raised his ears, and she wondered what he'd heard. He settled back after a moment, but the pause made Serena wonder. What if—what if this was Richard's fox? That is, the fox the hounds were after? No, it couldn't be; there were any number of foxes in these woods. And if he was, well, she would protect him, she thought defiantly. She'd climb the nearest tree if she had to!

Richard was not enjoying this hunt at all, as he should have done and, indeed, always had. As usual, the hunt was a major event in the countryside, with Charlie and his guests in the lead, the local gentry following, and then the usual tumble of farmers and stable boys bringing up the rear. Sir Digby Elkwood, bucolic, cherub-faced squire that he was, served as huntmaster, just as had his father before him, and that allowed Charlie time to play host. Which he did, with

242

his usual smooth and genial charm.

Richard knew most everyone, but Charlie introduced him to those few he didn't. Richard was so pleased to be able to inform all who asked that his father was indeed recovering. But he was increasingly uncomfortable with having to explain time and again that the lovely lady at his side was *not* his bride but his sister's friend. Caroline did not at all like this distinction and he wondered what the devil else she wanted him to call her. No, his wife was not ill, he assured one well-wisher after another; they would all meet her at the ball tonight. Some peered a little too keenly at Caroline, who preened a bit too much and kept making eyes at Richard in a way most unbefitting their respective positions. At one point Caroline sweetly pointed out to the Dowager Lady Willoughby that the new marchioness did not care to hunt. As that lady retreated in puzzlement, Richard cast an angry glare at Caroline, who managed to look innocent and quite confounded by his reaction. His look softened; at all events, it was at Serena that he was most furious. Why the hell wasn't she here with him, where she belonged? Caroline, he noted with vexation, might look delightful in the saddle when trotting at a sedate pace, but hung on for dear life when they rode to hounds.

The fox was lightning fast and the hounds were wild in their pursuit. After a while Caroline dropped back in the ranks, which did not displease Richard at all. The chase was exhilarating, and had taken them far from Atwater Manor, until finally Richard realized that they had come to a corner of the Luntsford woodlands. And then the hounds began behaving strangely, yelping no less vociferously but seemingly in a welter of indecision as to whether the fox had gone east or west. The master of the hounds quickly brought the majority under control, however, and a westerly direction was decided upon.

"Tally ho!" came the cry from Sir Digby, and the hounds were off, save the few who seemed bent on racing east.

Richard thought the whole decidedly strange; it was almost as if there were *two* strong scents. Indeed, perhaps there *was* another fox. Out of curiosity, and perhaps wishing for solitude, he dropped back and surreptitiously disengaged himself from the group, continuing on in an easterly direction. He could not say why. What could he hope to find sans the foxhounds? He had not long to ponder this, however, for he heard the familiar yelping behind him and turned to see Charlie following him, accompanied by his groom and four maniacal hounds quite determined to follow Richard's direction.

"Sir Digby's gone with the rest, but these fellows wouldn't give up," Charlie called as Richard drew rein. The groom struggled to hold the determined, clamorous hounds in check. "Have you seen anything?" Charlie shouted above the din.

"Not at all. I was merely curious and—"

"Beg pardon, my lords," interrupted the groom, "but I reckon we're bein' followed."

Both men turned to see a small group coming toward them, Lady Willoughby and Caroline among them. "Well, I guess it's a contest then!" Charlie exclaimed and Richard tried to look enthusiastic. He waved politely to the ladies and several gentlemen who had accompanied them, then urged his horse on.

He and Charlie took the lead with the groom and four errant foxhounds. It was only a few minutes before the hounds began jerking at the leashes and barking with such intensity it was clear they were on to something.

"Sir Digby will be in high dudgeon," Charlie declared with a grin.

"Unless there is more than one fox, Charlie," Richard reminded him as they rode on.

The groom had all he could do to hold on to the dogs, so feverish had they become. At a signal from Charlie, he let them go and they surged forward, eyes bright and tails straight in the instinctive pointing posture. Richard and Charlie galloped after them, over several hills and through tall oak and elm trees, the small contingent of riders following tenaciously behind. Shortly, they came to a small copse of thickly wooded terrain, and he and Charlie could barely keep up with the hounds. It was only the surefootedness of Richard's stallion that allowed him to charge through the copse just inches behind the dogs, and it was then that Richard saw the flash of yellow skirts. What the— Richard did not wait to figure it out, but without thinking spurred Corinthian forward. And then he saw her, standing atop a rise, some bundle in her skirts and a look of sheer terror in her eyes as the frenzied hounds leapt toward her. God Almighty! Serena! What the hell—

She turned and ran, stumbling on those damned long skirts, but kept on to the nearest tree. Little fool, did she really think she could climb in those skirts? The dogs were at her heels, tearing at her dress. What the bloody hell could they want with Serena? he wondered as he charged ahead. He drew abreast of her and jerked back on the reins. Then, leaning over as far as he dared, he grabbed her round the waist and scooped her up onto the stallion.

"Oh!" she exclaimed swivelling her head to see him. "Oh, Richard, I—"

"Hush, it's all right," he rasped, clutching her to him with a shaking hand.

He could feel Serena's body shaking as well, and would have kept on riding, but that a thick wall of trees blocked them on one side and the hounds on the other. They were baying fiercely, clamoring on hind legs to reach Serena. And why—suddenly he recalled the bundle she carried.

"Serena, what—"

"Serena, are you all right?" Charlie shouted, riding up to them and trying to kick the dogs away, even as Richard's stallion began to buck and bray.

"Yes, I—I—" she began.

"What is it, Serena?" Richard demanded, tugging at the reins to steady Corinthian. "What do they want with—"

But he never finished the sentence, for as he and Charlie looked down at her, they noted a certain movement from within the folds of her skirts. And then there appeared a quite unmistakably bushy red tail.

Richard could hardly believe what he was seeing and he felt a surge of fury, which, mingled with his fear of a moment ago, engendered such a tumult of emotions as he'd never felt. "Goddammit, Serena! Is that a—"

"Beg pardon, milords. Oh my stars! Can't think what maggot's got into these blasted canines! Oh! beg pardon, my lady!" interrupted the groom, reining in and now attempting to calm the nearly apoplectic hounds, who had not the slightest notion of giving up.

And no wonder, Richard thought, nearly apoplectic himself. He wanted to strangle Serena. "Serena," he growled, "get rid of the damn—"

"Oh my goodness, what's happened?" came the high-pitched voice of Lady Willoughby, and Richard turned to see her rapidly approaching, Caroline and the others at her heels.

Richard groaned and his eyes blazed as the bundle in Serena's skirts seemed to jerk up and down. "Serena, get rid of the damn —"

"Lady Egremont!" Charles exclaimed, ruthlessly cutting him off and leaning over to tuck that bushy tail back into the flounces of her skirts, and slipping Serena's left hand inside as well, "I hope you are not too badly injured," he went on, in a voice loud enough to be heard by the assembled company.

"No, I—I—" Serena stammered, but Charlie ignored her.

"No wonder the hounds are after you—all that blood! However did you contrive to injure your arm?"

"I—I—er—"

"Anderson!" Charlie bellowed at the groom. "Call off these cursed hounds, so Lord Egremont can take his lady home!"

"Oh, my poor dear," gushed Lady Willoughby, peering over Richard's shoulder. "Is there anything I can do? Here—here is a handkerchief to staunch the blood." She fluttered a delicate handkerchief of embroidered lawn that would not have been sufficient for a pinprick, and Charlie took it and thanked her. The groom had already leashed two of the hounds, and was working on a third, but all four continued to lurch boisterously toward Serena's lap.

"How strange," Caroline suddenly chimed in, "*I* don't see any blood."

Richard stiffened, but Charlie replied cheerfully, "That's because Lady Egremont had the good sense to staunch the worst of it with her skirts."

There was a murmur of admiration from the company, before Caroline pointed to the rise and ventured, "Oh, look! There is Serena's sketch book!"

Richard tightened his arm furiously around Serena, thinking they were done for, but once more Charlie stepped into the breach.

"So it is!" he concurred, and before anyone knew what he was about, he jumped from his horse, skirting the hounds, and strode to the rise. Flipping the sketch book safely closed, he came back and handed it to Serena. "My lady," he said with a twinkle in his eye, and she smiled back gratefully.

Richard was too stunned to say a word, and in any case, too enraged to trust himself to speak, and Serena was still quaking. He was ever thankful that Charlie suffered no such difficulties.

"Come now," Charlie encouraged the group, "we must find Sir Digby's trail once again. The hounds have led us a merry chase, I warrant. Lord Egremont will see to the marchioness." he said firmly, just as

248

Anderson succeeded in restraining the last of the hounds. He could not keep them from clawing at the stallion's flanks, however, their glazed eyes fixed on Serena's suspiciously lumpy lap.

"Take care of her, Richard," Charlie commanded, winking at Serena and throwing Richard a speaking glance.

His face glowering, Richard only nodded and, the hounds notwithstanding, turned Corinthian and urged him out of the copse. He passed Caroline, who seemed to have nothing further to say, but the look in her eyes made him uncomfortable.

Never mind, he thought, and spurred his horse on even as his own anger coursed through him once more. How dare Serena endanger herself, and embarrass him this way!

He waited till they were out of the copse, a little way from the others, and then demanded in a low sharp voice, "Let him go, Serena. I don't know what in hell you think you're about, but let that damned fox go or I swear I'll—"

"No, Richard," she answered tremulously. "I will not allow him to be mangled by those awful hounds. He's a very gentle creature and—"

"Gentle! You little idiot, don't you know if I hadn't come the hounds would have mangled *you*?"

He could feel Serena shaking again and this time he suspected she was crying. But he refused to give in. This was even more outrageous than the swimming incident.

"I—I didn't expect the hounds to come here," she stammered.

"That's no excuse. You *knew* there was a hunt today. And whatever are you doing with that—that—oh—never mind—just let him go!"

"No, Richard. Not until we spy a foxhole—somewhere he'll be safe."

Richard had never felt such boiling fury. Serena was jolted against him, and his strong arms held her captive. But he resolutely kept both hands tightly on the reins, lest they go instead to her neck, which he had a powerful urge to wring.

Richard clenched his teeth and tried to smile as he took Serena's bandaged arm and led her into the ballroom of Atwater Manor. It would not do to announce to half the coutryside that he and his bride were not on speaking terms. But that was no more than the truth, Richard thought grimly, remembering their interview this morning. This being a masquerade, there was no announcement of their names as they crossed the threshold, and so they were spared the surge of curious well-wishers that Serena's first public appearance in the neighborhood would have engendered. As it was, Richard surveyed the already crowded ballroom with dismay. Despite the disguises, the various knights and princesses, the shepherdesses, pirates and even a berobed friar, Richard recognized many people. And just how were he and Serena to appear the companionable couple after this morning's heated set-to?

Livvy and Caroline, who was breathtaking in her Grecian gown, had already been greeted effusively by

Lady Atwater and Charlie. Richard and Serena had fallen behind in the receiving line, and as they waited, Richard glanced surreptitiously at his wife. He might have known she'd dress as a gypsy, he thought, peeved. He did have to admit she looked quite fetching in the large gold earrings and brightly colored scarf he'd bought for her at the fair — God, that seemed ages ago. But why did she have to wear her hair down loose? It was too enticing by half. So was the deep blue loo mask that covered only her eyes and left her dainty nose and soft pink lips exposed. And her blouse — he knew exactly where he'd seen that white lawn shirt before and he didn't like it one bit! It hugged her figure no less suggestively than it had yesterday. Her multi-tiered, multi-colored skirt was obviously a concoction of several of her gowns which were probably best off cut up. But the skirt did not even cover her ankles, for pitysakes! And — and — he looked down and his eyes boggled as he saw that she had somehow discarded her shoes and stood now in bare feet. He supposed it was authentic, but still and all, dammit, it was not at all the thing! And that thought brought his mind forcibly back to this morning.

She had finally relinquished that blasted animal into a foxhole, and when they'd arrived home he'd marched her straightaway to their chambers. But Serena had not been at all contrite, insisting she'd done nothing wrong, and his seething fury had not made a whit of difference. Lord, how could he ever have thought her a timid little mouse? He looked down at the bandage wrapped around her non-existent injury and felt his anger rise again. But Lady Atwater, resplendent as

251

Queen Elizabeth, was greeting them now, and Richard forced himself to smile as she gushed over his new bride. And he tried very hard not to strangle Charlie, or rather Sir Walter Raleigh, as he inquired solicitously of Serena whether her arm pained her overmuch.

"No, Charlie," she replied levelly, "it is not my *arm* that pains me." Charlie roared with laughter, and Richard wanted to throttle them both.

Richard did not enjoy watching Serena dance a country set with a certain pirate whom he knew to be Lord Willoughby, Lady Willoughby's all too handsome son. He had a reputation as a hardened rake, much to his mother's chagrin, and Richard did not wish Serena to be overmuch in his company. Nor did Richard care for the way Mrs. Babbington pointedly eyed Serena's naked feet and then whispered animatedly to several of her cronies. He groaned inwardly, remembering Serena's previous meeting with the vicar's wife.

As if her wayward tongue were a warning, Richard claimed his wife at the end of the set and squired her about the room, introducing her to those neighbors whose disguises he could penetrate.

Everyone expressed delight at meeting the new marchioness and concern over her injury, which she blithely tossed off as a mere trifle. Richard was not best pleased, but he *was* glad to report to all who asked that the duke was indeed recovering.

Inevitably they came round to the vicar and his wife. "How wonderful to see you both!" Mrs. Babbington exclaimed, removing her mask after they'd greeted each other. "Such a bother, these things, don't you agree? Why, everyone knows who everyone is at all events. Here in the country we are so close, aren't we, Oliver dear? And I daresay I am the only Viking princess here tonight, and so am persuaded my identity is well known by now. Not but what I'm afraid I've got the headdress all wrong. 'Tis so difficult to set it right with these braids, you see. What do you think, Lady Egremont?"

Serena murmured that the headdress looked just right, and quite perfect with the flowing robes, but she needn't have bothered, for Mrs. Babbington went right on. "I vow I spent hours considering my costume, but dear Oliver *will* insist on wearing his clerical collar as always. But he looks so handsome, don't you think?" The vicar turned pink and his lady went on. "As do you, Lord Egremont, so dashing in your black domino! And my dear Lady Egremont, may I say that your costume is—well—it is quite original, isn't it!" She finally paused for breath, looking Serena up and down, her eyes coming to rest at her very bare feet. "But then, so are you, my dear," she added, and despite her kindly tone, Richard was decidedly piqued. "Shoes are so restricting, aren't they?" she went on. "Always pinching one—oh, but do watch out for the Turkish sultan, my dear. He trod twice on my toes during the last quadrille!"

On this note Richard and Serena escaped and he signed Serena's card for the first waltz, because he knew it was expected. In truth, he did not wish to dance with her at all. He was still smoldering and she had been stiff and formal with him all evening. The prospect of the waltz seemed not to please her either and he wished wholeheartedly that his infernal evening were over.

He relinquished her to her next partner, the berobed friar with the balding head, and he was unreasonable irked that she seemed most eager to go. He accepted a drink from a passing footman and glanced around the ballroom. It was adorned in Lady Atwater's usual style, with profusions of palms and hothouse flowers. His gaze lighted on Livvy, surely the loveliest shepherdess here tonight.

He was pleased to see her enjoying herself. She'd not yet sat out a single dance. Now she was dancing with Charlie, and she erupted in a cascade of giggles at something he said. From the mischievous look on Charlie's face Richard half expected him to tug at her pigtails, and Livvy to stomp merrily on his foot. Really, Livvy had two big brothers, Richard mused, and he was glad.

A while later, Richard danced a Roger de Coverly with Livvy, and then stood up with Caroline for a quadrille. She flirted outrageously with him, and despite her enchanting appearance, he found himself not at all wishing to tighten his arms around her whenever the steps of the dance brought them together. He wondered why—she was not only beautiful but always had a smile for him, which Serena decidedly did not.

Serena next stood up with a tall blond medieval knight, and Richard decided he'd had enough of the ballroom for a time. He repaired to the cardroom but found he could not escape Serena there either. It seemed his wife was the primary topic of conversation this evening. His presence had not yet been noted when he overheard a retired colonel and Sir Digby, attired as a Scottish chieftain, conversing in bemused tones. "A taking little thing, isn't she?" the colonel was saying.

"Who?" asked Sir Digby, seemingly intent on his cards.

"Why, Lord Egremont's little gypsy, of course."

Sir Digby lifted his eyes. "Ah, yes, very fetching, indeed. Egremont will have his hands full, if I don't miss my guess."

"Oh? What makes you say that?" the colonel asked, and Richard stiffened.

"Didn't join the hunt, you know. Doesn't care for it. Deuced strange, you must own."

The colonel did and Richard fumed. Damned tattle-mongers! They were just as bad as a gaggle of women! He quietly slipped from the room, resigning himself to the ballroom for the duration.

Caroline's mind was churning, even as she danced gaily with one partner and the next as if she had not a care in the world. Her plans with Marco to discredit Serena were proceeding excellently, but she must not pass up the opportunity tonight's ball had thrown into her very lap. Her mind whirled even as her partner — an inconsequential lawyer's clerk got up as a court jester, of all things — whirled her around in the dance. She'd seen Serena dancing with a handsome, danger-ous pirate a short time ago. Richard had not seemed overly pleased, and while Caroline did not care to ponder the reasons for *that*, she did see that the situation had possibilities.

A masked ball had its distinct advantages, she reflected when the dance ended and she made her way to Pirate Willoughby. For, of course, one need not be formally introduced before striking up an acquaintance. Helen of Troy would do what she must to lure the pirate onto the terrace, and then she would watch the drama unfold.

As the orchestra struck up the first chords of the waltz, Richard strode purposefully across the large ballroom to claim his wife. He was tired of seeing her with other men, for all he did not really want to dance with her himself. At first he held her rigidly, several inches away from him. But he noted many curious eyes upon them and so he pulled her closer. He reminded himself that he was most justifiably angry with Serena, but still she felt so good in his arms. She smelled of roses, and he liked that. She was small enough so that her head came just to his chin, and he liked that too. Unwittingly, he found his anger dissipating and wished that *she* were not so tense.

"Relax, little gypsy," he whispered. "We might just as well enjoy it, you know."

The gentleness of his voice, the warmth of his body so close to hers, quite disarmed her, and all thoughts of this morning fled. Still, she could not be comfortable and found herself smiling ruefully and replying in all honesty, "I — I have never waltzed before, Richard." At his curious look she added, "My parents did not approve, you see."

"Ah, yes, I might have known," he said dryly, slowing their pace in time with the music. "Well, I am glad I am the first, Serena." His dark eyes held hers and she could not look away. "And I trust you find it—pleasurable. It is my privilege to teach you to enjoy the—er—waltz."

Serena flushed and finally lowered her eyes. His meaning was all too clear and—dammit! Why did he have this effect on her? She must not forget that this was the same man who rung a peel over her at every opportunity. And then there was Caroline. No one was more beautiful, more elegant than Caroline tonight. But Caroline was not dancing with him now, and when Richard's large hand began to gently caress her back, she found herself relaxing against him.

A small sigh escaped Serena's lips, and Richard could feel her body mold to his. He felt absurdly happy, enjoying himself for the first time all evening.

Charlie watched Richard and Serena and smiled to himself. Perhaps there was hope for Lord Egremont and his gypsy, after all.

He was not so sanguine a few minutes later when Lord Willoughby solicited Serena's hand for the next dance. Richard frowned prodigiously, and even without being able to hear the exchange, Charlie knew that he'd denied the request. It would have been her second dance with the pirate, Charlie recalled. Instead, Serena went off to the punch bowl with Willoughby, and Richard fumed. He was doing a great deal of that lately, Charlie mused.

Matters did not improve when they all went in to supper. "I was merely being polite," Serena whispered to Richard, as he seated her at a table near the center of the room.

"You do not have to be polite to rakes," Richard said through clenched teeth and then stalked off to the buffet table.

Oh Lord, here we go again, Charlie reflected, as he escorted Livvy to the same table. Willoughby and Miss Lister joined them but minutes later, and Charlie groaned to himself. It needed only this.

He and the gentlemen heaped plates of cold glazed meats, succulent hothouse fruits, and lobster patties, and conveyed them to the table. They all removed their masks to eat, as had others. Indeed, many of the guests seemed to recognize each other at all events, and Charlie thought it would have all been quite cozy had it not been for the complex undercurrents at this particular table. Richard and Serena were stiff with each other once more, and Caroline fluttered her eyelashes at Willoughby. Willoughby flirted quite unabashedly with her, and Richard eyed the pair with a distinct frown. Now what was that all about? Charlie wondered, and then decided that Richard must simply be trying to protect his house guest. But then Caroline flashed Richard a most dazzling smile, and Willoughby eyed Serena with an intensity that caused Richard to transfer his glowering countenance to his wife.

Livvy chatted amiably throughout it all, quite in awe of the splendor of her first ball. Thank goodness she was too young for all this nonsense, Charlie mused, and thought longingly of Scotland and the simple affections of the innkeeper's daughter.

It was almost midnight, almost time for the unmasking, and Caroline thought her scheme would best be carried out before. And so she sought out Lord Willoughby and, blushing prettily, suggested that they might take a breath of air on the lower terrace. His lordship appeared startled for a moment, and then, smiling knowingly, agreed. He must go first, Caroline ventured, and she would follow in but a few moments.

So far so good, she thought when he'd gone, and she went in search of Livvy. "Oh, there you are, Livvy, dear!" Caroline exclaimed. "I declare I am fagged to death with all this dancing. But isn't it wonderful?"

"Oh, my yes! I cannot think when I have enjoyed myself so!" Livvy rejoined.

"Come, let us take a glass of punch," Caroline said, linking her arm with Livvy's. But a moment later she gazed down in great distress. "Oh, my dear Livvy, you must forgive me, for I fear I've trod on your gown and quite torn it. Oh, but come, I shall take you to the ladies' withdrawing room. No doubt the maid will have it repaired in a trice!"

Livvy entreated Caroline not to feel so guilty about a mere accident, and Caroline left her safely with the maid and went in search of her other quarry — Serena. It was a simple matter to tell Serena that Livvy seemed quite overset about something and desired Serena to come to her at once on the lower terrace. "You know, Serena, the dark and quiet terrace, just beneath the main one up here." Serena asked no questions, merely said, of course, she would go, and headed for the French doors. A small smile played about Caroline's lips as she counted the minutes before locating Richard. And now she must proceed carefully, so as not to give the game away—not tonight's or any other.

"Oh, Richard," she pleaded, her amber eyes limpid, "I declare I am much in need of a breath of air. Might I prevail upon you to accompany me out to the terrace?"

Richard was all solicitude and escorted her to the upper terrace straightaway. She had no idea whether the voices from below could be heard, or if she would have to contrive a way to get Richard down to the lower level. She hoped not. Subtlety was key. As it was, luck was with her. There was only one other couple on the upper terrace, silently gazing at each other, and the voices from below filtered up more clearly than she'd hoped.

"Whatever the reasons, my dear," Willoughby was saying, "the fact remains that fate has brought us together. And you need not worry, we are completely private here."

Richard frowned at the words and made to lead Caroline back inside, but the next voice stopped him cold in his tracks. "But—but Lord Willoughby, I—"

"Hush," he replied, and Richard heard no more, but with an ominous growl dropped Caroline's arm and stormed toward the stairs.

Charlie had always felt it was his duty as host to look after all of his guests, and tonight, certain guests in particular. And so he noted that the terrace was becoming a bit too populated, and something about it disturbed him. He disengaged himself from Mrs. Babbington's bird-witted monologue as soon as he could and strode to the French doors. The upper terrace was empty, save for one couple, and he heard footsteps on the brick stairs that led to the lower one. He raced downstairs; Richard and Miss Lister were just ahead of him, and he froze at the scene that met his eyes. Willoughby stood on the far side, not inches from Serena! It was obvious that he had cornered her and she darted gratefully to Richard, but he was fairly shaking with fury.

"How dare you, Serena!" he seethed. "And you, Willoughby—I ought to—"

"My dear Egremont, I assure you—" began Willoughby, but Richard advanced on him, taut with rage.

Charlie deemed it time to intervene. "Richard," Charlie interrupted firmly, startling everyone. "Lady Egremont was in need of a breath of air, and a bit of privacy. She came out here quite alone, you must know. Is that not so, Serena?"

Serena's eyes flew to Caroline's. The triumph there was unmistakable. And how could she explain? Richard would never believe her. But she must try. "I did come here alone, but I came because I was led to—"

"Spare me, Serena," Richard growled derisively, and Charlie saw Serena visibly wince.

Charlie turned his attention to Willoughby. "What you do in your private life is not my concern, Willoughby. What you do under my roof *is*. I cannot, I *will* not, have you offering insult to any of my guests."

"Nor would I think of doing such, Atwater. Lady

Egremont came out for a breath of air, as you said, and I was merely regaling her with an amusing *on dit*. And now gentlemen, ladies, as the hour grows late, I shall bid you good evening." He bowed and exited, and Richard made no move to detain him. But his body was as rigid as ever. Charlie had seen that clenched jaw before and knew what it meant.

"Richard," he began, puting a hand to his friend's shoulder. "Surely you must—"

"No, Charlie," Richard interrupted, his voice low. "You have averted a scene, and for that I am grateful. But as to the rest—well—it is a private matter, and must remain so."

Charlie nodded and dropped his hand. He cast an encouraging smile at Serena, and watched helplessly as Richard clamped his hand on her wrist and led her away. Caroline Lister followed meekly, several paces behind, and Charlie sighed deeply. Richard was right in one thing at least. No one, no matter how close a friend, could interfere between a man and his wife. They must work it out for themselves, and he hoped to God they would.

They had not been able to leave the ball straight-away. Richard knew they would have to wait at least until the unmasking were their departure not to be remarked upon. Besides, Livvy, who had thankfully been absent from the scene on the terrace, had been enjoying herself enormously and he did not wish to spoil her fun. And so he tried to appear as if he, too, were having a capital time, but in fact he spoke to almost no one, until finally he, Serena, Livvy and Caroline found themselves in the carriage lumbering home. Livvy and Caroline prattled gaily about who had worn which costume, and how many times the Turkish sultan had trod upon their feet. Richard was silent, trying very hard not to glare at his wife. Serena said little but gazed curiously at Livvy and Caroline, and never glanced at Richard at all

Caroline kept Livvy engaged in merry chatter during the ride home; she did not want anything of moment discussed. Not that Richard and Serena seemed much inclined to listen, nor speak, but later they would, and that worried Caroline. For though Serena had kept silent several days ago about the missed hour's vigil with the duke, Caroline suspected she would not be so reticent this time. Caroline's mind tossed about for possible schemes, but it was Livvy, naive little gudgeon that she was, who gave her the opening she needed.

For when the carriage finally drew near the Court, Livvy invited Caroline to her room for a comfortable cose. This was her first ball and there was so very much to talk about! Livvy exclaimed with glee. Caroline hesitated, her mind carefully considering the options, much as a chess player anticipated future moves. Caroline knew she did not wish to be occupied with Livvy, but if Serena were . . . It was not a good idea to give Livvy and Serena a chance to talk, but it was more important to keep Richard and Serena apart. And *that*, if Caroline were particularly clever, might be accomplished quite thoroughly.

Caroline yawned delicately and declared that she

was positively fagged to death. Might she and Livvy review it all on the morrow? Livvy looked most disappointed, whereupon Caroline quite innocently suggested that Serena might sit with Livvy instead. Richard's eyes flashed and Caroline smiled sweetly at him. "It will only be for a little while, Richard. And dear Livvy is much too giddy with excitement to sleep just yet," Caroline pointed out.

Richard nodded his approval, and Serena rose to the bait, for, of course, she wished to question Livvy. But it wouldn't signify, Caroline reflected smugly, not after Caroline was through with this night's work. Actually, she realized, Serena's temporary absence provided several interesting opportunities, and Caroline was never one to pass up an opportunity.

It was just as well that Serena was not here yet, Richard thought as he submitted to his valet's ministrations. It would give his ire a chance to cool. He wanted to thrash Serena! How dare his wife make such a mockery of him! First the swimming incident, then the hunt, and now Willoughby. Innocent though she may have been in that last, it was all of a piece. She was constantly flaunting the proprieties, oblivious to his position and hers, to say nothing of the danger in which she blithely placed herself. Well, by God, he would put a stop to it! He and Serena must talk straightaway; he hoped she would not tarry long in Livvy's room.

When Watkins had finished, Richard sashed his dressing gown and went to the sitting room. He was flipping through a book whose title he did not even know, when he heard a knock at the corridor door. "Who is it?" No one answered but the door clicked open and Caroline slipped inside. "Caroline!" he dropped his book and rose. "What on earth are you doing here? I thought you were quite exhausted." He noted that she still wore her evening gown, and was relieved.

"I—I am, but—oh, Richard, I just *had* to see you."

"What's wrong, Caroline? You know you shouldn't be here. It isn't at all the thing."

"Oh, my dearest Richard. I—I just wanted to tell you that I know what you must be suffering," she said softly, advancing to him.

"Caroline, I don't know what you're talking about," he replied tautly.

"Oh, Richard, do not pretend with *me*," she purred, sidling up to him. "I was *there*, and I saw it all. I am so sorry, Richard. And then—there was yesterday—those wretched boy's clothes! And what with her absence from the hunt and that rather unusual brouhaha in the copse—not but what it *might* have been the blood, as Lord Atwater said."

"Caroline," Richard began warningly.

"Oh, I suppose I have no right to speak thus," she breathed, her eyes full of concern, "But it—it simply tears at my heart." One delicate hand fluttered onto his arm. Richard felt himself stiffen. He did not want her here, but her words disturbed him greatly. "That you, a man of such eminence," she went on, her voice soft, "should be saddled with a wife who has no regard at all for your consequence—why, it is not to be borne!"

Richard took a deep breath, trying to still the tumult of emotions assailing him. "Caroline, this is not something I am prepared to discuss with you. What is—"

"Richard. My love. I do wish I could console you," she whispered, winding her arms around his neck and pressing close to him. "Tell me how I can comfort you."

"You don't know what you're saying," Richard chided with some difficulty. "You don't belong here, Caroline," he added firmly, disentangling her arms from his neck and stepping back. "If you have something to discuss with me, something which does not concern my wife and my marriage, well, then, we can speak about it tomorrow, in the library. For now, it is late. And you should not be seen here."

"But Richard, I—"

"Goodnight, my dear," Richard said pleasantly, and went to open the door.

Caroline edged her body close to Richard as she slid through the doorway, whispering a throaty "goodnight" in his ear. As soon as the door closed behind her she tiptoed to the next room, the one she knew Serena occupied. She listened for any approaching footsteps and, hearing none, slipped inside. This next bit of business would be the crowning touch. Even Marco would be quite impressed with her cleverness this evening. She padded quickly across the room and into the dressing room. Her task took her only a moment, and then she darted back into the corridor, sighing with satisfaction.

It was all going rather well. And if Richard had seemed a bit less than warm tonight—well, she *had* surprised him after all, and she'd always known he was a bit high in the instep. And even if his ardor *had* cooled somewhat—well, it didn't signify; she would simply fan the flames again. For after tonight the message would be unmistakably clear. Caroline was available and Serena was not.

Serena walked slowly down the corridor from Livvy's room to her own. Livvy had been so full of bubbling high spirits that Serena had been hard put to interrupt her gleeful review of all her dance partners. The evening seemed to have been quite perfect for her. At first Serena had considered questioning Livvy or voicing her own suspicions. But to what purpose? Serena already knew the truth and Richard did not want to hear it. Livvy could not help her, and Serena had no wish to shatter the girl's illusions. At least not tonight.

And so she had taken her leave, and was so lost in thought that she did not notice Caroline in the corridor until they had nearly collided.

"Oh, Serena, how lovely to see you again," Caroline cooed. "I've just come from Richard, you know. Such an intensely emotional man, isn't he? So very—loving."

Serena felt sick in the pit of her stomach. Caroline's insinuations disgusted her, and even though she did not truly believe there had been any intimacy between them, the thought of Caroline alone with her husband made her furious. And how dare he be so angry at *her* when he was so obviously enamored of Caroline! Serena strode to her room, determined to remain calm and not to let him see how much he had overset her.

Richard paced the floor of the sitting room, and downed too much brandy. Damn Caroline! Why was she behaving this way? Thank God Serena hadn't seen her, or there would be the devil to pay! Richard knew he had got to set Caroline straight on certain matters. It would be easier, however, to do so after he and Serena had come to—well—work things out.

And where the devil was Serena? Richard did not stop pacing until at last he heard her enter the bedchamber. He waited for Hannah to retreat, and then gulped the rest of his brandy and marched to the connecting door. The time for a reckoning had come. She was the Marchioness of Egremont, and he would make clear, once and for all, just what sort of behavior was expected of his wife. And then—Richard took a deep breath—and then he would teach her the more interesting things a wife should know.

He tapped at the door. When she didn't answer he turned the handle. It was stuck. Puzzled, he tried again, more forcefully. The handle would not turn and then he realized—by God! It wasn't stuck. It was locked! Serena had locked him out of her bedchamber! "Serena!" he called, banging loudly on the door. "Serena!"

He heard her come into the dressing room. "What—what is it, Richard? What's wrong?"

"What's wrong? Blast it all, Serena! Don't come the innocent with me! Unlock this damned door!" He did not even attempt to keep his voice down.

"What do you mean, unlock—who, who locked it?"

"Pitching it too rum, my girl. Now open the bloody door!"

"I'm — I'm trying, Richard. But — but there's no key."

Lying again, was she? "Devil take you, Serena! I'll not abide this! I demand that you open this door!"

"Richard, there *is* no key. Why do you not use the corridor door if—"

"How dare you! How dare you lock this door to me!" he exploded. "I'll enter my wife's bedchamber when and if it pleases me! And I'll not use the bloody corridor door to do it! Now, will you open this door or must I break it down?"

"Richard," she cried. "Please, be reasonable. It must be some mistake. I didn't—"

But he didn't hear whatever else she said, for he lunged at the door several times, throwing his whole weight against it. He was too furious to feel any pain. On the third try the door gave, flying open and sending splinters of wood scattering.

Serena stood several feet back, her fist in her mouth. He was in a towering rage, that dwarfed even his prior anger. He stormed to her and seized her by the arms. "You are my wife, Serena," he seethed. "Don't you dare *ever* lock your door to me again. Do you understand?"

When she didn't answer he shook her, and yelled louder. "Do you understand?"

"Y-yes, Richard," she finally choked.

"Good, and don't ever forget it!" he spat back, and then brutally shoved her away from him, sending her sprawling across the room. The chaise broke her fall and she collapsed against it. He turned his back and strode from the room, deliberately shutting out the sound of her quiet sobbing.

269

Chapter Twelve

Serena did not sleep for many hours, and when she did it was a sleep tormented by unpleasant dreams. Upon waking she remembered very little of the dreams — only dancing flames and the sound of drums. But her encounter with Richard last night she remembered all too well. She had never seen him in such a passion; indeed, never had she seen *anyone* so angry. And it was so unjust — Serena had no idea how that door had come to be locked.

Now in the cold light of morning, when passions receded and reason stepped forward, Serena could see that perhaps his rage was fed by more than just the locked door. There had been the hunt, and then Lord Willoughby on the terrace, even the swimming incident of the day before. And, if she were perfectly honest with herself, in the cold light of morning, she supposed that perhaps it was not just Richard's offended sense of propriety that had prompted his reaction each time. Perhaps he *did* have a care for her safety as well. But dammit, he had a strange way of showing it—always flying into such a taking! And could he really believe her capable of making an assignation with—oh, damn him! He was autocratic and unreasonable and his behavior last night in their bedchamber was inexcusable!

But she could not help comparing that picture with the youth who had saved Charlie's life, and with the grown man who showed such care for his tenants, and such ingenious enthusiasm for his study of insects. And then there was the man who had held her in his arms during the waltz—No! She must not dwell on any of it. Nor on the fact that sometimes he spoke to her ever so gently, for those times were few and far between! She winced inwardly, supposing that most of Richard's kind words were reserved for Caroline. Well, so be it, Serena sighed. All she wanted from Richard, she told herself, was to be left in peace.

And she certainly had no wish to encounter her husband this morning, nor at all this day, for that matter. She rang for Hannah, dressed quickly and requested a breakfast tray in her room. She ordered a great deal of food, much of which she pocketed for the afternoon. She breathed a sigh of relief when she had escaped the house without encountering any of its inhabitants.

Today she determined to go back to her little dell, but nonetheless, when she arrived there, she looked about her warily. She did not like the feeling that her private hideaway had been invaded. She kicked off her shoes and sat down. Still, it took her some time to settle down with her sketch pad, for she kept looking over her shoulder. But after a time the stillness soothed her, and she caught sight of a goldfinch feeding on thistle-seed in the nearby brush. She picked up her pencil and forgot everything else.

"You very good artist, Serena," came a whisper from behind her.

"Thank you, Gaya," Serena said, looking back for a moment, "although my subject was not quite so patient as you. He left me some time ago." Gaya sat down beside her and Serena put a few more touches to her sketch before closing the pad.

Gaya sat with her knees drawn up, her dark hair spilling down her back and over her shoulders. "I could not come back yesterday. I have fight with Marco. He not allow me to leave vardo," she said abruptly, then plucked a blade of grass and slid it between her teeth.

"I'm sorry."

"We yell very much. It very loud brangle."

"Oh, dear."

"Yes. Marco find a new man for me. Gregory. He comes all the way from Cornwall, Marco say, just to marry me."

"And? Do you not care for him?"

"No. He is too skinny. Not like George. Marco say I am a child. I cannot have George. I must marry someone else. I say, if I am a child, why do I have to marry?" Serena choked on a laugh and Gaya added, "Besides, I think Gregory have black temper. Like Marco."

After a moment Serena said, "You know, Gaya, sometimes our first impressions about people are too rash. With men especially, it is hard to know them at first. I think they hide much. Perhaps they are afraid of being too soft."

Gaya dropped the blade of grass and gazed intently at Serena. "I have fight with Marco. You have fight with young lord, is not so?"

Serena blinked, then smiled faintly. "Yes, Gaya. I had a dreadful row with Richard, I'm afraid. Several, in fact."

"Why?" Gaya demanded without a qualm.

"I—well—" Serena began, not certain how much she wished to confide, but Gaya, as usual, anticipated her.

"Oh! The little fox!" Gaya gasped. "Young lord find you with the fox!"

"How did you—oh, never mind," Serena sighed. "Yes, 'twas the fox."

"I make trouble for you," Gaya said quietly.

"No, Gaya! You must not think it was your fault. Why, how could either of us know the hounds would come after—"

"The hounds come too?"

Serena's lips curled in a half smile. "Yes. The hounds too." Serena did not really wish to go into it, but at Gaya's look of intent curiosity she said ruefully, "Perhaps I ought to tell you the whole."

"Oh, yes," Gaya said simply, and waited.

Serena recounted the tale, half expecting Gaya to burst out laughing at any moment, but she did not. Instead, when Serena had done, Gaya regarded her pensively.

"He have black temper, too, the young lord. But— but I think—not always."

Serena looked down at the hands clasped in her lap. "No, not always," she echoed in a muffled voice.

"And you went to gorgio ball with bandage on your arm. Young lord not like that either," Gaya added and Serena's head jerked up in surprise. She had never mentioned the ball, nor was she wearing the bandage now. Then a reluctant smile tugged at her mouth.

"No, Gaya, he didn't like that either." She hoped Gaya would not question her further about the ball. For some reason Serena did not want to tell Gaya what costume she had worn, nor—

"What else you brangle about with young lord?" Gaya asked abruptly.

Serena blinked, then recalled saying they'd had *several* rows. But she did not wish to discuss the ball, nor the locked door. Then she remembered Monday, and her missing clothes. How fortunate to have so *many* clashes to choose from, Serena reflected with bitter irony. "Richard—ah—well, Richard does not wish me to swim alone," Serena replied, not wanting to say more.

Gaya eyed her keenly for a moment, then shrugged. "Then swim with me."

Somehow Serena doubted that Gaya would qualify as an adequate chaperone. In answer, she merely smiled and said, "Would you like a biscuit?"

While they were munching biscuits and apples, Gaya said, "Marco not angry today. He say Serena come to camp. Mayhap take lunch with us. You will come?"

"Oh, I should love to, Gaya!" How kind your brother is!" Serena exclaimed, glad to put her mind to other

274

things. "But first, I want to see you dance. Will you show me?"

Gaya eyed her intently again, then nodded. "I show you," she said, popping the last bit of biscuit into her mouth.

Then she stood and moved a few feet away from Serena. Today Gaya wore a bright blue blouse that fell in a deep V to expose her throat. Her skirt of blue, yellow and red was sashed with a wide red scarf that emphasized her tiny waist. Without a word she began to move her head in slow circles and at the same time lift her bare feet in tiny, delicate steps. Her eyes were closed and her hair fell gracefully, first down her back, then over her face. And then she began to chant, a haunting melody that almost sounded like it was coming from far away. Gaya clapped her hands to the beat of her own melody, and motioned for Serena to do the same. It was a strange rhythm, soft and slow one moment, staccato the next, and it took Serena some minutes to master it. When she finally picked up the rhythm, Gaya stopped clapping and instead began to move her body, her entire body, in time to the faraway chant issuing from her lips.

Serena watched Gaya's torso sway and her bare feet tap the ground lightly. Her body moved in a slow and sensual motion, almost languid. And then her feet began to stomp the ground as the rhythm became faster and her brown legs seemed hardly to touch the ground at all. Her colorful skirt swirled around her, her hair flew about her face, and her body moved in ways Serena had never thought it possible for anyone to move. Serena could not help thinking of the very proper dances of last night; even the waltz could not compare to this. There was an intensity and passion in the Romany dance that was exhilarating.

Serena sat mesmerized, her hands automatically clapping the beat. The little dell was filled with music, as if a dozen drums and violins were playing. And then Gaya's chant began to slow, and with it her stirring movements. And then suddenly she was still, her head bent, face hidden by the curtain of her hair, the chant ended. For several moments Serena merely stared at her, unable to speak. And then abruptly Gaya straightened and came to sit near Serena.

"I think I would like another biscuit now," Gaya said in that matter-of-fact tone of hers.

Serena blinked. "Y-yes. Of course." She reached into her pocket and handed Gaya a biscuit. "Gaya, that was wonderful."

"Now you," Gaya said.

"Oh—oh, no. I couldn't."

"Yes you can. I will make music and when the music start, your body tell you what to do."

"No, I—I—am content merely to have seen you." Which wasn't true at all, Serena admitted to herself. She very much wanted to try, but somehow the dance frightened her.

Gaya cocked her head as she chewed the last of her biscuit. "You dance now. Someday, you dance for young lord."

Serena felt herself blush. "Oh, no Gaya, I—I could never do that."

Gaya merely smiled enigmatically. Then she sprang to her feet and pulled Serena up alongside her. She began to chant another melody, this one more lilting, lighter than the other. She clapped and her body moved in lively swirls. Serena found herself tapping her feet and when Gaya took her hand, she began to move in time with the music. She dipped when Gaya did, let her arms and head and shoulders sway and her feet flirt with the grass below. Where the first dance had been passionate, this was filled with a joyous gaiety, and Serena enjoyed herself enormously.

She was quite winded when they stopped and they fell to the ground laughing.

"It is in the Romany blood, the dance," Gaya said, suddenly serious. "But anyone may dance, if he listens to his heart."

Serena did not care to pursue that particular bit of wisdom, and readily fell in with Gaya's suggestion that it was time to leave for the camp. Serena made a half-hearted attempt to pin her hair back up and, reaching for her shoes, followed Gaya out of the dell.

Richard spent the morning trying, with little success, to work. He kept thinking of Serena last night. Other than yesterday, when he'd gone off to the hunt, today was the first day since their marriage that they hadn't breakfasted together. He hadn't needed to feel at all guilty about reading his newspaper, and yet he'd missed her. Missed her soft, early morning chatter and her secret smile as she gazed out the window looking for things to paint. Yes, he *had* missed her, but blast it all, *she* had been in the wrong, many times over! And he'd be damned if he'd be the one to apologize!

277

Abruptly he picked up the morning's correspondence, but it was Serena's image that swam before him. Her wild and glorious hair, her deep blue eyes, her perpetually bare feet. Damn and blast it all! Where was Serena?

She was not in their chambers, nor the morning room nor family drawing room, nor any of the myriad public rooms on the main floor. Nor, a quick glance out the window told him, did she seem to be in the gardens.

He did encounter Caroline, however, in a most unlikely pose. She was in the picture gallery, standing precariously on a spindly-legged chair. The chair was drawn up nearly to the wall and Caroline was intently studying the large portrait of his great-great grandmother—a formidable woman with frowning countenance, double chin, and an enormous, ornate diamond and emerald pendant at her bosom. He'd never thought the portrait particularly good, and what Caroline had found to fascinate her so he could not for the life of him imagine.

"Caroline, what on earth are you doing?" he asked, trying to remember just when he'd said that before.

His words startled her and she nearly toppled from the chair. But she had righted herself and climbed down by the time he reached her.

"Oh, R-Richard, how nice to see you," she said breathlessly. "I—I was just wandering about and I saw this portrait and well—I just had to have a better look. It is so very interesting, is it not?"

He didn't think so at all, but refrained from saying so, merely gazed intently at her. She slid her arm through his. "Picture galleries just fascinate me, Richard," she purred. "I would so much like to learn more about your family. Would you walk around with me and introduce me to all your noble ancestors?"

He did not know what it was, the fact that he wanted to find Serena, or something about Caroline's tone of voice, but he found himself impatient with her. And there was something in her eyes — something that made him think she was lying. Why, he couldn't say, but he didn't like it one bit.

He disentangled himself and remembered to inquire after her ankle. He had forgotten all about it at the ball and it seemed that she had, too. She replied that it was much improved and only then did he recall Serena's sarcastic words about Caroline's injury. Confused, he took his leave, gently admonishing her to have a care lest she do worse than sprain an ankle in her efforts to become acquainted with his ancestors.

He found Livvy emerging from his parent's suite. She had no idea why Caroline was behaving so oddly, nor did she know Serena's whereabouts.

"No, Richard, I haven't seen her at all this morning," she answered his query. "But I shouldn't worry about her. She goes off like this most every day. She sketches, you know. She'll be home later."

"But — but it's nigh onto luncheon. Doesn't she come home to eat?"

Livvy shrugged. "One never knows with Serena, does one? I don't suppose she particularly likes schedules."

"No, I suppose not," he said absently, before thanking her and going on his way.

Schedules or not, Richard was more than perturbed.

Much of this, he knew, was his own fault. He had left her too long to her own devices. And given recent events, there was no telling what she might get herself into next. Where the hell did she go every day, when she wasn't catching foxes, and for how long could a person sit and sketch? He supposed she *did* have a special way with animals, and a fine, artistic eye, but still and all . . . A thought struck him and he hurried to the stables. Her horse was still there, and it was some relief to know she was on foot. At the least she couldn't go too far.

He shuddered when he remembered Monday's escapade. He hoped she'd have enough sense not to go back to the same place. And as to swimming—well—if he caught her at *that* again he'd break every bone in her body. He thought fleetingly that perhaps he ought to demand she take a groom with her wherever she went. But he knew she'd balk at that, probably tear the very rafters down objecting. And besides, it oughtn't to be necessary, dammit! She was a married woman and she was on Gower land. She ought to be able to contrive to stay out of trouble . . .

Richard decided that a brisk ride would do him good. He marched back up the stairs to change into his habit. He didn't care to face Watkins with his cheeky grin just now, and so searched the dressing room himself for his things. A hairbrush slipped from the dresser top and he bent to retrieve it. And there, on the floor, wedged between the dresser and the wall, was what seemed to be a rather large canvas, covered with a cloth. Richard had not looked at Serena's work since Gateshead, and that had been a fleeting glance that

280

he'd stolen guiltily. He'd been impressed, but they hadn't known each other very well, so he'd said nothing. And since then, she'd never once invited him to view a work in progress, and so he didn't think he had the right to look. Nor did he care to ask. But somehow, he couldn't resist this covered canvas, which almost seemed to be deliberately hidden.

He lifted it up and gently removed the cloth. He stared wide-eyed at a partially done portrait of a girl. Even in its half-finished state, it breathed with a life all its own. There was a stark beauty, a grace and innocence in the girl's countenance and in her stance — a feeling of freedom, of a creature at one with nature and at peace with herself. It struck him that whoever this was, the painting was in a sense a portrayal of Serena herself, of what was inside her. He wondered if Serena knew that. Then he grinned. His little gypsy was very talented indeed. Gypsy! Richard gasped and cocked his head at the portrait. The subject was no figment of Serena's imagination and was definitely a gypsy! Oh, Lord, had Serena really got herself mixed up with gypsies? He thought of her costume, so authentic, and knew she probably had.

Gently he replaced the cloth and set the canvas down in its place. It was long past time that they had a very long talk, even if it needs must wait until tonight. He liked to call her "little gypsy," even liked to think of her that way. But dammit, he only meant it as an endearment, not to be taken as carte blanche to go out and become one!

There were more people in the camp today and Serena was dazzled by the veritable flood of color created by the wagons and by the women in their sashes, shawls and three-tiered skirts. Several women were tending the fire in the middle of the camp, stirring the pots and joking with people who milled and sat about.

Marco stood when he saw Serena and Gaya and came forward. He greeted Serena warmly, too warmly, she thought and felt her heart begin to pound a little too loudly. He led them to the campfire, where they each received a plateful of food, and then to a pleasant grassy area a little way off, where they sat down to eat.

Marco played his role of host very charmingly, Serena thought, and one glance at Gaya told her it was not always so. She could not help but be flattered and found she was enjoying herself immensely. Marco spoke of his love for the English countryside and asked Serena about Luntsford Court—what it looked like, how many rooms it had. She wondered at his pointed questions, but other than that he kept the conversation largely impersonal, for which she was grateful. But there was nothing impersonal in the way he kept looking at her, and several times she felt herself flush.

She took refuge in her food. It all looked—well—interesting would be the best way to describe it. She did not ask what anything was until after she'd eaten and was agreeably surprised when what she thought was asparagus turned out to be stewed shoots of bracken fern. But she was not particularly pleased to learn that the delicious meat dish was claybaked hedgehog stuffed with boiled and pounded beechnuts. She prudently did not comment and instead took another sip of the warm, thick mead someone had given her. She did not know what that was either, but it made her feel pleasantly lightheaded and she accepted when Marco offered a refill.

"You like our food. I knew you would," Gaya said confidently. "You not like other gorgios."

Serena wondered just how other gorgios *would* react to eating claybaked hedgehog, but was saved a reply by the approach of a tall, lanky man with a long, very determined stride. The way he looked at Gaya made introductions almost unnecessary; Serena knew this was Gregory. Gaya offered him some food and when he sat down Marco rose to leave and motioned for Serena to do the same. She glanced briefly at Gaya, but her friend was already totally absorbed in Gregory. With a faint smile Serena stood up and followed Marco.

He led her past clusters of people, who stood aside to let him pass and stared unabashedly at Serena. They wended their way through a dozen half-naked children scampering about, not to mention the dogs and chickens. Serena knew she was causing a stir and did not much like it. She wondered if that was why Marco kept walking until they were clear of the camp and well into the woods.

He turned to face her, standing very close. "I be thinkin' you very smart, for a gorgio," he said seriously. "Gregory make good husband for Gaya."

"I hope so," was all she said.

Then he took a step closer and stared into her face with eyes that were too intense. "You be very beautiful, Serena," he said softly. His large brown hand came up to finger her loosely pinned hair. "I am glad Gaya bring you here."

"Th-thank you, Marco," she stammered. She felt very warm, and wondered if all the mead she'd drunk had anything to do with it. She knew he was flirting with her and could not help being flattered. Yet suddenly she felt very nervous about being out here alone with him.

"You have seen the dance? Did Gaya show you?"

"Yes, I have seen the dance."

"Good. Tonight Gaya will dance again. And I too. Late. When the moon is high. I invite you to come and see," he declared, and she had the feeling this was a royal summons, one very rarely given.

She chose her words carefully and with true regret. "I should love to, Marco, but I cannot. I cannot leave the Court at such a late hour."

"I reckon that is best time. No one will know."

Serena shook her head. "Thank you, but I—I couldn't."

"Hah! Marco glad to hear you be such an obedient wife. The rai be very fortunate. A man is so reasonable but a woman—hah! A woman can drive a man to his very grave, a-yellin' and wantin' her own way. I hope Gaya be so obedient with Gregory."

Serena did not much like being called an obedient wife. She was not at all sure she was a wife and the very thought of blind obedience horrified her. And as to Richard, well, after last night about the last thing in the world she would call him was reasonable.

"I am persuaded that men are not all so very reasonable, Marco. And as to wifely obedience, well, I believe a woman has to make her own decisions, to follow her heart and do what she thinks best. I hope you will allow Gaya to do so."

She thought his eyes glittered with anger for a moment but then his expression softened. "And you, Serena. Do you always make your own decisions?" His hands moved to her shoulders and she felt her heartbeat race.

"I—I try," she replied, and then, remembering herself, she stepped back from his grasp.

"And what does your heart tell you now?" he whispered, leaning close but not touching her.

She swallowed hard, awash in confusion. She did not know what her heart told her now, and her body was treacherous. "I—I think we should go back now," she managed after a moment.

His finger traced the line of her lip. "Yes. We go back now. But you come tonight. Never again will you see such dancing," he said huskily.

She knew he was right. And she was fascinated by him. There was a certain intensity about him that drew her, but frightened her at the same time. She *had* to see him dance, and to see Gaya dance with him. And as to Richard, she didn't really owe him anything. Besides, no one at the Court need ever know. Just this once, she would go. Then perhaps later she would think about being more obedient.

"I—I will try," she breathed and then he smiled, a dangerous, devastating smile.

She was relieved to go back to camp, but had no opportunity for private conversation with Gaya. Gregory had gone but her friend appeared rather distracted, a glimmer of a smile playing about her lips. She and Marco walked Serena to the edge of the clearing.

"Goodbye, Serena. I see you very soon," Gaya said, and then at a look from Marco, took her leave.

Marco gazed down at Serena and flashed that smile again. Then he raised her hand to his lips. "Until tonight," he murmured, and she could not meet his eyes.

Serena's mind was churning all the way home. She wanted, desperately wanted to see the dancing tonight. She knew it was not quite the thing, but what harm would there be if no one were the wiser? It was not as though there were any danger in it. She *would* be on the duke's land, after all. She shuddered to think of Richard's fury should he find out about such an expedition, but she refused to be cowed by her husband's temper. Besides, she would contrive a way to leave and return undetected. It should not be all that difficult. As far as she was concerned, she and Richard were not on speaking terms. Nor would they be until Richard apologized for his outrageous display of temper last night. That, she knew very well, was highly unlikely. And Richard could not very well expect her to have brandy by the fire with him if they were not even speaking to each other! No, she would retire early, and alone. She would listen for the sounds of his settling in for the night and then, when the moon was high, she would leave.

As it was, Richard made it very easy for her. She was in her bedchamber, soon after she arrived home, working on the watercolor of the caterpillar, when he tapped at the connecting door. "Just a moment, please," she called.

She dabbed one last time at the eyes of the fuzzy fellow and then stepped back. Yes, it was done. And quite life-like and pleasing, she thought. Quickly, she took the painting off the easel and set it aside, replacing it with a blank page. Then she hurried to the door. Richard did not come in, however, merely requested an interview in the sitting room.

She cleaned her hands and followed him in, seating herself in a tapestried wing chair. He paced the floor, frequently running his hand through his dark brown hair. "Serena, I wish to talk with you. I had thought to wait until tonight, but perhaps it is best to start now."

Serena sat bolt upright. My goodness, could he be about to apologize? She could hardly credit it, and didn't know whether to be pleased or disappointed. He looked at her expectantly and when she said nothing, he went on, drawing himself up in front of her.

"Now, Serena, I realize that you cannot have thought out the implications of your recent behavior, especially last night in our bedchamber. So if you will simply apologize, then we can, I am persuaded, have a most comfortable cose."

She stared at him for a moment, at the dark eyes and unyielding jaw, not knowing whether to laugh or cry. Instead she screamed. "Apologize? You want *me* to apologize?" She jumped from her chair and faced him squarely, her temper rising with every second. "*You* have ranted and railed at me and made absurd accusations! And last night, *you* shook me and shoved me and screamed at me! You—you became violent! Never have I been subject to such Turkish treatment! Why, you broke the bloody door down! And *I* should apologize? No, my dear husband, it is not *I* who should apologize. I fear we are a long way from any comfortable cose. And what's more, when I retire tonight it shall be alone! I bid you good afternoon, my lord!" she declared and flounced from the room, leaving, she knew, an astounded and nearly apoplectic husband behind.

Chapter Thirteen

Richard treated Serena with an attitude of silent fury all through the evening, and she did not feel at all guilty excusing herself early and going to her room to wait. Richard's anger was a relief, actually, for now she could go to the gypsies without any remorse. In fact, the only thing she felt guilty about at the moment were the covert glances that had passed between the duke and duchess at dinner. She would very much have liked to please them. But unfortunately, there seemed to be no pleasing their son.

She let Hannah put her into a nightgown, so as not to arouse any suspicion, but as soon as the maid left Serena took shoes, a brown walking dress, and a shawl from the wardrobe and secreted them in her room. Then she sat down with a book to wait for the household to put itself to bed. Most of all she waited to hear the sounds of Richard retiring. She heard him come in a short while later, and then heard Watkins join him in the dressing room. She tried to lose herself in the book she held, but instead kept listening for footsteps. Watkins retreated and then she held her breath when she heard Richard approach the bed-chamber door. She did not want to confront him now. But whatever his intention, he seemed to think better of it, for he retreated to the sitting room. She heard the door close and breathed a sigh of relief.

She sat still in her chair for a very long time, not wishing to make a sound that might arouse Richard. When the candles guttered in their sockets she rose quietly, stretching her stiff muscles. The house was utterly still and there had been no sound from the sitting room for a very long time. Silently, she pulled off her nightgown and tugged on her clothes, very pleased that she'd had the presence to take her clothes from the dressing room earlier. Throwing the shawl over her shoulders, she tiptoed out of the room.

The corridor was quiet, nearly dark, and she care-fully made her way to the stairwell. She stopped to reassure herself of the comforting silence around her, and continued on her way. When she emerged from the back door into the gardens she sighed with relief. She was not sure she had even drawn breath in the last thirty paces, so anxious had she been to reach the door undetected. It fleetingly occurred to her that perhaps she had ought to take Firefly, but she dismissed the notion. There might still be someone lurking about the stables, and besides her feet knew the way very well; her horse did not.

The moon was bright, almost full, but even so Serena was grateful that she had tramped through these woods so many times before. She heard the music long before she could see anything. The beat of drums and the strains of a fiddle rent the stillness of the night.

The drums grew louder and louder, and as she stepped through the woods to the clearing she could see a huge fire in the open pit.

The camp was alive with people, some milling about, drinking, others sitting on the ground, clapping hands and swaying to the mood of the music. Suddenly Serena was seized by a momentary panic. She didn't belong here; she was a stranger. And then a man and woman ascended the dance platform. The fiddler began to pluck a lively tune and as the drumbeat picked up, the couple began to move. Serena watched their dancing gradually accelerate into a frenzy and knew very well why she was here.

She hadn't realized she'd been stepping closer to the center of camp until Gaya appeared, almost out of nowhere. "Serena! What you doing here? What young lord going to say?"

"Oh, Gaya. The young lord isn't going to know. Marco invited me and I—I just had to see the dancing. You do understand, do you not?"

"Oh, yes. I understand. You feel the magic. Come with me."

Gaya led her close to the stage, and Serena was glad that everyone seemed too intent on the dancing and general gaiety to notice her. She was not surprised, however, when Marco materialized quite suddenly before them. He wore a black shirt, unbuttoned nearly to his waist. Serena tried not to stare at the hard, muscular chest, thick with dark hair.

"Ah, Serena, you have come," he said in a low, husky voice and raised her hand to his lips. His familiarity disconcerted her but he gave her little time to think on it. "Gaya, take Serena to the vardo. She not watch dancing in gorgio clothes."

"But Marco—" Gaya began.

"Silence," he hissed in a tone that frightened Serena. "You will do as I say," he said to his sister. Then he turned to Serena. "You want to see dancing, is not so?"

"Yes, of course."

"Good. You go to vardo." His tone brooked no argument and Serena thought it would be silly to quibble over such a trifle as clothes. It was not at all proper, she knew, for her to appear in gypsy garb—this was not a masquerade, after all. But then again, to these people it would seem less strange than what she now wore. And besides, no one from her own world would ever know.

Gaya was curiously silent as she rummaged through a drawer and handed Serena a red blouse and multi-colored skirt. Then she tactfully withdrew so that Serena might change. Serena removed her shoes and dressed hurriedly, thinking this was quite an improvement over last night's garb. Her hair was already down, Hannah having brushed it out, and Serena relished it. For once she would be less conspicuous this way, she mused, and went to join Gaya.

"You do not approve, do you Gaya?" Serena asked after a moment.

Gaya smiled. "I think my clothes suit you. You very beautiful. It is Marco I not understand."

Though Serena would have pressed her, Gaya said no more but let the way back to the dancing. Marco seated them right in front of the stage, handing them each a mug of the warm mead Serena had drunk this afternoon. Gregory came and sat next to Gaya, fully claiming her attention. Serena knew she and Gaya would have no further opportunity for private discourse this night.

The mead was thick and sweet, a bit more heady, perhaps, than it had been earlier. Serena sipped it and concentrated on the dancing. She loved the swirl of color as the dancers moved and she could not help tapping her feet to the music. Several fiddles played now, and tambourines jingled to the beat of the drums. As soon as her mug was empty Marco refilled it, and sat down much too close to her. The drink was making her feel warm and relaxed all over and his presence was warming too. She inched away and he smiled enigmatically at her.

And then she turned her attention to Gaya, who stood and walked slowly to the stage. Her sleek black hair gleamed in the firelight and her white blouse made a stunning contrast to her dark skin. The drums had stopped, but now started up again, a slow beat as Gaya ascended the platform. She stood still, head bent as she had in the dell. But instead of her chant the fiddles began a haunting melody and Gaya began to move. Her body swayed and then as the drumbeat accelerated her feet picked up the rhythm. The tambourines and fiddles joined voices and the air was filled with a strange tension. The drums beat loudly; the flames of the campfire danced even as Gaya did, her body bending and dipping, her skirts flying and exposing her long brown limbs.

Serena watched transfixed. Perhaps the mead had made her lightheaded; she did not know. But everything outside of the fire, the music, the dancing, ceased to exist for her. She was only dimly aware that Marco had left her side, and then suddenly he leapt onto the platform. He took Gaya's hand and twirled her around. The drums slowed a little. Then the dancers separated, moving several feet apart. They began to dance to each other, twisting, undulating, one answering the other. The rhythm of the music became faster, and the dancers swirled and swayed and bent to its beat. If Gaya's movements were lithe and sensual, Marco's were bold, throbbing. As the pace increased, their bodies moved in wild gyrations that seemed to Serena utterly primitive and passionate.

Serena felt beads of sweat break out on her brow; suddenly she was excessively hot. Sister and brother were dancing now in a wild, provocative frenzy. Instinctively Serena knew that the tension in the air had nothing to do with brothers and sisters. She wondered if it were the mead making her so dizzy and sending ripples of heat through her body. And then for the first time she became aware of Gregory, several feet away from her, staring with mouth open at the stage. His body was rigid, his breathing labored. Serena turned away from the raw emotion on his face.

The dance was slowing now. Gaya and Marco swirled gracefully to a halt as the fiddles and drums subsided. The crowd erupted into tumultuous cheers as Gaya descended the platform. Gregory immediately stepped forward to take her hand, and they disappeared into the shadows. Serena fleetingly noted that Gaya had danced with no man but her brother. Even her dance with Gregory would have to wait, Serena knew, until her wedding.

The drumbeat picked up again, and a woman in a multicolored peasant dress, large gold earrings dangling from her ears, rose to join Marco. This time

Serena watched only Marco. His muscular thighs seemed to strain against his britches as he moved, and the bare flesh of his chest flashed in the firelight. Someone refilled her mug and she drank deeply. Time ceased to exist. Several women followed the one in the peasant dress, and still Marco danced with an intensity that intrigued and frightened Serena.

Now the fiddles and tambourines had grown silent. Only the drums beat in a slow, sultry rhythm that seemed to match the dancing flames of the fire. Fire and drums, she thought, suddenly remembering Sibella's words. "Fire and drums and violence and sunshine." And then she recalled her dream last night—fire and drums again. She closed her eyes and a shudder coursed through her, but she shook it off. There was nothing to fear of the sunshine, and as to violence, there would be none here, after all. Here there was only laughter and gaiety and a love of life. Very slowly, Serena became aware of a silence surrounding her, and she opened her eyes. People seemed to be staring at her, and now she turned to the stage. Marco was leaning toward her, beckoning her.

"Come, Serena. You will dance with Marco," he commanded softly, his hand outstretched.

Serena gasped and shook her head slowly. She couldn't. It was unthinkable. But the silence deepened and Marco stood still, his eyes boring into hers. Somehow, those eyes compelled her and a part of her thrilled to the thought of dancing with him. She knew it was not at all the thing, not for an English lady. But she was also aware that she, a gorgio, had just been tendered a great honor by the Romanies. She would never again have such an opportunity. And would she not shame Marco if she refused?

The fiddles struck up a lively melody and Marco bent down and reached for her hand. She was lightheaded from the mead, but she felt exhilarated. Just this once, she would do it. No one but the gypsies would ever know, after all.

Richard sat slumped in a wing chair drawn up to the hearth in the sitting room. The nearly empty decanter of brandy stood on the table to his right as he downed yet another glass. He stared with burning eyes at the empty grate.

Damn and blast it all! he thought as he slapped the glass down on the table. She made him so angry that he didn't even know himself. But God help him, he missed her. She'd avoided him all day—that much was obvious. And when finally they *had* spoken, it had quickly degenerated into a nasty brangle. That was not at all what he wanted, but there it was.

Richard knew he could not fall asleep, despite his half-foxed state. He wanted, needed a warm, soft body in bed beside him. A very particular warm, soft body. But dammit, *she* was in the wrong. He couldn't back down now. The issues at hand—especially the locked door—were just too important. A man had to take a stand, after all.

He sloshed more brandy into his glass and slugged it down. It took several moments for the soft knock on his door to penetrate his consciousness. When it did he felt a glimmer of a smile touch his lips. Serena had come to her senses. But why the corridor door? Surely Watkins had repaired the other.

"Come in," he called, rising.

"Caroline!" he blurted, none too pleased.

"Oh, Richard forgive me for intruding at this late hour," she breathed anxiously, darting to him and taking his hands. "Indeed, I—I did not wish to come at all, so much does it grieve me to bring you such news as may distress you. But I could never live with myself if any harm befell her . . ."

"Caroline, whatever are you talking about?" He disengaged his hands from hers and studiously kept his eyes from the folds of her dressing gown.

"I—I'm afraid 'tis Serena again. I couldn't sleep, you see, and so I sat by the window and then suddenly I saw a figure dart across the lawns. I wasn't sure who it was and it frightened me. And—well I know it was wrong of me but I went down and followed her. It was Serena, Richard. I could tell by the hair, you must know. She kept walking, toward the woods and I came back here."

Richard could feel that now familiar mixture of fear and anger rising in him. Where the hell could Serena have gone in the middle of the night? But then his eyes narrowed and he eyed Caroline skeptically. She was the picture of concern and innocence and yet . . . Too many things flashed through his mind—the miraculously healed ankle, Caroline's strange behavior in the picture gallery and his sense that she was lying, her entrance into his room last night. Was it possible that she was lying now? Of course, it must be. Serena would never be so foolhardly as to venture out at night. She was safe in her bed, where she belonged.

"Wait here," he said gruffly to Caroline and stalked, none too steadily, to the connecting door. The dressing room was empty and he knocked at the door to the bedchamber. His heartbeat accelerated when there was no answer but he willed himself to calm. He opened the door and stepped in. The candles still burned in the sconces and it took but a moment for his eyes to scan the room, including the bed. The empty bed!

Oh, my God, he thought, racing to the dressing room. Had he driven her so far away from him that she would do something like this—something so utterly shocking and dangerous? He threw open the wardrobe doors and yanked out breeches and a shirt. "Go to bed, Caroline," he called into the sitting room, "I shall take care of everything."

"Very well, Richard," he thought she said and heard her retreating footsteps.

He was dressed in minutes, despite a somewhat foggy brain and hands less than nimble for all he'd drunk. He nearly catapulted out of his room and down the stairs. He ran through the corridors of the main floor in the faint hope that she might be here. She wasn't. He had no idea where she had gone, but she could not have gotten far on foot in so short a time. He would find her. He hoped to God he would find her, and soon! He would never forgive himself if any harm befell her!

There was no one in the stables and he thought it just as well. Serena would not thank him if the whole house was roused on her behalf, as would surely happen if word got round that she was missing. He threw the saddle over Corinthian but it took some minutes to set it right. Oh God, he couldn't be foxed now, he just couldn't be. He mounted quickly and set off. The cool night air swept over him and he hoped it would clear his head. It was not until he was halfway across the lawns that he realized he was being followed. He turned around and reined in.

"Caroline! Where the hell do you think you're going?" he shouted.

She was riding Livvy's gelding and drew to a halt next to him. Fully clothed, he noted, and wondered how she'd done it so quickly.

"Oh, Richard, please allow me to come. I couldn't let you go out alone in the middle of the night. Lord knows *what* might befall you. Besides, you don't even know where she's gone."

"Do *you*?" he asked with deadly quiet, a strange prickling at the back of his neck. He was feeling less and less inebriated.

"No—no, of course not, Richard. But—well—oh, no. That has nothing to say to the matter."

"What is it Caroline? Out with it!"

"Well—I—I am persuaded this is fair and far off, but, well, Serena and I were having a comfortable cose this afternoon, you must know. And—and she began talking of gypsies, Richard, and some of their strange customs. I thought it a most singular discussion at the time, but, well . . ."

Richard's eyes were narrowed to mere slits. He could not imagine Caroline and Serena having any sort of a cose, let alone that Serena would discuss gypsies with Caroline. Caroline was lying, he thought in a flash. She had to be, for what purpose he would not ponder now. Now he had to think of Serena. Where in blazes would she—suddenly he remembered the half-finished portrait of the gypsy girl. There might well be a grain of truth to what Caroline said. Richard did not doubt that somehow Serena had got herself mixed up with the Romanies. But had she gone to them now? He had to admit it was a possibility. Damn! If only he'd been able to speak to her this afternoon, he might have prevented this mad flight tonight.

Caroline sat very still on her horse and Richard's eyes pierced hers. He grabbed the reins of the gelding. He had the uncomfortable sense that she knew more than she was letting on. "Do you know where she's gone, Caroline?" he asked with deceptive calm.

"Oh, would that I did, Richard. But please let me help you find her. Two pairs of eyes and ears are better than one, after all. And I do know what you must be going through."

Like hell you do, he thought, dropping her reins in disgust. Perhaps she didn't know Serena's whereabouts, but she was dissembling, nonetheless. He would wring the truth from her tomorrow, but he would not waste more time on her tonight. As to finding Serena, well—he supposed two pairs of eyes *were* better than one. Without a word he spurred his stallion forward, and was not at all surprised when Caroline followed him into the woods.

"I think I hear drums, Richard," she called ahead, not long after.

"I don't hear a thing, Caroline." Indeed, the night was deathly still. Too still.

"Well, I do. It's coming from over there," she said. Typical woman, he grumbled inwardly, to assume he had eyes in back of his head. He slowed his horse and then turned about to see which way she pointed. "Don't gypsies play drums?" she asked ingenuously.

Yes, gypsies play drums, he thought, but by this

time he had no idea whether she was telling the truth or not. Having nothing else to go on, however, he turned his horse in the direction she indicated.

He could hear nothing for some time and began to grow apprehensive. Then Caroline drew abreast of him. "Oh, Richard, I'm so frightened here in the woods at night. It's so dark and cold. I—I fear you were right. I should never have come." Richard reined in and gazed at her for a moment. This was the Caroline he knew, soft and vulnerable; some of his suspicion abated. Of course, she oughtn't to be here, but he could not take the time to escort her back. "I know the way home well enough from here, Richard. I shall go back now," she said. Richard started to protest but she forestalled him. "Pray do not trouble about me. Godspeed, Richard," she whispered and turned her horse and was gone.

He did not like her going alone, no more had he liked her following him at first stop. But he must, above all, concentrate on finding Serena. He still had not heard any drums but kept on in the same direction. What else could he do? And then, very faintly, came the sound of drums! He kept riding and finally the strains of a fiddle wafted toward him. And what the hell were gypsies doing on Gower land, he wondered, but knew that was the least of his problems.

The drumbeat grew louder and louder as he followed its call. Richard thanked God he was intimately acquainted with these woods, else he would have had a hard time tracing the exact source of the music. Perhaps it was Corinthian, with his fine ear, who was the greatest help, and Richard stroked the stallion's mane each time he turned closer to the music.

The first thing Richard became aware of as he approached the camp was the sound of cheering voices and raucous clapping to the staccato beat of the music. He reined in and dismounted, knotting the reins over a tree branch. He approached stealthily; the gypsies would not take kindly to having their camp invaded, the fact that this was *his* land notwithstanding.

The periphery of the camp was bathed in darkness but even at his considerable distance he could see that it swarmed with people. At its center was a platform of sorts, behind which blazed a campfire. Two people, a man and a woman, were dancing. They wore traditional gypsy garb, but their faces were in shadows and he could not see them. It seemed that everyone in the crowd watched the dancers intently, and Richard found himself doing the same. They were dancing close together, never quite touching but their bodies moving suggestively to the sensual, pulsating rhythm. Never had Richard seen such dancing and he could not understand how the Romanies could let their women display themselves so. As the woman dipped and swirled her long mane of dark hair flew about her face. It reminded Richard of Serena and he once more scanned the crowd. How the devil was he to find her without making a scene?

He edged his way closer to the stage, trying to be as unobtrusive as possible. It was a mark of the fascination the dancers held that no one seemed to notice him. Involuntarily, his eyes lifted to the dancers again. There was something utterly wanton in the dance, generating a palpable excitment in the audience. Good God, he thought, his body suddenly very tense, was Serena actually watching this?

He kept searching the crowd and somehow found himself very close to the stage. The blood pounded in his temples even as the firelight blazed and the drums beat louder and louder and then, abruptly, he looked up. He gasped for breath and felt such a blinding flash of pain and fury as he had never known before. For he looked up at the woman dancing and gazed clearly into the face of his wife! It must be some bizarre nightmare, he thought. It must be all the brandy. He closed his eyes and shook his head to clear it. But she was still there, dancing like a harlot with a tall dark gypsy. And then suddenly, the gypsy pulled her to him and ground his lips down onto hers.

Richard saw red spots in front of his eyes and his heart pounded painfully in his chest. He could hardly breathe; he felt as though he would choke on his very rage. He was beyond thought and beyond speech.

"Arrr," he roared, a kind of animal cry as he lunged onto the stage and grabbed his wife, tearing her from the gypsy's embrace.

He turned murderous eyes on the blackguard, wanting to hit him but not willing to let go Serena. He was dimly aware of the shock on Serena's face, and in the Romany's eyes, a mocking gleam and something else — the utter *lack* of surprise. Richard wanted to kill the bastard, at the least beat him to a bloody pulp, and certainly expel him from his land. But all that would wait until tomorrow. It was his treacherous wife that he wanted now, and by God he would have her!

"R-Richard, please let —" she began, but he silenced her with blazing eyes, his breathing too ragged for speech.

He dragged her from the stage, inwardly damning

303

her to hell with every step. He ignored the uproar in the crowd, hardly noticed that they parted to let them pass. He held tightly to Serena's wrist, his fingernails digging into her flesh as he yanked her after him. For one fleeting moment he thought he glimpsed Caroline in the crowd, a strange, triumphant gleam in her eyes. He blinked, knowing it must be his imagination. And then the image was gone. Nonetheless, he felt sick and bewildered, and pulled Serena even harder.

He tossed her savagely onto his horse and mounted behind her, ignoring her second attempt to speak. He jabbed his knees cruelly into the stallion's flanks, his arm snaking around Serena's waist in a viselike grip when the horse bolted. He could hear the drums as they rode off, and he saw the fire in his mind's eye. He felt as if his very soul were on fire. Fire, he thought. Fire and drums. Was that not what the gypsy woman had foretold for Serena? He wondered bitterly what the rest of the fortune had been, and then he remembered his own. Some nonsense about sapphires and the deceit of a woman. Willoughby was child's play compared to this! God damn her! he cursed inwardly. Denying *him* and then giving herself to some thieving gypsy libertine. She was *his*, and it was high time he proved it!

Chapter Fourteen

The ride home seemed interminably long, but it did not cool Richard's fury one iota. He was only vaguely aware that he was riding Corinthian much too hard. When they finally arrived at the Court he reined in abruptly, dismounted and nearly tumbled Serena from the horse. He clamped his fingers around her wrist even as he led the horse into the stable, did not relax his grip for a moment as he yanked her up the stairs to their suite. He shoved her into the bedchamber and slammed the door with his boot.

"Richard, please, let me explain."

"Explain? What is there to explain?" he roared, having found his voice and feeling a resurgence of the raw, searing anger that had seized him in the camp. The bright moonlight streamed in through the windows, and he advanced on her, ignoring the fear in her eyes. "That you prefer a gypsy to your own husband? That you lock me out of your room but run to the arms of that—that Romany swine?" Serena backed away, but he stalked her, like a lion stalking his prey; she would

305

not get away from him this time. She backed into a chair and stumbled; he grabbed her arms and pushed her toward the bed.

"Richard, it isn't like that."

"No, then what *is* it like?" he snarled, backing her closer to the bed. "Didn't you like being in his arms? You damn well seemed to be enjoying it, up there on that stage for all the world to see."

"No!" she cried, shaking her head. "No!"

He ignored her and shoved her back so that she staggered against the bed. "And did you enjoy his bed, Serena?"

"No, Richard. Please, I never—"

"*Did* you, my little gypsy jade?" He grabbed a clump of her wild hair and jerked her up, then, taking her arms, lifted her and tossed her savagely onto the middle of the bed. Then he lunged after her, straddling her prone body with his knees. "All these nights I've wanted you, but I waited while you played the frightened virgin," he growled, wrenching off his neckcloth and unbuttoning his shirt. "Damn you to hell, Serena! *I* am your husband and *I* am going to have you!" he raged.

She struggled beneath him but he held her fast with his knees as he yanked off his shirt. "No, Richard. Please," she implored, her hands pushing at his now bare chest. "Don't do this. Not this way. We—"

But Richard hardly heard her, her resistance only fanning his ire. "Lock your door to me, will you?" he demanded. "And then run off to that dark Romany!" He swung one leg over and bent to wrench off his boots. She squirmed away, rolling to the edge of the bed. He clamped his hand over her wrist and dragged her back. She kicked and clawed at him but he easily pinned her hands above her head and heaved himself on top of her.

The feel of her warm, writhing body beneath him sent waves of desire through him. "Your husband's kisses weren't enough for you — is that it, Serena? Well, let's just see if we can change your mind!" he seethed, his voice growing hoarse with lust.

His mouth came down brutally onto hers, his teeth biting her lips, his tongue trying to force them apart. She tried to twist away but he held her fast, one hand still at her wrists, his powerful thighs pressing hers into the bed. He tasted blood from her lips but still he would not let her go. He wanted to hurt her just as she'd hurt him. His free hand slid to her throat and down to her breasts. He kneaded them roughly, and the feel of them nearly burned his hands even through the thin fabric of the blouse she wore. He tore at it savagely, his large hand rending it from her body easily. He lifted his head and cursed inwardly at the sight of her chemise, still covering her. He slit it in one fierce stroke and drew a ragged breath as her breasts, gleaming white in the moonlight, were exposed to him.

"Richard, please, let me go," she rasped, still struggling. "In the morning we—"

"Never, Serena," he muttered, lowering his mouth to hers again. His hand moved desperately over her breasts, and down her side. When his hand encountered her skirt he tugged it down, tearing the chemise off in the process. She flailed at him and succeeded in twisting her mouth away for a moment. She uttered a somewhat feeble protest, which he smothered with his lips, finally releasing his hold on her wrists. And then

307

with both hands he continued his fierce exploration of her hips and thighs.

Richard's strong, relentless hands seared her bare flesh, and Serena told herself she must make one last protest, must use her newly freed hands and all of her strength to push him away. But somehow she couldn't. His lips burned a trail down her throat, his cruel hands were making her insides feel all watery and fiery at the same time. Her own hands somehow found their way round his neck and she moaned deep in her throat.

Marco, and the dancing, had stirred passions in her tonight, she knew that now. But they were passions that belonged to Richard. Only Richard. And it was much more than passion. Oh, God, how could she not have known how much she loved him? And he hated her now. He was saying it with every brutal touch of his hands on her body. But she didn't care. She wanted him anyway, even if it would only be this once. She clung to him, her hands gripping his broad shoulders. And when his mouth clamped down on hers again, she answered his kiss.

Richard never knew when his rage turned to something else entirely. Perhaps it was the feel of her silky, pliant body, finally naked, under his, perhaps it was the way, miraculously, she seemed to be kissing him back. He did not know. But he wanted her more than he had ever before wanted a woman. And, oh God, he did not want to hurt her. He loved her, he thought suddenly, he loved her desperately. He could not stop now; it was too late. But he would not hurt her, he vowed. He gentled his touch, one hand softly caressing her breast and the other coming up to stroke her brow. "Serena," he rasped. "God, Serena."

308

"Richard," she cried in answer.

Somehow he removed his breeches, the last impediment to their love, and when she arched against him he knew she was ready. He brought them together in one quick thrust. She cried out and he kissed her tenderly. Could he really have doubted her virtue? How drunk must he have been? He lay still for several moments and then began to move, very slowly, his eyes questioning. She nodded, smiling tremulously. He wound his hands through her hair, her beautiful hair, willing himself to be gentle, respectful of her innocence, though he felt his control near breaking. But then he realized she was urging him on, her hips moving, her hands at his back, pulling him closer. He groaned into her mouth and finally gave way, letting himself take her hard and fast, with a shattering frenzied need such as he'd never known before. And when he felt the wild shudders course over her, he took his own pleasure, and together they danced to the flaming, throbbing rite of passion until the flames subsided, and the dance ended.

He shifted his weight from her, kissing her eyes and the tip of her nose. Oh, God, what had he done? Would she *ever* forgive him? He turned onto his side and pulled her into the curve of his body. He could not think straight. He only knew that she felt soft and warm against him and that he must savor the delicious moment.

"Richard," he heard her whisper, "I think—"

"Hush, little gypsy. Tomorrow we shall speak," he mumbled, his voice already thick with drowsiness.

So much to say, Serena thought, but not now. Now she was so exquisitely tired. And so she snuggled very close to her husband's warm, naked body, shutting out the thought that she might never do so again, and promptly fell asleep.

Chapter Fifteen

Serena awoke just after daybreak. It took her a moment to realize that she was, indeed, wrapped in her husband's arms. She smiled contentedly and burrowed further under the covers. But then, in a rush, all the events of last night came to her. She remembered the feel of Richard's hands on her body, remembered his feverish kisses and felt once again the burning, aching sensations he invoked. He had been furious, had wanted to hurt her, she knew that. But somehow he hadn't. Somehow his cruel assaulting hands had become soft and caressing. And though she knew he'd taken her out of hatred and not love, yet she loved him, and it had been a wondrous awakening.

She also knew, as she lay in bed feeling the strength of Richard's lean hard body behind her, that she had provoked him foolishly and wantonly. It was one thing to befriend the gypsies, even visit with them. To go at night had been at worst foolhardy, reckless, perhaps.

But to have ascended that platform, to have danced with Marco, and in such a manner — *that* was unforgivable, no matter how much sweet mead she'd drunk. She bit her lip, and tried to keep the tears from escaping her eyes. She had shamed Richard; she did not deserve to bear his name, let alone his heirs.

She had known last night, just as she drifted to sleep, that she would have to leave. She saw it even more clearly now. For aside from the disgrace she'd brought to Richard, there was the fact that she loved him and wanted him to be happy. And happiness for Richard lay with Caroline Lister. He might desire his wife, but it was at Caroline that he looked with adoration and love. Serena had seen that time and time again. And now she must face it, with all its implications. For all she was spiteful and scheming, Caroline would make a much more proper marchioness, and eventually duchess, than Serena ever would. And all of her machinations had, after all, been born of her love for Richard. Or so Serena hoped, else she would personally come and scratch the cat's eyes out. At all events, knowing Richard's heart, she would have to leave the way clear for him, and leave him with a clear conscience as well.

She lay in bed a few minutes more, mentally composing the letter she would leave Richard. Then she slithered out of his embrace, rose noiselessly from the bed, and tiptoed to the dressing room. She wondered fleetingly what Hannah and Watkins must have thought last night, then shrugged. It really didn't matter. Nothing did.

She dressed hurriedly and threw a minimum amount of clothes and essentials into the smallest bandbox she could find, sparing, as she did so, only a thought as to where she would go. There was little choice really. She had few relations, and certainly none who would take her in at all events. Her parents were out of the question. As were her few girlhood friends, for whether they still lived with parents or now with husbands, none would be at liberty to take in a runaway wife. No, there was only one place she could go, where she would be accepted without question. And when she came into her inheritance, she could repay them for their kindness.

She took down a satchel from the cupboard and packed what painting materials she could. Her easel, of course, and the portrait of Gaya, she would have to leave. She regretted it but there was a limit to what she could carry through the woods, after all.

She stole a glance into the bedchamber to assure herself that Richard had not stirred. Then she sat down at the vanity in the dressing room to write her note.

"My dearest Richard," she wrote. "I am sorry for the disgrace I brought upon you last night, and for the distress I have caused you. I shall never be a fitting marchioness, nor duchess, for you. I know that you have loved Caroline for a long time and it is right that you should marry her. No one need know about last night, and I am persuaded you can obtain an annullment of our short, ill-fated marriage. Please do not trouble yourself about me, nor try to find me. I shall go where I am safe and welcome, and in three years' time, when I come into my inheritance, I shall be independent.

"Pray give my fondest regards to your parents and Livvy. I shall write them soon; they have been very kind to me.

"As to last night, you are not to suffer pangs of conscience nor remorse. You were justifiably angry, and as to the rest—well—" here Serena smiled as she wrote, "I would not for all the world have missed it. It was quite wonderful, Richard. I shall remember it, and you, always.

"Goodbye and God be with you.

Serena."

Then on impulse she added a postcript.

"Please accept this watercolor of a fuzzy little fellow I met in the woods one day. I hope he will be helpful to you in your classifications. Perhaps someday you will recall these last weeks with a certain kindliness."

She sealed the note, wrote Richard's name on it and then went to retrieve the caterpillar painting. She stole back into the bedchamber and ever so quietly propped the note and the painting on the bedside table.

She looked down at him, at the dark brown hair, tousled on the pillow, at the strong nose and those full, generous lips. They had held a hidden warmth, after all. "Goodbye, my love," she whispered at his sleeping form, and then tiptoed out.

Richard awoke to the sensation that something in his life was different today. He realized that he was in the middle of the bed, not at the very edge, and remembered what it was. Sleepily, eyes still closed, he reached for Serena. He knew they had to talk today, but perhaps first he might, gently and quite without talk, convince her of his love. His arms couldn't reach her and he moved over, groping among the bedcovers. Then he opened his eyes. She wasn't there, he realized, disappointed. He wondered where she'd got to. Had she merely gone to the garden to paint, or was she, perhaps, too embarrassed to face him? Or worse, was she angry? She had reason to be, God knew, but still, she had, in the end, enjoyed their lovemaking and he supposed he'd hoped she'd not quit his bed quite so soon.

Richard sat up and it was then that he saw the note on the bedside table. A sick feeling descended on him. She could not forgive him for last night. She would not, and she was leaving him. He sat at the edge of the bed and broke the seal with shaking fingers.

He read the letter once, twice, then three times. There were tears in his eyes when he finished. There was no anger in her words, none, except for herself. And yet she was leaving. And what was all this about Caroline? Could she really believe he loved Caroline? He glanced again at the letter. Serena forgave him completely and utterly, and never in his life had he felt a more complete and utter bounder. She was worth ten of him, and it had taken this disaster for him to realize it. He glanced over to the bedside table and picked up the painting, which lay face down. It was a beautiful delicate and faithful rendering of the larva of a—a— oh, he couldn't remember *which* butterfly. His eyes welled up again as he contemplated a future without Serena and her endless sketch books and water colors.

No, there could be no future without her. He shook his head with the irony of it all. He had used all his wiles in trying to seduce his wife. And instead, it was she, enchanting, free-spirit that she was, who had seduced him, quite differently and quite irrevocably.

He stood up, determined to pursue her. But first he read the letter one more time, trying to read between the lines. Was there no hint of affection for him? She had not spoken of love, but then, she had wanted to ease his conscience. The missive was not a play for sympathy. And yet she had responded to him last night, quite passionately in fact. Why, she alluded to that in the letter. Called it wonderful, in fact. And she had left the painting, and said she would remember him always. Surely not the words of a woman who was indifferent? It wasn't all that much, he supposed, but perhaps there was a chance. At all events, if he could convince her of his own feelings, he might also persuade her to come back to him, for in time she might come to return his regard.

He strode to the dressing room, hoping he might contrive to don his habit before Watkins appeared. He was sorely disappointed, for the blasted valet was sitting there waiting for him! He ignored the twinkle in the man's eyes as he told him that the Lady Serena had gone riding and Richard wished to join her without delay. He strove to contain his impatience and maintain an impassive countenance as Watkins carefully shook out his breeches and brushed his riding coat. Only when the valet seemed to take an inordinate amount of time deciding on which side to part Richard's hair did his control finally snap. "Get on with it, man!" he barked, and then fell silent as Watkins continued his ministrations at a faster pace.

Today at least, the question of where Serena had gone was simple. It wasn't even a question, for there was only one place he could think of that she would go.

That she would be welcome there, he did not doubt, but safe? Not for long, he thought, remembering the tall, dark Romany. But Serena was probably too naive to realize that, and he knew that the sooner he reached her the better. Besides, the Romanies were not about to remain long in his own back woods, not when they harbored his wife! He wondered how long Serena had been gone, and hoped to God he'd reach her before the gypsies decamped.

Watkins finally let him go, and Richard bolted from the suite. He tried to keep a decorous pace as he made his way down the corridor and the stairs, his mind reviewing Serena's letter and coming to rest on the part about Caroline. How could Serena have so miscon- trued the situation as to think he was in love with Caroline? He supposed he had once thought he was, but that was *ages* ago, for heaven sakes! And then he recalled when, just a few days ago, Serena had accused him of deceiving her with Caroline. He thought he had dispelled the notion then, but obviously he hadn't. He ought to have tried harder, but he remembered being sidetracked by the sight of Serena in breeches.

Suddenly he recalled that it was Caroline who had alerted him to Serena's arrival home that afternoon, even Caroline who had led him to the terrace. And it was she who had seen Serena leave last night. He thought of Caroline coming into the library and his bedchamber, Caroline summoning him to her. What exactly had she been about? And what the devil had she been doing with his great-great-grandmother's portrait?

Damn her! he cursed inwardly as he attained the bottom of the stairwell. For he finally admitted to himself that Caroline had tried to drive a wedge between Serena and him. He wanted to wring her cold, beautiful neck, he thought savagely as he pushed open the rear door and headed for the stables. Caroline had a great deal to answer for, and he suspected he didn't know the half of it. But Caroline would wait. Serena must come first.

But apparently, Caroline couldn't wait, for she accosted him just inside the stable door. He did not wish to waste time with her now, but he certainly did not want her following him, so perhaps it was best to get it all over and done with. Besides, he wouldn't want Serena to have to deal with her later. Caroline wore a thin, lemon yellow muslin dress that stretched enticingly across her breasts. Her silky hair was caught up in a topknot, with a few tendrils artfully escaping to graze her cheeks. He stared at her impassively and felt not the faintest stirring.

"What is it, Caroline?" he said without preamble. There was no one about, fortunately, and where once he had thought she smelled of lavender, now he smelled only the horses, and the hay.

"Oh, Richard, I—I just wanted to assure myself that you had arrived home safely."

"As you see. I trust you met with no mishap on your way?" His voice was icily polite.

"None at all," she said, her clasped hands fidgeting at her waist. "And—and Serena?"

"She is quite safe," he replied with a hard edge to his voice. Caroline apparently did not find his answer satisfactory, for she pressed him further.

"I'm glad to hear it, Richard," she said, smiling sweetly, a smile that did not reach her eyes. "Then, she

318

was not, of course, with the gypsies."

What the hell, he thought. She could do no harm now, and he would have a bit of amusement at her expense. "Yes, actually, she was. I think Serena has an affinity for them. Even looks like one half the time. She's a free spirit, like they are," he said jauntily, and had the pleasure of seeing her eyes widen, even if for just a moment.

Then she put her hand on his arm. "Oh, Richard, you are such a good sport, and a gentleman, to make light of it, when I know it has all been a sore trial for you. Surely you must see that she will never make a proper duchess, or even a marchioness. And running such a grand estate as this will be quite beyond her, I fear." Her voice was soft; there was sympathy and concern in her eyes. She was either a consummate actress, or perhaps she really did care for him. Not that it mattered, or excused her behavior.

He sighed. "I fear you are right. The manner of a duchess does not come naturally to her. She is much too — spontaneous. And as to the running of an estate — she will have much to learn. But she will, I am persuaded, have the love and loyalty of all her dependents."

"Perhaps, Richard," she admitted, inching closer to him. "But can she give *you* the love that *you* deserve?" She pressed her breasts close to his chest and turned limpid amber eyes to him. "*I* would never lock my door to you, Richard."

And then suddenly everything became chillingly clear. He felt his body go rigid and removed her hand from his arm, taking a step back. "How did you know about the locked door, Caroline?" he asked with deadly quiet.

He had to give her credit. Not by a flicker of the eye nor a facial muscle did she betray herself. But she could not help the sudden paling of her complexion. "Oh, well," she said lightly, "servants talk, you know."

"Not my servants, Caroline," he said coldly, his fists clenching as the enormity of her actions began to sink in. "And it wasn't just the locked door, was it? No, you have a good deal more to answer for, do you not? Like the disappearance of Serena's clothes that day, and Willoughby, *and* the locked door, *and* — and, last night. Heard drums, did you? Remarkable hearing you have, my dear Miss Lister," he spat scathingly, deliberately keeping his distance. He wanted to strike her but didn't think she was worth his so demeaning himself.

"Richard, please," she interjected. "You are overwrought. If you —"

"Oh, you were very clever; I'll grant you that," he interrupted brutally. "I still am not certain how you did it. No —" he put up a hand when she appeared about to speak, "do not enlighten me. Pray spare me the sordid details," he drawled contemptuously, thinking that she had to have the cooperation of that Romany cur for last night's display, and not wanting to know how she contrived to get it. "But," he continued grimly, stepping close and taking her chin in his hand none too gently, "You have not been so very clever, after all, Miss Lister. Did you really think that after you had done everything in your power to destroy my wife and my marriage, that I would turn to you?" He released her with a disgusted flourish. "Once," he added, his voice barely audible, "I thought I loved you. I was wrong."

And without a word, he turned from her and strode

to the stalls. She ran after him and he stopped just before the one he wanted. Turning to face her he said, his face a mask of icy calm, "Oh, and by the by, from this moment you are no longer welcome at Luntsford. You have until ten o'clock to pack your bags and leave. And if you ever come near Serena, or Livvy, or any of my family or retainers again, Miss Lister, I shall ruin you. Oh, and don't look so haughty and disbelieving, my dear. A few words in the right ears about certain nocturnal visits to my bedchamber would do the trick, I should think. No, the game is up. I suggest you journey now to those distant relations of yours in the north, else go to join your brother on the Continent. There is no place for you in Kent, anymore." And with that, Richard entered the stall, and slammed it in Caroline's face.

She was standing in the stableyard when he emerged astride his stallion. As he passed, she trained on him such a cold look of malevolence as made him shudder. Any last vestige of belief that she might have cared for him more than his title died with that look. It behooved him, he reflected as he rode out, to thank God, and his parents, every day of his life for his narrow escape.

This time, Richard strode into the gypsy camp as if he owned the place. As, indeed, he did! He looked quickly about him and instinctively headed for the most elaborate looking caravan, which stood at the far end. He recognized the tall dark man standing near it when he was still several yards away. He crossed the space between them in record time, whatever sense of calm he'd willed into himself during the ride com-

321

pletely deserting him.

"Where is she?" Richard demanded. "Where is my wife?"

"A Romany does not steal gorgio wife," the gypsy said disdainfully. "Even if her own husband cannot control her. She is not here, Egremont."

"I know she's—" Richard stopped, for a girl emerged from the wagon. She came to stand before him. This man's wife? No, the resemblance was too strong. Sister, then, he thought, and realized that he knew her. "Why, you—you're the girl in the painting!"

"I am Gaya," she said simply.

"Where is my wife?"

"Mayhap you come walk with me," Gaya said.

"Dammit Gaya!" The man exploded. "I *told* you not to mix in gorgio business! This time I—"

"I be back soon, Marco. Come, my lord, you come with me."

Richard followed reluctantly, wondering at the girl's quiet defiance of her thunderous brother. She led him into the woods, then abruptly turned to face him.

"Where is she? I want my wife back," he demanded.

"You make Serena very unhappy."

He sighed and spoke more softly. "I know that."

"I think you very foolish."

He grinned sheepishly. "That, too. Gaya, is she here? I wish to talk with her."

"In Aunt Violet's vardo."

"What in the world does that mean?"

"I think Sibella right."

"Sibella? What do you know of Madame Sibella?"

"Oh, she my aunt, too. She tell Serena 'fire and drums.' And 'violence and sunshine'."

322

Fire and drums—my God, he thought, last night. There had been fire and drums and, God knew, there was violence.

"I think," Gaya was saying. "I think today the sun shines, yes?"

He gazed intently into her eyes and then grinned with relief. "Yes, Gaya, today the sun shines."

He followed her back to the camp, and he could not help thinking of his own fortune. "A jewel in the house of Gower"—"a fortune in sapphires." He still had no idea what that meant. But "the deceit of a woman"—that was Caroline, and had been all along.

"She in Aunt Violet's vardo," Gaya said again when they reached camp.

"What the devil is that?" he asked, but Gaya only smiled and led him to a small, beautifully decorated wagon. She knocked and a rather huge woman emerged. Aunt Violet, Richard surmised. Gaya stepped up into the wagon and moments later Serena came down. She was barefoot and her hair hung loose, secured by the scarf he'd given her. Little gypsy, he thought, bemused. The earrings flashed at her lobes, but what drew his attention were her eyes. They shone a brilliant deep blue, sparkling in the sunlight, almost like—oh, my God, how could he have been so blind?

"Serena," he said uncertainly. "Come walk with me a pace." He extended his hand and together they walked into the woods.

Marco watched them go in quiet fury. He too had seen the sunlight catch in Serena's deep blue eyes. He had much knowledge of beautiful jewels—diamonds and emeralds and—sapphires. Damn her eyes! He should have known. He cursed under his breath and stormed up to his vardo, slamming the door behind him.

Richard didn't stop until they were deep into the woods, well out of sight and earshot of the camp. Then he turned to face her. They stood several feet apart and he had to steel himself not to stride to her, to reach up and tug her scarf off. He longed to see her hair fall freely about her shoulders.

She looked at him with unreadable eyes. "You should not have come, Richard."

He cocked his head at her. "Shouldn't I, Serena? But I had to, you know. I couldn't go without explaining about last night," he said, taking a step toward her.

"There—there's nothing to explain," she said nervously.

"I think there is, Serena. I had drunk rather a bit too much, I'm afraid—er—not that that excuses my behavior, you must know."

"So—so had I, Richard. Not—not that that excuses my behavior, of course."

"Of course," he echoed, lips beginning to twitch. He stepped closer.

"What I did was inexcusable, Richard," she said, moving back. "I know—"

"You seem to have no trouble excusing me, Serena, if your letter is any indication. And my offense was, you must own, far greater."

"No, Richard, I—"

"Serena, let us have done with this useless self-recrimination. Come home with me, Serena," he breathed, advancing on her. "I—I really cannot let you

324

go, you know, for I—" here he brought his hands up to brush her cheek, "I love you, little gypsy, most desperately."

She shook her head and stepped back from him. He sighed. "I do not expect you to feel the same, Serena, but, given time, such a feeling may grow." And then an uncomfortable thought registered in the back of his mind. Reluctantly he brought it forth. "Serena, I must know. Do you hold this man, Marco, in any special regard? Oh, I do not accuse you of any wrong-doing, but sometimes we cannot control what is in our hearts."

She shook her head again, a tremulous smile at her lips. "Oh, no, Richard. There was never anything—anything between us. Except—"

"Yes, Serena?" His voice was tense.

She took a step toward him and spoke very slowly. "Except perhaps that he—he made me feel a—a desire that I—I was afraid to feel for you."

He moved very close to her and placed his hands gently on her shoulders, his eyes gazing into hers. "Why, Serena? Why did you—keep me at arm's length?"

She shrugged away from him. "Because of Caroline," she answered, her voice low. "It was *she* you loved, even though I came to understand that you wanted me. I could not let myself respond. It—it wasn't enough, you see."

"Ah, yes, I see. Oh, my love, do you really imagine I could give my heart to that—that cold, scheming viper? Truly, I had hoped you thought better of me." He began advancing on her again.

"B-but you—she—"

"Serena, can we not consign my infatuation with

Caroline to the dustbin of youthful folly? For that is all it was, you know—a very foolish adoration as insubstantial as the air. Based on nothing, for I did not really know her at all, you see." He kept walking to her, and she kept retreating.

"But she—"

"And when I did come to know her, well, suffice it to say, Serena, that much of our difficulty can be laid at her door: the disappearance of your clothes, the locked door, even last night. Someday, when I've figured it all out, I shall bore you with the sordid details. Though what she was doing sidling up to the portrait of my great-great-grandmother, I'll be damned if I know," he mused, just a foot away from her.

"The jewel, Richard," she said suddenly. "Sibella's jewel. I—I saw Caroline studying several portraits, you must know. Always ladies with big—er—bosoms and necklaces to cover them."

Richard threw back his head and laughed heartily, and then he regarded her affectionately. "Ah, the jewel. Those elusive sapphires. Someday I'll explain that too, my love," he murmured, his expression sobering.

He backed Serena into a tree, a large oak, and put one hand to its trunk, just grazing her cheek. "But all that is fair and far off, Serena. The only question now is whether you—you think that, in time, you might come to care for me."

She did not hesitate, but stood perfectly still, her back to the tree. "No, Richard," she replied firmly. He stiffened and felt his stomach plummet to his toes, but he waited for her to continue, this time in a much softer voice. "I—I do not think time will help the matter any. For I am already hopelessly in love with you, you see." A slow smile spread across his features and he bent his head to hers. But she stayed him with a hand, adding in a rush of words, "But I am not at all the thing, you know. I have no sense of—of consequence whatever. Why, I should always want to run barefoot, and I fear I shall forever be getting into scrapes and—"

"And I shall always be there to rescue you, little gypsy. And I have never actually seen you swim, you know. I should very much like to correct that omission," he interrupted. And then he took her face into his hands and began to kiss her, very gently. Or at least, that was what he intended. But somehow, it didn't turn out that way. It was a fiery, hungry embrace, and he was not quite sure who was kissing whom.

When finally they parted, he drew a ragged breath. "I think, my love, that we ought to go home. Better still, we ought to return to Gateshead. It's much more—private there, is it not? If we do not tarry, we can of a certain be there by nightfall," he added with a rather wicked gleam in his eye.

"Yes, Richard," she whispered. "I—I should like that very well."

He chuckled deep in his throat, then swung her around and hugged her close. "I'm glad, little gypsy. Now, come, my horse is waiting." And with his hand about her waist, he began to propel her back.

But she hesitated. "Oh, Richard, my things. They are in—"

"We'll send someone for them later, my love," he interjected, urging her on, but she refused to budge.

"Very well. Ah, Richard—there is one thing more. The Romanies have been—that is—I would not wish to think—"

Richard turned to face her. "Do not tease yourself, love. I've far more important things on my mind just now." His eyes swept lecherously over her and she giggled.

"Then let us not tarry, Richard."

Suddenly, a voice rang out from above. "You forgot your shoes, Serena," someone called.

"Good God," Richard blurted, "has someone actually been—" But Serena merely laughed, interrupting him, and looked up into the trees. He followed her gaze and smiled ruefully. "We'll send for those too, Gaya," he called.

Gaya watched the young lord take Serena away, holding her very close all the while. Gaya sighed deeply. Mayhap I marry Gregory after all, she thought.

Chapter Sixteen

Marco stood atop a grassy knoll, gazing down at the grand circular drive of Luntsford Court. Swarmin' with gorgios, it was. Two vardos they were loadin', one heaped high with luggage. The gorgios were fools, he thought; the Romanies could teach them a thing or two about how to travel, he reckoned. Caroleen paced the grass right next to him.

"Damn!" she cursed again, maybe for third time.

"So, Caroleen, your little plan, it has gone astray, I think."

She glared at him. "Not all of it, Marco. I will find the jewel and I shall have my revenge."

Marco shook his head. Such fools, these gorgios. He looked down and saw Egremont leading his rawnie to the vardo. "Ah, Caroleen," he said softly. "Do you *still* not see? He has *found* the jewel. And mayhap, I help a little. That is some satisfaction, I think."

Richard tried very hard to ignore the gloating

expressions of Hannah and Watkins as they stood in the drive. They looked so smug that one would have thought Richard and Serena's role in recent events quite negligible. Richard chuckled inwardly, and then turned to Serena, noting that she was dewey-eyed as she bade his parents and Livvy goodbye. But he was anxious to be off and drew her toward the waiting carriage.

"Richard, are you sure you will not stay to luncheon?" the duchess asked. "That hamper Cook packed will hardly sustain you, I am persuaded."

"I assure you it is ample, Mother. And now if—"

"Oh, do stay a while longer, Richard. Whatever is the great rush, after all?" Livvy pleaded.

The duke stepped forward. "No, my dears, I do think Richard is in the right of it. They will want to reach Gateshead before—er—nightfall, after all," he said, casting a meaningful look toward his wife. Richard watched his mother blush.

They bid perfunctory farewells this time. "You must forgive my eagerness, love," he murmured into Serena's ear as he opened the carriage door, "but we do want to arrive before we are too tired. I want very much to show you that I can be gentle as well."

Serena smiled and her voice was a mere whisper. "I should like that, Richard. But I would not mind if sometimes you—you were not so very gentle, after all."

A very wolfish grin suffused Richard's face and he gathered Serena to him, right then and there. And without a thought for one coachman, three footmen, four maids, a cheeky valet, the duke, the duchess, and a very shocked sister, Richard kissed his wife deeply and thoroughly.

"Richard!" his father's booming voice recalled him to himself, but only a little. "You can either take your wife upstairs or get into that carriage and be off to Gateshead, where you belong! But I will not have you standing here before my ancestral home making a spectacle of yourself!" he roared, trying very hard, Richard knew, to keep a stern countenance.

Richard released his wife reluctantly and then breathed into her ear, "It seems I am not so very proper after all, am I, little gypsy?" and was delighted to see her blush.

With a parting grin to his family, he handed Serena up into the carriage and promptly followed her. They sat across from each other, she with her hands demurely folded in her lap, he politely commenting about the weather. But as soon as the carriage rolled out of sight of the ancestral home of the Dukes of Luntsford, Richard stopped talking. His eyes swept the length of his lovely marchioness with a less than proper gleam. And then Richard Gower, Marquis of Egremont, reached over and pulled his lady wife right into his lap.

"Damn the prorieties, anyway!" he growled, and then added, more softly, "Kiss me, little gypsy." And she did, for a very long time.

THE BEST IN REGENCIES FROM ZEBRA

PASSION'S LADY   (1545, $2.95)
by Sara Blayne

She was a charming rogue, an impish child—and a maddeningly alluring woman. If the Earl of Shayle knew little else about her, he knew she was going to marry him. As a bride, Marie found a temporary hiding place from her past, but could not escape from the Earl's shrewd questions—or the spark of passion in his eyes.

WAGER ON LOVE   (1577, $2.50)
by Prudence Martin

Only a cynical rogue like Nicholas Ruxart would choose a bride on the basis of a careless wager, and then fall in love with her grey-eyed sister Jane. It was easy for Jane to ignore the advances of this cold gambler, but she found denying her tender yearnings for him to be much harder.

RECKLESS HEART   (1679, $2.50)
by Lois Arvin Walker

Rebecca had met her match in the notorious Earl of Compton. Not only did he decline the invitation to her soiree, but he found it amusing when her horse landed her in the middle of Compton Creek. If this was another female scheme to lure him into marriage the Earl swore Rebecca would soon learn she had the wrong man, a man with a blackened reputation.

DANCE OF DESIRE   (1757, $2.95)
by Sarah Fairchilde

Lord Sherbourne almost ran Virginia down on horseback, then he silenced her indignation with a most ungentlemanly kiss. Seething with outrage, the lovely heiress decided the insufferable lord was in need of a royal setdown. And she knew the way to go about it . . .

Available wherever paperbacks are sold, or order direct from the Publisher. Send cover price plus 50¢ per copy for mailing and handling to Zebra Books, Dept. 1997, 475 Park Avenue South, New York, N.Y. 10016. Residents of New York, New Jersey and Pennsylvania must include sales tax. DO NOT SEND CASH.

THE BEST IN GOTHICS FROM ZEBRA

THE BLOODSTONE INHERITANCE   (1560, $2.95)
by Serita Deborah Stevens

The exquisite Parkland pendant, the sole treasure remaining to lovely Elizabeth from her mother's fortune, was missing a matching jewel. Finding it in a ring worn by the handsome, brooding Peter Parkisham, Elizabeth couldn't deny the blaze of emotions he ignited in her. But how could she love the man who had stolen THE BLOODSTONE INHERITANCE!

**THE SHRIEKING SHADOWS OF
PENPORTH ISLAND**   (1344, $2.95)
by Serita Deborah Stevens

Seeking her missing sister, Victoria had come to Lord Hawley's manor on Penporth Island, but now the screeching gulls seemed to be warning her to flee. Seeing Julian's dark, brooding eyes watching her every move, and seeing his ghost-like silhouette on her bedroom wall, Victoria knew she would share her sister's fate—knew she would never escape!

THE HOUSE OF SHADOWED ROSES   (1447, $2.95)
by Carol Warburton

Penniless and alone, Heather was thrilled when the Ashleys hired her as a companion and brought her to their magnificent Cornwall estate, Rosemerryn. But soon Heather learned that danger lurked amid the beauty there—in ghosts long dead and mysteries unsolved, and even in the arms of Geoffrey Ashley, the enigmatic master of Rosemerryn.

CRYSTAL DESTINY   (1394, $2.95)
by Christina Blair

Lydia knew she belonged to the high, hidden valley in the Rockies that her father had claimed, but the infamous Aaron Stone lived there now in the forbidding Stonehurst mansion. Vowing to get what was hers, Lydia would confront the satanic master of Stonehurst—and find herself trapped in a battle for her very life!

Available wherever paperbacks are sold, or order direct from the Publisher. Send cover price plus 50¢ per copy for mailing and handling to Zebra Books, Dept. 1997, 475 Park Avenue South, New York, N.Y. 10016. Residents of New York, New Jersey and Pennsylvania must include sales tax. DO NOT SEND CASH.

BESTSELLING ROMANCE
from Zebra Books

CAPTIVE SURRENDER (1986, $3.95)
by Michalann Perry

When both her husband and her father are killed in battle, young Gentle Fawn vows revenge. Yet once she catches sight of the piercing blue eyes of her enemy, the Indian maiden knows that she can never kill him. She must sate the desires he kindled, or forever be a prisoner of his love.

WILD FLAME (1671, $3.95)
by Gina Delaney

Although reared as a gentle English lass, once Milly set foot on the vast Australian farm, she had the Outback in her blood. When handsome Matthew Aylesbury met Milly, he vowed to have her, but only when the heat of his passion had melted her pride into willing submission.

WILD FURY (1987, $3.95)
by Gina Delaney

Jessica Aylesbury was the beauty of the settled territory in Australia's savage Outback, but no one knew that she was an adopted part-native. Eric, the worshipped friend of her childhood, now an outlaw, was the only man who made her burn with desire. She could never let anyone else teach her the pleasures of womanhood.

TEXAS TRIUMPH (2009, $3.95)
by Victoria Thompson

The Circle M was most important to Rachel McKinsey, so she took her foreman as a husband to scare off rustlers. But now that Rachel had sworn that they be business partners, she could never admit that all she really wanted was to consummate their vows and have Cole release her sensual response.

TEXAS VIXEN (1823, $3.95)
by Victoria Thompson

It was either accept Jack Sinclair's vile proposal of marriage or sell the Colson Ranch. Jack swore, if it took till dawn, he'd subdue Maggie Colson's honey-sweet lips and watch her sea-green eyes deepen to emerald with passion.